A Funeral
in Mantova

Books by David P. Wagner

The Rick Montoya Italian Mysteries
Cold Tuscan Stone
Death in the Dolomites
Murder Most Unfortunate
Return to Umbria
A Funeral in Mantova

A Funeral in Mantova

A Rick Montoya Italian Mystery

David P. Wagner

Poisoned Pen Press

Copyright © 2018 by David P. Wagner

First Edition 2018

10 9 8 7 6 5 4 3 2 1

Library of Congress Control Number: 2017946815

ISBN: 9781464209512   Trade Paperback
ISBN: 9781464209529   Ebook

Poisoned Pen Press
4014 N. Goldwater Blvd., #201
Scottsdale, AZ 85251
www.poisonedpenpress.com
info@poisonedpenpress.com

Printed in the United States of America

For Bill Oglesby, fellow writer, intrepid travel companion, and *zuppa inglese* expert, with thanks for all the help and encouragement, right from the beginning.

The body rolled off the planks and slipped into the water with barely a splash. It sank a few inches, bobbed back to the surface, and was immediately embraced by the river's steady current. A man stood watching, his form casting barely a shadow in the weak light of the morning. He took in three short breaths, gaining his composure after the exertion of the struggle. The fishing pole lay where it had been placed, ready to be stowed in the boat that was tied a few feet away. He moved his eyes from the body, now almost invisible in the dark water, and surveyed the scene. Leave it as it is. He turned and walked away.

The small wooden dock jutted out at a point where the Mincio widened before turning into a virtual lake at Mantova. After passing the city it would squeeze back to normal size before emptying into the mighty Po for the final kilometers to the Adriatic Sea. Once the border between Venice and Milan, where the armies of those two powerful city states clashed in mortal combat, the river ran through land now known more for food than violent history. This was the eastern tip of the region of Lombardy, its point shaped like a local cheese knife.

On this morning, like so many mornings in the northern Italian winter, the water and the land were covered with dense Lombard fog. It made driving treacherous, sometimes nearly impossible, but the Mantovani accepted it as a fact of life. The locals also believed, with some justification, that the moist air contributed to the quality of what the land produced, and helped age the cheeses and cure the meats for which the area was famous. Stumbling through zero visibility in the winter was a small price to pay.

The body glided under the layer of fog as it moved into the center of the river. It was too early in the day for any boats, which was why the dead man had always found this hour, just before dawn, to be the perfect time for fishing the dark waters. Usually his first cast was at a small bend where trout often congregated. They were huddled there now, just above the mud, but on this morning there would be nothing to tempt them.

In the distance a string of lights outlined the Via dei Molini causeway which connected Mantova's medieval center with flat farmland to the east. The water of the Lago Superiore narrowed toward the single passage under the causeway, taking the body with it. The lifeless figure swept slowly over the small dam that ran under the roadway, twirled for a few moments in the eddy below, and continued toward the middle of the Lago di Mezzo. The next barrier was another causeway, the last obstacle of any length between the city and the Po. But the capricious currents in this part of the river would keep the body here, as if they had decided the man should not be allowed to stray far from his home, even in death. The dark figure floated toward the shore and came to rest against the rocks below the walking path along the river's edge.

The grim ramparts of Castello di San Giorgio looked down on the scene. Even in its modern role as a museum, the gray stone exuded cold malevolence. There was a time in Mantova's history when a body floating past its walls had been as normal as a farmer trudging to market—but this was not the fifteenth century.

The young jogger who found the body would have nightmares for weeks afterward.

Chapter One

Rick felt the faint vibration of his cell phone before hearing the ring. He pulled it from his pocket and saw that the number was from the States, though not an area code he recognized. Given the hour in Rome, the caller had to be an earlier riser—very early, if calling from the West Coast. He moved to the side of Piazza Navona and took a seat on one of its stone benches.

"Montoya."

"Mr. Montoya, my name is Alexis Coleman. I am in the employ of Angelo Rondini."

The voice was smooth and efficient. "In the employ" was an expression more appropriate for use in a nineteenth-century British novel than by a woman whose American accent Rick could not place. He prided himself on detecting accents, both American and Italian; it came with being a professional interpreter. But he couldn't decide what part of the country she was from. More intriguing was her tone. It implied that he would know who Angelo Rondini was.

"Good morning, Ms. Coleman. How can I help you?"

"Mr. Rondini would like to contract your services."

"I'm always glad to hear such words. How did he find out about my services? If I might ask."

"It is a perfectly reasonable question. The chief of the economics section in the embassy recommended you."

The economics counselor at the embassy in Rome was a good friend of Rick's father from an earlier assignment in their careers. It always helped to have friends in high places.

"Mr. Rondini spoke with Mr. Treacy?"

"Mr. Rondini spoke with the ambassador, who gave him Mr. Treacy's name. I called Mr. Treacy."

Aha. Not just anyone, Rick knew, could pick up the phone and talk to the American ambassador in Rome. Perhaps, like the ambassador, Mr. Rondini had been a major contributor to the president's election campaign. Whoever this Rondini guy was, he had clout. And he was above speaking to anyone lower than the ambassador in the embassy pecking order.

"What kind of interpreting would Mr. Rondini like me to perform for him?"

"Can you please hold for a moment, Mr. Montoya?"

Before he could answer she was replaced by classical music. Boccherini. Rick kept the phone to his ear and looked around the piazza. It was the usual mix of tourists and locals, most on their way to lunch, many stopping to watch the waters of the four rivers noisily recycle through Bernini's fountain. After a full three minutes, she returned.

"Sorry about that. Mr. Rondini is making a trip to Mantova, Italy, to attend a funeral and make contact with his family there. You will be his guide."

Not would, but will. He also noticed that she used the Italian "Mantova" instead of the anglicized "Mantua" that would be found on most maps in the States. The woman must have done her homework.

"It sounds interesting, Ms. Coleman, but I'm afraid that kind of thing is really not my usual—"

"I checked your website and saw your daily rate, Mr. Montoya. Mr. Rondini will double that. And cover your expenses, of course."

He looked at the phone and decided he'd heard right. "When will Mr. Rondini need me, and for how long?"

"The funeral is next Thursday, so he is planning on arriving that morning. He can't be away for more than a week. I will send you the logistical details by e-mail today. I trust that will work with your schedule?"

At that moment Rick was working on a series of academic translations. It was boring sitting over his keyboard with a dictionary trying to make sense of someone's turgid Italian and then transforming it into equally turgid English. He was anxious to have a live interpreting job, and this one sounded intriguing as well as lucrative.

"Certainly. I'll juggle my schedule, but it can work."

"Excellent. My e-mail will have contact information, but you can call me at this number if absolutely necessary. Good-bye, Mr. Montoya." She was gone before Rick could think of any other questions, let alone return her good-bye.

He looked up at the gray sheet of clouds that covered the city, perhaps portending another afternoon rain. The call had partially brightened his day, which needed some brightening. Not only was his work at the moment dull, his relationship with Betta Innocenti had been sliding into a predictable routine. Is this what happens when two people spend too much time together? A trip alone to Mantova might be just what he—and Betta—needed. She was immersed in a case of stolen paintings with the art police, so she might not even notice he was gone.

He kept the phone in his hand and scrolled through the numbers in his address book before hitting the one for the embassy. After talking to the switchboard operator and one secretary, he got through to the counselor for economic affairs.

"*Ciao*, Rick. I thought you might be calling."

"First, John, thanks for the recommendation. But tell me who this guy Rondini is. Besides being a friend of the ambassador."

Treacy laughed. "You found that out. They were both on the board of the U.S. Chamber of Commerce, but I don't think they're close friends. That Coleman woman's a piece of work, isn't she? Like talking to some kind of automaton."

"You think? I found her quite charming. Especially when she told me what Rondini was going to pay me. Listen, I'll look up Rondini on the Internet so as not to waste your time. You have better things to do. But thanks again for giving her my name. I'll let you know how it goes."

"Please do. And give my best to your mom and dad next time you Skype with them."

Rick promised he would. A few minutes later he was in his apartment, searching on his laptop for information about Angelo Rondini. He didn't have to go far, and began to scribble notes on a yellow legal pad as he read the screen.

Angelo Rondini, 78, born Voglia, Italy, widowed, one daughter, residences in Chicago and Marco Island, Florida, semi-retired from Rondini Enterprises (malls and shopping centers), serves on boards of directors at numerous corporations and national charities, art collector.

The photograph on the screen showed a man in a tuxedo with two other people who looked equally wealthy and of the same age, all holding champagne flutes. He had thinning but long white hair and wore glasses which were lightly tinted yellow. The event was a fund-raiser for the Chicago Symphony Orchestra, and these three looked like just the type of persons any community organization would kill for to have in attendance at their events. Nothing could be deduced from the expression on Rondini's face, not in this photo or any of the others that came up in the search. No kindly smile, but no stony expression either. Rick would have to wait until he actually met his temporary employer to make an assessment of the man. What was most intriguing was that Rondini had been born in Italy. There had to be a story in that.

Rick called his uncle. Commissario Piero Fontana was not at his desk at police headquarters, but the call was answered by his faithful secretary, Signora Rocca. It was a running joke in the building that she had started working in the *questura* when Rome became capital of Italy in the nineteenth century, using family connections to King Vittorio Emmanuele to get the job. She wasn't quite that old, but she did have connections, something Piero used sparingly and only when dealing with the most sensitive issues.

"Your uncle is out on a case, Riccardo. You can call him on his *telefonino*."

Not when he's working a case. "Thank you, Signora, please tell him that I'll be going to Mantova on Wednesday. He can call me when he's free and I'll explain."

"I'll tell him. And how is that lovely little friend of yours?"

It was another of Signora Rocca's traits, an interest in the personal life of everyone she met. Not that she was nosy; it was a benign interest, like that of a maiden aunt or a grandmother. Importantly, she didn't share what she knew with others, which meant that police in the building came to her with personal problems, knowing it would go no farther than her desk. Her advice was usually sound. The Ann Landers of police head-quarters. Today, Rick was not in the mood to share.

"Betta is fine. Working hard."

"You must bring her by some time so I can meet her."

After he hung up, Rick reluctantly returned to his transla-tion. An hour later he put his computer on sleep and pulled out his red guide book for Lombardia. As he expected, there was a long entry on Mantova.

Rick's overnight train from Rome arrived in Verona on time, saving him any worry about making his rendezvous with Rondini. The sleeping compartment gave him what he needed: a firm mattress, the regular clatter of the rails to put him to sleep, and a sink for him to wash up and shave when he awoke. The porter had tapped on his door at exactly the time he'd requested, holding a *caffè latte* and *cornetto* on a small tray. So much more civilized than flying. Poor Rondini would be a basket case after a flight from Chicago, with a plane change somewhere else in Europe before arriving in Verona, the nearest airport to Mantova.

Even without his morning run, Rick was in excellent spirits when he stepped off the car and started walking along the platform. Everyone else coming off the train seemed to be in more of a hurry. They rushed past him, suitcase wheels rumbling along the pavement, leading him down the steps, under the tracks and into the terminal. Like most Italian train stations, it was cavernous and bustling with people. The only ones not hurrying along had stopped to scan the massive schedule board or were talking on cell phones. He immediately spotted a strategically placed man in a blue suit holding a hand-lettered sign: MONTOIA. Close enough.

"I'm Riccardo Montoya." Rick extended his hand.

The handshake was firm, the smile genuine. "*Piacere*, Signor Montoya. Marco Bertani."

The driver was older than Rick by at least a decade. Gray streaks had begun to work themselves in among the long, dark hair, and there was the hint of a stomach. He was clean-shaven, and his shoes were shined to perfection. He wanted to make a good first impression on Rondini.

"You can be more formal with our employer, Marco, but please call me Riccardo."

"Riccardo it is." He gestured toward the door. "I'm parked just outside. Do you need help with the bag?"

"I'll get it, thanks. Are you from here, Marco? I'm always trying to identify local accents."

"In fact I was born in the Verona suburbs south of the city, but I've lived here in Verona most of my life. So I suppose my accent is more Vernonese city than of the countryside around it, not that there's much difference."

A large modern square greeted them when they emerged into the open. The day was cloudy with patches of sky, and the temperature noticeably colder than what it had been when Rick had left Rome. That would be expected this far north of the Apennines and in the shadow of the Alps, especially in late autumn. He tightened the wool coat that he wore over his blazer. They reached the parking lot and Bertani led Rick to a shiny black Mercedes S-class sedan parked away from the other vehicles. The car was a few years old, but had been so well kept up that looked like it had just rolled off the line at Stuttgart. Bertani popped the ample trunk and stowed Rick's bag. He went to the rear passenger door to open it but Rick waved him off, opened the front door, and climbed in. The driver brought the diesel engine to life and they eased into the street.

"You are making me look like a country bumpkin, Marco," Rick said. *Burino* was not a word he used often in his interpreting work, and he was pleased to have remembered it.

The driver glanced from the road to Rick. "I hadn't noticed anything but your cowboy boots. Are you from Texas? I've always wanted to visit there."

"I lived close to Texas. I went to university in New Mexico, the next state west of Texas."

"I had clients once from Santa Fe. That's in New Mexico, isn't it?"

"*Bravo.* The state capital. You have a lot of clients from America?"

"Yes. I suspect Mr. Rondini found out about my company from one of them. The word gets around."

"So your English must be fluent."

"Not totally fluent as is your Italian, Riccardo, but I am able to defend myself."

Less work for me, Rick thought. The car began to weave its way through the city as only a local driver could do, sometimes on major streets, other times getting off them to avoid traffic. They crossed the river, passed railroad yards, and moved into the suburbs which, as in most of Italy, were more drab than the upscale historic center. This may have been where Marco had grown up, but Rick didn't ask. They drove parallel to the *autostrada* and went underneath it as airport signs, with the international airplane symbol, began to appear.

"I was told you would have the flight information, Marco."

The driver grunted an assent as he wheeled off the street toward the terminal. His Mercedes passed the terminal entrance and the parking lot, coming up to a gate manned by a uniformed guard. He rolled down his window but the guard merely greeted him with a "*Ciao*, Marco," and waved the car past. Rick was impressed, but noticed they were parking far from the terminal. Just ahead, the tarmac spread out in front of the windshield. A mid-sized Lufthansa plane had just pushed away from the terminal and was making its way out to the runways.

"We can wait here," said Marco. "I'll check on their arrival, but it should be in just a few minutes." He got out of the car, pulled a cell phone from his suit pocket, and walked a few steps before dialing.

Rick opened his door and stepped to the cement. He stretched and looked around, his nostrils taking in the coarse odor of burning airplane fuel that always hung over runways. After so many plane trips as the son of a diplomat, he knew it well. They were close to a door at one end of the terminal where, he assumed, they would go in to meet Rondini at the gate. Better than going through a crowded terminal. Marco clearly knew his way around; he must have done this countless times when meeting other clients. Through a break in the clouds, Rick could see snow on the mountains, making him think of the upcoming ski season. Perhaps he could meet Flavio again for a ski vacation. The clouds closed in and his thoughts returned to the present. The Lufthansa plane was now at the end of the runway, gunning its engines, almost close enough to make Rick cover his ears. It lurched forward, picked up speed, and suddenly climbed sharply into the air. After it disappeared into the clouds, Rick heard the distant sound of another plane coming from the opposite direction. As he was turning to find it, the driver came back to the car.

"I have a friend who works in the control tower." Marco gestured toward the terminal. "The plane should be here at any moment."

"It's probably the one I just—" Rick's sentence was interrupted by the sound of the Lobo Fight Song coming from his pocket. He extracted his cell phone and flipped it open. "Commissario Fontana, it is an honor to speak with you." It was his standard response when receiving a call from his uncle.

"And how is my nephew?" said the voice at the other end of the line. "Have you been to the castle yet?"

"Still in Verona, Zio. At the airport. The man's plane should be here momentarily. Did you solve the case that has kept you so busy the last few days?"

"I'm afraid not, and we are running out of time." He paused. "Riccardo, did you speak with Betta before you left last night?"

Rick rubbed his eyes. It was the kind of question a mother would have asked, but perhaps Piero had begun thinking that he should be his sister's stand-in. Despite his affection for Piero, he was annoyed by this kind of meddling. Or was he annoyed because the relationship with Betta was going sour?

"I left her a message."

Even over the phone Piero could sense that his question was not appreciated. He let it drop. "Everything is on schedule up there in the north?"

"With typical northern efficiency, Zio." Rick turned away from the tarmac, hunched over, and raised his voice as the engines from the arriving plane got closer. "The driver is waving at me; it must be time to go into the terminal. Talk to you later. *Ciao.*"

Marco was gesturing for Rick to return to the car. When Rick got in, he put it in gear.

"Are we driving back to the terminal, Marco? I thought we'd be going in through that door."

"No terminal for us, Riccardo."

The Mercedes drove through an open gate onto the tarmac as the plane was directed to its parking place by an airport employee wielding two brightly colored paddles. Rick chuckled and shook his head as they parked off the left wing. He didn't know much about private jets, but he knew this was a Gulfstream, that it could easily fly direct from Chicago to Verona, and that if you had to ask what it cost, you couldn't afford one. The name RONDINI ENTERPRISES was centered under the seven oval windows, large enough to read but small enough to be tasteful. As they sat waiting for the plane engines to stop, a small Fiat Panda with a flashing light on its roof pulled up next to them and a man in a blue suit holding a briefcase got out.

"Passport and customs," said Marco without looking at Rick.

The two engines whined to a stop and the door of the plane opened. As soon as the stairs dropped to the ground, the official scurried up into the plane holding tightly to his briefcase. Rick and the driver got out of the car and leaned against its hood while they waited.

"Nice way to travel," Rick commented.

The formalities didn't take long. The man came down the steps, got back into his car, and drove off toward the terminal. As the car departed, a woman dressed in blue slacks and a white blouse looked out from the plane door. She gazed at the snow on the mountains to the north before noticing Rick and giving him a wave. He waved back. A few more minutes passed before Angelo Rondini himself appeared, shaking hands with the pilot and copilot. Rondini slapped one of them on the back and took in the mountain view before starting down the steps.

The society photo had not flattered or aged him. Except for a brown suit and tie rather than a tuxedo, it was the guy in the picture, down to the yellow-tinted glasses. He looked like he had recently lost some weight but hadn't bothered to get himself a suit that fit better. An Italian with that much money would have worn a perfectly tailored suit, but, apparently, appearance was not that important to Angelo Rondini. His eyes locked on the two men on the tarmac who now moved toward the plane, and Rick could feel himself being sized up.

"You must be Montoya," Rondini said as he shook Rick's hand. "There's a certain American aura about you. I haven't seen boots like that since I opened a shopping mall in San Antonio. The person wearing them almost cost me the deal. And this guy is our driver, I suppose?"

"Yes, sir."

He was about to make introductions, but Marco took the cue and stepped forward to offer his hand. "Marco Bertani, Mr. Rondini, at your services. It is my pleasure."

The English was accented but clear.

"Sounds to me like this guy speaks good English," Rondini said. "So tell me, Montoya, why did I hire you? I'll have to have a talk with Lexi. That's all right; I'll find something for you to do."

"Mr. Rondini, if you want to end my services now—"

The man clapped Rick on the shoulder just as he'd done with the pilot. "I always like to throw a curve ball when I first meet people. See how they react. It's never failed me in business, and as you can see, I've done all right." He didn't feel the need to gesture toward the plane to help make his point. "I think we'll get along just fine, Montoya. Despite the cowboy boots. Now if we can get Lexi off the plane, we can get the hell out of here."

"I didn't realize Ms. Coleman was coming along. She never mentioned that in her e-mails."

"Probably didn't think you needed to know. That's just like her. But I never go anywhere without Lexi, even to a funeral. Plus, she keeps contact with the office. Never know what trouble those assholes back there will get themselves into."

Rick looked up at the empty airplane doorway. Great. Not only do I have to deal with a millionaire with an ego, I have to put up with his supercilious special assistant. Perhaps I should have negotiated for three times my usual fee.

A male crew member came down the steps carrying bags and stowed them in the trunk of the car. He hustled back up the stairs and returned with another set. Angelo Rondini walked toward the tail of the plane to get a better look at the mountain. Rick pulled out his cell phone and checked the time.

Finally, Alexis Coleman appeared at the top of the steps, gripping a leather briefcase as if it held the nuclear codes. Jet-black hair in a natural cut framed an oval face, its smooth skin the color of a *caffè macchiatto*. The frames of her glasses subtly matched the burgundy hue of her lipstick, and if there was other makeup, it had been applied with perfection. He had been unable to estimate her age from the few words she'd spoken on the phone, but now Rick guessed mid-thirties, or perhaps younger, given the perfect complexion. He moved his eyes from the face to a slim figure which showed itself through the opening of a long wool coat.

Had it not been for her all-business manner, he might have looked forward to working with Alexis Coleman.

She extended her hand when she reached the bottom of the stairs.

"I assume you are Rick Montoya." It was a serious handshake, matching her expression.

"My pleasure, Alexis."

"Everyone calls me Lexi." It sounded more like an order than a clarification. "And this is our driver, Mr. Bertani?"

Marco mumbled a few words and shook her hand.

Rondini watched it all with a large smile on his face. "Can we get this show on the road, Lexi? The only funeral I want to be late for is my own."

Chapter Two

The drive from the airport to Mantova was short and mostly quiet. Rick was expecting Rondini to ask questions about the area of his birth, but instead he spent most of the half hour looking silently out the window at the flat countryside on either side of the *autostrada*—which made sense if he hadn't been back to Italy in a while. Or had he been back at all? Rick had a few questions of his own for Rondini, many about the reasons that his family left Italy for America. Italian emigration was something that had always fascinated Rick, the personal histories of desperation and hope. He would wait for the right time to ask.

While Rondini, deep in thought, watched the farms zipping by, Lexi tapped away at her tablet, sending and receiving e-mails that had stacked up during the flight. A question sneaked into Rick's head, but it was one he would never ask: how much of the operation did she run? Rondini had complete trust in the woman, that was clear, but what was the extent of her real power? Rick recalled something his father had told him about working in the bureaucracy of the State Department: the trick was knowing when to make a decision yourself and when to consult your boss. Lexi, it appeared, knew the trick. The personality of the boss was the key, and while Rondini did not strike Rick as a micro-manager, he was definitely in charge. So how much leeway did Ms. Coleman have? It would be fascinating to watch the two interact.

Marco eased the car off at the Mantova exchange, paid the toll, and headed west into town. As they neared their destination, the number of buildings increased—low boxy structures that included factories and gas stations along with residences. Beyond clumps of trees and bushes on both sides of the road, the lake suddenly appeared, stretching in both directions and dotted with floating patches of morning fog. They drove onto a long, two-lane causeway that separated the Lago di Mezzo on the right from the Lago Inferiore on the left. In the distance the skyline of Mantova began to appear through the morning mist, the round dome of Sant'Andrea and a medieval tower its first identifiable shapes. Halfway across the water the squared-off lines of the Gonzaga castle took form, and eventually overpowered the view. The Mercedes turned left when the causeway ended, drove between the fortifications and the lake, then eased into Mantova itself. Once inside the historic center, it passed over a narrow canal and started down a long, straight street before pulling to a stop in front of the hotel.

Rick estimated the buildings on the street dated from the nineteenth century. All were two to three stories with plain stucco fronts, neat and well maintained. As they entered he found that the interior of the hotel was very much of the present century, starting with the reception area. White walls contrasted with a décor of glass, shiny metal, and dark wood, the result of a restoration that was so spotless it could have been finished the previous day. Rick was certain that the efficient Ms. Coleman was not one to dip under five stars when choosing accommodations for her boss, so this place had to be the best in Mantova. The reception staff was young, spoke passable English, and fully checked them in while Rondini was still standing out on the street talking with the driver. When he got inside, Lexi handed him his key card.

"You are in the suite on the third floor, Mr. Rondini, and I'll be a few doors down. Rick is one floor below. Our bags are being taken to the rooms. The funeral is set for eleven, an hour and a half from now. I assume it will start on time?" She looked at Rick.

"The ones I've been to always have," Rick answered.

Rondini did not appear to have heard what was being said. His eyes were on a framed abstract print on the wall. "I was just chatting with our driver and he seems to know his Mantova art. Comes from taking tourists around the town over the years. That will come in handy." He turned to Lexi and Rick. "I'm going to rest for a bit and change into a dark suit. I'll see you down here at quarter to eleven. Knock on my door if I'm late." He turned and walked to the elevator.

"Mr. Rondini is very interested in art," Lexi said to Rick. "It is another reason he wanted to make the trip, besides attending the funeral of his cousin, of course."

"Lexi, that's the first I've heard whose funeral we're attending. Why don't we have a cup of coffee and you can tell me about what's going to happen during the next few days?"

She looked at her watch and then studied Rick's expression. "I suppose you're right. You don't really know much about all this. I have to make some calls so let's do it quickly."

They walked into the breakfast area where a couple was finishing their coffee and rolls. A girl appeared and Rick ordered a *caffè latte* for him, a *cappuccino* for Lexi.

"Do you want something to eat?" Rick asked as they sat at one of the tables. The buffet was so well stocked it looked as if it had just opened.

"No, I was well fed on the plane. But you go ahead."

He did, taking a yogurt and sweet roll from the groaning board. It had been a while since the train and he wasn't sure when he'd see food again. He walked back to the table and saw that Lexi was stealing a look at her cell phone. She glanced up at him and slipped it into an outside compartment of her briefcase.

"The funeral is for Mr. Rondini's cousin, Roberto Rondini," she began, as if making a presentation to a board. "Obviously, their fathers were brothers."

"Were the cousins very close?"

"On the contrary, they'd never met. Mr. Rondini came to the U.S. as an infant and has never felt very close ties with Italy. His parents thought it important that he embrace his new nationality, and they made a point of speaking English in front of him when he was growing up. Not that he feels any ill will toward his native country, but the whole Italian-American thing was never his style."

"So he doesn't wear a baseball cap that says 'Kiss Me, I'm Italian.'"

She looked hard at Rick, then shook her head. "No."

The coffees arrived and Rick stirred sugar from a small bowl on the table into his. She sipped hers without adding anything.

"Roberto Rondini's daughter, whose name is Livia Guarino, called the morning he died and I spoke to her. Her English is halting. She wanted Mr. Rondini to come to his cousin's funeral. She was very compelling and I put her through to him."

Rick swallowed a bite of the sweet roll. "So he was convinced."

"Yes. He didn't tell me what she said and I didn't ask. He just told me to make the arrangements."

"You said something about his interest in art."

"Yes." She took another sip of her coffee. "Mr. Rondini is an art collector, and lately his interests have shifted from modern to more classical genres. Not that he can afford to purchase any Botticellis or Raphaels, but he wants to see some of the great Italian painters other than those in museums in the States. So he sees this trip as a way to do that. Naturally, we won't say that to the family."

"But he must have some interest in his roots."

She gave him a faint shrug. "I know him as well as anyone outside his family, but I'm not sure."

"Perhaps the art thing is just an excuse to find out about his family, rather than the other way around."

Lexi brushed back her hair and he caught sight of one of her earrings, gold with a pearl pendant. "I never thought of that." She drained her cup and got to her feet. "I really have to make those calls. I'll see you in the lobby in about an hour."

Rick watched her walk away, still clutching her briefcase. Her coat had been sent up to her room with the luggage, so he could get a full view of her slender figure. The elegant pants suit fit perfectly, but Alexis Coleman would have looked good wearing a sweat suit three sizes too large. If only her temperament was as attractive as her looks.

• ● ● ● •

On the way to the church, the driver gave his passengers background on what they were going to see, but since it was just a few blocks away, Marco wasn't able to say very much.

"Even though the Duomo is the city's cathedral, Sant'Andrea is the more famous because it was designed by one of the greatest architects of the fifteenth century, Leon Battista Alberti. In fact, it was the last work designed by Alberti. Construction on it started in 1472, the year he died. You will see immediately how Alberti used classical elements, beginning with the Roman arch. The facade of Sant'Andrea is filled with them."

"Is there any art of importance inside, Marco?" Rondini asked. "I couldn't care less about architecture."

"The tomb of Andrea Mantegna is decorated by his *aiuti*— what is it in English, Riccardo?"

"His assistants," Rick said from the front seat.

"You finally earned your pay, Montoya," said Rondini. "I should let you take the rest of the day off, but I may need you at the funeral, and it looks like we've arrived."

The car parked across the piazza from the church where people dressed in dark clothing were beginning to climb the steps.

"You want to come in, Marco?"

"I should remain with the car, Signor Rondini. And the funeral would be a painful memory of one I attended recently."

The three of them got out and walked across the pavement. Rondini was dressed in a black suit with a gray tie over a white shirt. Lexi had changed into a blue print dress, covered by the same long, wool coat, but for the first time since getting off the plane she was without her briefcase. Rick wore his only suit, with a suitably somber tie, and his dress cowboy boots.

He looked at the facade and understood what Marco had meant about the architect's use of classical design—the arches and columns could have been taken from a building in imperial Rome. Because of the buildings which hemmed in the basilica, he was unprepared for its cavernous interior. A barrel vault ceiling covered with deep, square coffers seemed miles above their heads, and tall chapels running along the sides under their own vaults added to the vast sense of space. It was also empty, or at least most of it. The single-wide nave was bare of seating until directly in front of the main altar where rows of chairs had been set up. Rick, Rondini, and Lexi walked slowly toward the chairs that were starting to fill with silent mourners. Unlike the others who kept their eyes on the ground, the three could not help but take in their surroundings as they walked. When they were close to the chairs, Rondini spoke into Rick's ear.

"How am I going to find Roberto's daughter?"

Not many strangers would show up at her father's funeral with a black woman and a guy wearing cowboy boots, Rick thought. But he said: "I'm sure she'll find you."

At that moment they saw a woman quietly greeting people at the end of the aisle that ran between the rows of chairs. She wore a black dress and her head was covered with a veil of the same color. She smiled weakly at each of the people, who in turn embraced her and murmured into her ear. When it was Rondini's turn, he stepped forward, unsure what to say.

"My dear Uncle Angelo, I thank you for coming." She wrapped her arms around him and kissed him on both cheeks.

"You recognized me."

"How could I not? The resemblance with my father is…"

She searched for a word and found it. "Striking." She looked at Rick and Lexi.

"This is my assistant, Alexis Coleman," Rondini said, "and my interpreter for the visit, Mr. Montoya."

"My condolences," said Lexi as she took Livia Guarino's hand.

Rick was next, and offered his condolences in Italian.

She shook his hand and stayed in the same language. "I'm glad you're here. My English is abominable and it is nonexistent among my family." She said something about seeing them after the service and turned to the group forming behind them.

The three took seats in the fourth row from the front just as a voice began to sing in Latin from somewhere out of sight. The mournful words echoed off the walls and faded into the dome high above them. Ahead, between the rows of chairs and the altar, sat the dark casket, its top covered with a tight blanket of white carnations. Rick listened to the music and let his eyes move around the space. He remembered the few funerals he'd been to in Italy, starting with two for his Italian grandparents, who had died within months of each other in Rome. It had been a difficult year for his mother and uncle, and, by extension, for all the Montoya family. Those masses had been celebrated in the same parish church where he, his mother, and his sister had been baptized, and where his parents had exchanged vows. It could have fit in one corner of Sant'Andrea.

The priest and two altar boys appeared, and the mass began. The eulogy was full of vague descriptions of the dead man, and many allusions to the afterlife. In case Angelo might want to know what was said, Rick tried to remember them since taking notes would have been inappropriate. At the end everyone rose and the casket was rolled between the chairs toward the door, accompanied by six men and followed by Livia Guarino and several others. As they passed up the aisle, those watching began to applaud.

"What the hell is this?" Rondini whispered to Rick.

"Sign of respect. Italians often do it at funerals."

Rondini nodded and began to clap. "I like it."

As the casket took its slow journey toward the large doors of the church, the people emptied the rows and followed behind them, talking softly to one another. Rondini walked to one side and stopped to look into one of the chapels, Lexi at his side. Rick watched, remembering what Lexi had said about Rondini's interest in art. The man was starting already.

"Signor Montoya?"

The person who spoke must have been sitting behind them, since Rick had studied the profiles of everyone in the rows ahead while listening to the priest. The man's fatigued eyes were even with Rick's, putting him over six feet, and his plain, dark suit was well filled out. Too well filled out. *Could it be that this guy…?*

"I am Inspector Giulio Crispi."

He is. A cop.

"Your uncle and I worked together a few years ago, and I was speaking to him this morning. He mentioned that his nephew was in our city."

"That's right. I'm working as an interpreter for the American cousin of Roberto Rondini. He flew in this morning. Did you know the deceased well, Inspector?"

"Never met him."

No doubt the *questura* sent an official representative to the funerals of prominent locals, and Inspector Crispi had drawn the short straw. Rick was about to ask if that were the case, when he saw that Rondini was looking around for him.

"Inspector, it was a pleasure to meet you, but I must be on my way."

"Signor Montoya, we suspect that Roberto Rondini was murdered."

Crispi was a man of few words, but they got Rick's attention. "I…I had no idea."

"There is no reason you would. Since you will be spending some time with the family of Signor Rondini, I would be most grateful if you could be observant, now that you know of our suspicions." He handed Rick a card. "I can be reached at any hour at this number. The address of the *questura* is also there. Good day, Signor Montoya."

•••••   ⁋

When the Mercedes fell in line behind the hearse, clouds were beginning to move in from the west. They were the vanguard of a cold front that had originated south of Geneva, descended to Turin, and now widened as it moved through the Po River Valley toward the Adriatic. The weather system could eventually bring rain or snow, but, for the moment, served to remind the Mantovani that winter was on its way. The fields on either side of the road had given up their crops weeks earlier; for them a white winter blanket would be welcome. For the townspeople, not as much.

"Who were you talking to in there, Language Man?"

They were the first words Rondini had spoken since the car had driven across the lake. Rick had been fingering Inspector Crispi's card in his overcoat pocket while deciding how to handle the policeman's request. The inspector suspected foul play. What better way to gather information about the dead man and his family than from Riccardo Montoya, who was working for a member of the family? Crispi also must have known, from talking to Piero, that Rick had assisted the police in the past. The problem for Rick was his present employer. Working on the side with the police wasn't something he could keep from Rondini; that would be unethical, not to mention impossible. Now was not the time to explain, and there hadn't been time in the church to get any details of the case out of Crispi. Rick could meet the policeman later, when he had a break from his translation duties. Before that, he'd talk to Rondini.

"His name's Crispi, a work colleague of my uncle. He found out I was here and stopped me to say hello."

Marco kept his eyes on the road, and Rick wondered how much of the conversation he was getting, since Angelo had a fast, choppy way of talking. It was a speech pattern that many foreigners would have trouble following. That was likely what Roberto Rondini's daughter meant when she said how pleased she was to have Rick's assistance.

"You have a big family, Montoya?"

An interesting question from someone who'd never bothered to meet his own cousin. Was the funeral bringing out some feelings of guilt in Rondini? Well, that was fine; it wasn't too late for him to get to know what was left of his family. Rick turned in his seat to answer.

"The cliché would be that my Italian side, my mother's family, would be much more numerous than those on my father's American side. But in fact it's just the opposite. I have an Italian aunt and uncle, and one cousin, that's all. Back in New Mexico, there are Montoyas everywhere."

Rondini listened and nodded before returning his eyes to the countryside passing the window. As if mesmerized by the monotony of the terrain, he was still staring out when he spoke again.

"I suppose being an only child had its advantages, like getting all the attention from my parents. All my friends in the neighborhood had big families, so there was no lack of kids to play with or fight with. They even had grandparents, which I didn't, but the old folks didn't speak much English and I didn't speak any Italian, so I stuck with my own generation. When I went off to college, the size of your family was never something anybody talked about. Still isn't."

The Mercedes slowed, pulled over, and stopped, keeping its place in the line of cars which were now emptying of their passengers. The casket was removed from the hearse by eight of the men; there would be no wheeled cart as in the church. They carried it carefully through the iron gate of a tall, stone wall, followed by mourners who kept their eyes to the ground as they walked. Once inside, Rick saw that the wall was made up of horizontal tombs, like catacombs, most of them sealed by stone squares etched with names and dates. Beside the gravel path next to the wall, the ground held traditional graves marked by gravestones, many with small black-and-white photographs of the deceased. Wilting flowers drooped from metal vases attached to the grave markers on the ground and the wall. The only sound was the crunch of shoes on the gravel path as the procession walked to a far corner where the freshly dug grave awaited. Rick noticed that three graves in the same row had the names Rondini etched on their surfaces. From the dates below the names, he concluded they were the dead man's parents and wife. He whispered in Rondini's ear while he inclined his head toward the grave markers. Angelo looked at the names of his aunt and uncle and nodded. The priest began to speak.

Perhaps because of the ominous clouds, the ceremony was brief. The thick walls, filled with stacked tombs, protected the circle of mourners from a wind that stirred the air, bringing with it the scent of wet leaves. When the ceremony ended, everyone gathered around Roberto Rondini's daughter and exchanged more embraces. Rick and Lexi hung back while Angelo joined in offering his condolences. They watched Livia Guarino speak into Angelo's ear, after which he nodded and gave her another hug. Then he shook hands with the man whom Rick assumed was Livia's husband. The man's awkward demeanor indicated to Rick that he didn't speak much or any English, but he did pass something to Angelo, earning a nod.

"We're invited back to their farm," said Rondini when he got back to Rick and Lexi. He held up the card. "This is the name of the place. Our driver should know how to get there. It will be family and close friends, so Lexi, you can go back to the hotel and get some work done." He looked at Rick. "But not you, Language Man. Time for you to go to work."

Rick remembered Inspector Crispi.

In more ways than one.

Chapter Three

The driver knew exactly where the Rondini dairy farm was located. In an area of Lombardy where numerous cheese producers thrived, Rondini's was known by everyone as one of the largest and most successful. Much of its production came from its own cows, but it also bought milk from other farmers in the area. Rondini cheese could be purchased throughout Italy and was exported to other countries in the European Union, and while the farm's lead product was Parmigiano-Reggiano, it made other cheeses that were less regulated and less expensive. All this required acreage and equipment, and Latteria Rondini had more than enough of both. The farm's clean, white buildings lined one side of a large parking lot where trucks and tractors were neatly parked. Behind them, level fields dotted with cows stretched for kilometers. Marco drove past the farm entrance to a modern house separated from the business operation by a row of thick trees. Cars from the funeral were already parked in front and people were walking up to the house. The Mercedes slowed and entered a long, circular driveway, coming to a stop at the walkway that led to the door.

The driver got out and opened the door for Rondini, who disengaged himself from the seat with some effort. Rick stood and looked around him, taking in a rural smell that mixed the strong odor of hay with the fragrance of the few flowers that still bloomed along the driveway. The sky continued to threaten, but it was impossible to know if anything would come of it. Those who'd spent all their lives in the Po Valley might know, but he didn't.

Rondini leaned down and spoke through the open driver window. "Lexi, call me if there's any movement with the guy in Memphis, but I have the feeling it's not going to happen. If you talk to him, tell him we need the decision by yesterday." He stood up and looked toward the house. "Marco, you should have time to get something to eat before you come back. This may take a while."

Marco got back in the car and drove toward the road with Lexi in the back seat.

"Mr. Rondini, before we go in, I need to talk to you about something."

Angelo, who had been straightening his tie, stopped and eyed Rick. "You can't ask for a raise, you haven't done anything yet."

"No, sir. It's something else. The man I was talking to in the church? He's a policeman."

"He's not a friend of your uncle, like you said?"

"I said he's a colleague of my uncle, and my uncle is with the police in Rome."

"That could come in handy if I get into trouble on this trip." He chuckled while watching the Mercedes pull out onto the road. "So what's the big deal?"

Rick took a breath before answering. "Inspector Crispi thinks there is a chance your cousin was murdered."

"Whoa." He scanned the house, where the door was open and visitors were entering. "Does Livia know that?"

"He didn't give me any details, since there wasn't time to talk."

"Why would he tell you this?"

"I've worked with the police in the past. He knew that."

The man's face showed that what had been confusing was starting to make sense. "And he wants you to work with them again. He knows you'll be around people who were close to Roberto but might not be forthcoming with him."

"That's correct. But my contract is with you. If you don't want me to help him, I won't. Just say the word."

Rondini rubbed a hand over his chin and squinted his eyes in thought. "He really thinks Roberto was murdered?"

"That's what he said."

"Are they going to pay you?"

It was a logical question from a businessman, but something that never entered Rick's mind. He shook his head. "They haven't before."

Rondini had run out of questions. Rick guessed that this was not an issue he usually faced in his business dealings, most of which dealt with the bottom line. Complicating it was the new family connection, a foreign culture, and a little jet lag. But the man had not become successful by avoiding decisions.

"Yes, do it. He was my cousin, after all, the least I can do is not stand in the way of an investigation if he was murdered. But here are the conditions. It can't interfere with what you are doing for me. When I need you to interpret for me, you have to be there."

"Of course."

"And you will keep me in the loop with anything you find out from these people."

Rick agreed, but interpreted "these people" as the family and friends of Roberto Rondini, not the police. He didn't want to share what Inspector Crispi might know, unless forced to.

"And finally, Roberto's daughter must not know what you are up to. This is just between you, me, and the cops."

"Understood." Rick stretched his arm toward the walkway up to the front door. "Shall we go in?"

A man wearing an ill-fitting suit took their coats inside the door. Rick guessed he was someone who worked elsewhere on the farm and had been pressed into service for the event. They walked into an ample rectangular living room, beyond which he could see a dining room, its round table set with trays of food. The dining room chairs had been pushed to one side, under windows that looked out on the grass lawn and fields beyond. About two dozen people mingled between the two rooms, most with glasses in their hands, a few with small plates of food. The voice level was higher than it had been in the church, but still muted. Some looked up when Rick and Angelo approached, one being Livia Guarino, who had been talking with her husband and a man with the ruddy complexion of someone who worked in the open air. She walked over to them and took Angelo's hand in both hers.

"So good to see you, Uncle. May I call you that? It was kind of you to come all the way from America. I know you must be a busy man."

"I wish we had met under other circumstances, Livia. As I wish I had met your father."

Rick decided he wasn't needed and didn't want to listen in on their private conversation. He excused himself, encouraged by Livia to partake of the food and drink. After lifting a glass off a passing tray, he surveyed the group like an embassy officer at a diplomatic reception. Why not start with Livia's husband and the man with the tan? He was curious about both. He took an initial taste of his wine, a dry, dark red, and walked to them.

"You must be Livia's husband." Rick shook the younger man's hand.

"That's correct; Francesco Guarino," he answered, before turning to the man next to him. "Carlo, this is Riccardo Montoya, Angelo Rondini's interpreter. Riccardo, Carlo Zucari is the manager of the dairy farm." His eyes darted toward the door where an elderly man was making his way in from the hallway. "Can you excuse me a moment? Livia is busy and I should greet the new arrivals."

He hurried off, leaving Rick to wonder if the man was just shy and nervous, or thought he should greet an important visitor rather than mix with the hired help.

"This is quite an operation," Rick said as he shook Zucari's hand.

"It is the largest family-owned dairy in the area. With a few exceptions, all the others are cooperatives. We keep busy."

"Now the ownership passes to his daughter, I suppose?"

"You suppose correctly. Livia and her husband. I doubt if things will change much for the workers. Signor Rondini had not been very involved for years. He left it up to me to run the place. He only became involved if there was a long-range decision about the direction of the operation."

Rick looked around the room. "But he was here."

Zucari frowned in non-comprehension, then smiled. "Ah. You mean he lived here. Yes and no. One wing of this house is his, but he also had an apartment in Mantova. The last several years, since his wife passed away, he was spending more and more time in town. He would sometimes drop in to see me in the morning after fishing, but he didn't get involved in the day-to-day operation of the farm and the cheese-making."

"His death was sudden?"

"A fishing accident? I would say so."

"I don't know anything about the circumstances of his death. We only arrived here this morning."

"Of course, you wouldn't." He took a sip from his wine-glass. "He slipped on the dock and fell into the river. His body washed up near the castle in town."

"He always fished in the same place?"

Zucari's look made Rick wonder if he was probing too much.

"He tied up his boat at a dock at the edge of the property. I don't know where on the river he fished since I'm not a fisherman. Never had the time or the inclination. Running a place like this keeps me busy."

It was the second time the man had noted that he was busy, contrasting with the deceased owner, who apparently spent his time fishing or in Mantova. Rick had been keeping an eye on

Angelo, who now waved him over. He was standing next to Francesco Guarino.

"My *capo* is calling, Signor Zucari, and needs his interpreter. It was nice to meet you."

"Come back, if you have time, and I'll show you around the farm."

"I'd enjoy that, thank you."

As he walked to his boss, Rick thought about the times he'd visited relatives in the States when he was young. Being introduced to cousins and other relatives for the first time was always the same; they weren't quite sure what to think of him. Most had never met anyone who lived outside New Mexico, never mind another country, making him very exotic. Angelo wasn't getting any of that, these northern Italians were very much used to foreigners in their midst.

Rick noticed the relief on the faces of both his boss and Livia's husband when he reached them.

"I was asking Francesco here about what he does for a living, but I'm not sure he understood the question. I think he said something about cheese, so he must be part of the dairy."

"Signor Rondini was inquiring about your work," Rick said in Italian to Guarino.

"I think I understood that, but I could not explain well. I am an inspector for the Parmigiano-Reggiano Consortium. My territory is this part of Lombardy. But of course someone else inspects the cheese of Latteria Rondini."

Rick interpreted, and with him in the middle, a conversation began between the two men.

"The quality control is pretty tight for the cheese?"

"We have a most rigorous process to assure that the Parmigiano-Reggiano meets the highest of standards before it can display the stamp of the *Consorzio*. You can be assured that any cheese with the stamp burned into its rind has passed those tests." He pointed at a wooden board holding a large slice of the cheese. Protruding from it was the distinctive teardrop-shaped knife not used with any other kind of cheese. "You must try some. This is a *stravecchio* made here."

"Are you sure it's okay, even though you didn't inspect it?"

Even after Rick's translation, Guarino wasn't sure if Angelo had been joking or not. He wedged out two chunks and passed them to Angelo and Rick. He then got one for himself and popped it into his mouth. "It is one of the few foods we eat with our fingers."

"This is good cheese," said Angelo after eating his bite. "Now that your father-in-law is gone, Francesco, will you be leaving your inspector job and taking over the cheese-making here?"

The question took Guarino by surprise, and the nervousness he had shown to Rick earlier returned.

"I—I haven't thought about that. Livia is the owner now, so it will be up to her on how to proceed. With everything going on, we haven't discussed it." His eyes darted around the room, as if he were searching for an escape route. Rick provided it.

"I think Signor Rondini might want to taste some of the other cheeses."

"Yes, yes, of course. There are many good things to eat, please do."

Rick and Rondini stood by the table and surveyed the spread, which included small sandwiches, various kinds of salami and other cold cuts, and a variety of cheeses. Everything was local.

"Kind of a strange duck, that one." Rondini picked up a small plate and began to fill it. "Livia seems like a very intelligent young woman, but he doesn't seem like her type. Who were you talking to?"

"Carlo Zucari. He's the manager of the farm. He told me that your cousin had pretty much turned the operation over to him to run a while back. He'd show up occasionally but was hands-off on a day-to-day basis. He invited us to tour the place, by the way."

Rondini nibbled a miniature *panino*. "Livia did as well,

and we'll have to do that. These sandwiches are good. If I eat enough of them I won't need dinner."

Rick took another chunk of Parmigiano-Reggiano, noting its perfect consistency—an advantage of getting it at the source. "He told me that your cousin was drowned after he slipped on the dock when he was going fishing."

"She said that, too, but didn't go into details." He rubbed his eyes. The time change was starting to catch up with him. "She also asked a favor of me, which I found somewhat curious." He looked around to be sure no one was listening, though it was unnecessary since they were conversing in English. "Apparently her father was considering selling a plot of land to a developer. She said the people she trusts have no expertise on such things, and those who do have it, would have a stake in the decision. The manager of the farm is dead set against it, thinks it should be used to expand production. She knows that development is my business and asked my advice. I'm a bit bothered by her request."

"Why is that?"

"Don't you see? I thought she asked me to come over for the funeral because I was family, but she may just have wanted to pick my brain."

"Maybe a bit of both, Mr. Rondini, don't you think?"

Angelo had been giving his wineglass a hard look. "Yeah, maybe you're right. Way in the back of my mind is that my parents never talked much about my father's side of the family. Don't get me wrong, they never said anything against those who'd stayed in Italy. But I never sensed a warmth, if you know what I mean. Sometimes I wonder what was behind that." He glanced over Rick's shoulder. "Who's this guy?"

A large man holding a glass of red wine was marching toward them. His eyes indicated that the glass had been filled a few times, and his tie was slightly askew, something rare among Italians. Like the farm manager, his face was tanned and well creased.

"You are Mr. Rondini?" he said to Angelo, like it was an accusation. The English was as rough as the man's complexion, so Rick intervened in Italian.

"This is Signor Angelo Rondini, the cousin of the deceased. I am his interpreter. And you are?"

The answer was in Italian. "I'd heard there was a rich relative from America. I am Emilio Fiore. I own the farm to the east." He jerked his free thumb eastward before turning to Angelo and bowing dramatically. "My deepest condolences, Signor Rondini, on the passing of your cousin."

Rick translated, including the part about the rich relative.

"This guy's a piece of work," said Angelo to Rick as he returned the bow. "But since he's been softened up by Livia's wine, he may be able to answer some questions."

Rick managed to contain a smile. His concern that his employer would be against involvement in the murder investigation had been unwarranted; the man was embracing it. He went into his interpreter's routine.

"You must have known the deceased well, being his neighbor."

Fiore drained his glass and looked around for a refill. Fortunately for him, the girl with the tray was in the vicinity, and she swapped his empty for a full one. "I knew him well enough, but it is no secret that we didn't get along. But I will not speak ill of the dead, especially here, today."

"It is perfectly natural for neighbors to have disagreements," said Angelo after hearing the translation. "What was the nature of yours?"

"That is not a secret either. It was over his parcel of land on the river, quite a large number of hectares. It's been fallow for years, the same number of years I've been trying to purchase it from him so I can expand my dairy farm. Right now it's wasted, but he didn't care. Then word got out a few weeks ago that he was going to sell it to developers to build a factory, or something worse. We don't need any more factories creeping onto agricultural land. Agriculture is the backbone of our community, always was and always will be."

"What will happen to the land now?" Rick wasn't sure if Fiore had heard the question; the man was staring out the window at the expanse of flat fields.

"Let's just say I hope Livia has more sense than her father." He took another gulp of the wine.

"When did you see Roberto Rondini last?"

"Haven't seen him in weeks, but he was spending most of his time in town." A malevolent grin split his face, accentuating the wrinkles. "Can't say I blame him."

Fiore excused himself, shook hands again, and moved on. Rondini sidled back to the table to put more food on his plate, with Rick at his side.

"Did you catch that comment?" Rondini asked.

Rick nodded. "I did. But did it get garbled in my translation for you?"

"I don't think so. My cousin was spending time in town with someone, and it wasn't his priest."

Thanks to the wine and the lapsed time since the burial, the sound level in the room had risen, and serious faces had been replaced with normal ones and even smiles. People came over and introduced themselves to Angelo, ostensibly to pass on their condolences, but also curious to meet the *Americano* and his exotically booted interpreter. Many told him of relatives in the States, most asked how long he was going to be in Italy, and all encouraged him to see the art and architecture for which Mantova was known. He assured them he would.

Rondini was showing fatigue from the trip, despite sleeping on a real bed in his jet. "How long do you think we should stay?" he asked Rick during a break in the action. "You know the local customs."

"People are starting to leave, and Livia knows you've been traveling all night, so I think you can head back whenever you want. You'll be seeing her again, of course?"

"She wanted to have lunch tomorrow at a restaurant near here. I agreed but said I was inviting them. You'll need to be there since her husband hardly speaks any English."

They said their good-byes. Outside, Marco was leaning against the car and scanning the low horizon. Clouds still covered the sky but in a less-menacing manner, and the wind had died down to a light but chilling breeze off the river. When he saw Rick and Rondini approaching, he bent down and opened the rear door for his employer.

"Back to the hotel, Mr. Rondini?"

"Yes, Marco, but we're going to make a stop on the way. I need to check out a piece of land that may be for sale."

Rick noticed the bewildered look on the driver's face, and could almost hear the gears working in the man's head. The rich American comes back to his birthplace for a funeral and finds a parcel of land for sale. What better way to return to one's roots than to buy land where they were once planted? It made sense to Rick, but it might be the farthest thing from Angelo's mind.

"Go out to the road and turn left, toward the river." Rondini got into the Mercedes, followed by Rick and the driver. The car drove slowly along the driveway and stopped momentarily before turning onto the road. Fences lined both sides of the pavement, those on the left marked periodically with the R of the Rondini property. Just as the water became visible, Rondini tapped Marco on the shoulder.

"Pull up at that gate and we'll get out. I always like to walk when I'm looking at a property."

The driver obliged, slowing to a stop. The metal gate was a narrow one, opening on a path rather than a road. Farm equipment would have to get into this field from another direction, though it appeared that this part of the farm had not seen a tractor, or any other machinery, in some time. The ground was covered with a green stubble that looked like it was attempting to grow back after its last cutting. Perpendicular to the path, dirt rows ran between the green in the direction of the river, their lines blocked here and there by scraggly brown weeds.

Rondini emerged from the back seat, adjusted his glasses, and looked in all directions. He pulled the belt of his overcoat around him after a cold gust tried to force it open.

"Not exactly like the wind off Lake Michigan, though it's trying." The gate was closed but not locked. Rondini pulled the latch and it swung open with a low creak. "Let's check it out, Montoya." The two men walked through the gate into the field while the driver leaned against his car and watched. His face showed concern, which Rick assumed was worry that mud might find its way to the floor of his immaculate Mercedes.

As Rondini's eyes moved, he spoke. "The main factor, Montoya, is location, depending on what kind of business they might put here. If it's a factory, there has to be easy access to the highway to get the product out, and that road where we're parked could be widened to accommodate the traffic. If they're selling, the public has to have a way to get in, so the same concerns. Depending on what you're selling, you have to be close to your market. Is this place near enough to Mantova to get people here if they put up some mega-store? I don't know. You'd need a marketing study of the demographic. Or is there enough of a rural population to support a business here? The idea that you build it and they will come is crap. You'd have to know what you can expect before anyone would sink a dime into construction."

Rondini was in his element, making Rick feel like a young resident following a veteran doctor on his hospital rounds. They turned to the right and walked down between rows of dormant plants toward the river. The sky had darkened to a color that signaled a change in weather, but Rondini was oblivious to the possibility of getting wet.

"Assuming electricity, sewerage, and water are not a problem, this could work. Its flatness makes it very easy to build on. But there are too many questions that I can't answer. Look how scenic the river is from here."

They had reached the end of the row and ascended a small hill. Through breaks in the trees they could see the waters of the Mincio, its width beginning to open as it flowed toward the city.

"I can see why my cousin liked to come here. I've never been into fishing, or for that matter any pastime other than golf, and I only play it for the business contacts. But somehow, looking at that water, I get it. Ironic, isn't it, that it's here that he met his end? Or perhaps poetic is the right word. Come on, let's get back. I've done what Livia asked, but if I were her, I'd keep it as farmland."

As they turned to retrace their steps, Rick noticed, through a break in the trees, a small dock jutting into the river. It was at the end of the road where the car was stopped. Rondini didn't spot it, and Rick said nothing. Nor did he mention a pickup truck that was idling at the far end of the field on the opposite side of the road. It was too far away for Rick to make out the face of the driver, and as he was trying to do just that, the person drove slowly through the field and out of view.

The return drive was mostly silent except for a few drops of rain that hit the roof of the car. Rondini went back to staring out the window at the passing scenery, deep in thought. Rick mused about what little he had garnered from talking to the people at Livia's place, and decided it didn't amount to much. Roberto Rondini had lost interest in running his *latteria*, and spent perhaps most of his time in town. Did the widower have someone on the side in Mantova? The most curious tidbit was the sale of the acreage they had just surveyed. Was there a connection between that sale—or non sale—and his demise? The dock he'd seen through the trees—could it be where the murder took place? If it was, it couldn't be any closer to the plot of land. It wasn't much, but it was all he had to go on. Perhaps some of it would click with Inspector Crispi.

It was midafternoon when they walked into the lobby of the hotel.

"I'm going to check in with Lexi to see what's going on in Chicago, then get some quick shut-eye. I'll meet you down here in an hour. We're going to make a visit to the house of Mantegna."

"The painter."

"Good for you, Language Man. You don't just read dictionaries. I did some research on him and thought it would be fun to see where he lived before we see his masterpiece tomorrow. I should say Lexi did the research and I read it. The house is now a museum. You've got something to do until then?"

"I'll go talk to the inspector."

"Of course. You have things to tell him."

The woman at the front desk armed him with a map marked with a yellow highlighter to show him the route, insisting it would take no more than ten minutes. He was ready for a walk; it would give him a chance to get the feel of the town that peering from car windows couldn't provide. He could also try to plot a route for his morning run. He walked briskly, breathing in the heavy humidity in the air and enjoying the moisture on his skin. Fall was the best time of year in all the places he'd lived on both sides of the Atlantic. In New Mexico it meant aspens turning yellow on the mountains, and in Italy it marked the end of the harvest and meals with mushrooms and truffles. The street crossed the canal that had once been a defensive barrier, a piece of Venice dropped into a corner of Lombardy. He was now in the oldest section of Mantova, and the street narrowed accordingly before bursting into the open space of the Piazza delle Erbe that ran along the side of San'tAndrea, where they'd been for the funeral. The daily market held in the square had folded up and moved on hours earlier. Now its only inhabitants were two women pushing baby carriages.

Passing under an arch between buildings, Rick looked up to see a small door surrounded by a metal cage clinging high up on the side of an ancient tower. He'd seen them in other cities, a place of cruel punishment for criminals or enemies of those in power. It crossed his mind to ask Inspector Crispi if the police were still putting it to use, but the man had seemed humorless when he stopped Rick in the church. Probably not a good idea.

He turned the corner and found himself at one end of the magnificent Piazza Sordello. The city had banned vehicles from its cobblestones, keeping the long square—at least visually—in the golden age of the Gonzaga dynasty. The Palazzo Ducale, home of the dukes, ran along most of one side. Across from it was the cathedral which looked drab compared to Sant'Andrea—Marco the driver had been correct about it playing second fiddle to the more famous church. Immediately on Rick's right, at the corner, was the police station. It was simple to spot the *questura* in any city, since armed police were always stationed in front, and Mantova was no exception. He walked to the entrance and pushed through the doors.

Rick was expected. A uniformed corporal glanced at his identification and immediately took him up a set of steps to the second floor. Halfway down a drab corridor he tapped on a partially open door and looked in.

"*Ispettore? E' arrivato Signor Montoya.*"

The inspector ignored the policeman, but came around his desk and shook Rick's hand.

"Thank you for coming in, Signor Montoya. Please sit down."

Rick had not had much time in the dark church to size up the inspector, but he could see now that the man was, in his appearance, the complete opposite of his Uncle Piero. Crispi's unshaven face was not an attempt to be fashionable, but simply the result of not seeing a razor for too long. His suit looked to be a size large, but he was on his way to filling it. The hair needed cutting and combing, falling down on both sides of his forehead. At least his shoes were shined. Rick wondered how well Piero knew the guy.

"I hope I can be of help, Inspector."

"So do I," answered Crispi as they both sat.

"Perhaps you could begin by telling me what you know about Roberto Rondini's death. At the gathering I just came from, all I found out was that he drowned. No one said anything about foul play."

"I wouldn't expect his daughter to say something. I told her we were investigating, but she got it in her head that because of the nature of the death, such an investigation is a required formality. She dismissed any possibility other than a tragic accident." He paused. "The autopsy showed that Signor Rondini had a blow to the head, but that his death was by drowning. The medical examiner surmised that the head trauma caused him to lose consciousness, at which time he fell into the river and subsequently drowned. He frequently went fishing early in the morning, and kept a boat tied up at the river at one corner of his farm. We went to the dock and found blood stains on the wood. Given the fact that the dock was slippery from the morning mist, it is possible that he did indeed slip, lose his balance, hit his head, and fall into the water. He was in good physical health, but he was in his late sixties, so it could have happened that way."

"But you're not so sure."

"The wound analysis was inconclusive, the result of spending too much time in the water. The medical examiner could not say for sure if it was made only by impact on the dock, or if he was struck with something and then the head hit the wood, leaving the traces of blood. Or the head could have been purposely pressed to the dock to make it look like he slipped, after which he was pushed, unconscious, into the water to drown."

To Rick it seemed like thin gruel to justify the launch of an investigation, and he said so.

Crispi did not appear to be annoyed by his visitor's frankness. Nor was he pleased. The man was so lacking in emotion that he almost seemed to be on tranquilizers. His neutral expression never changed, including the eyes, which were locked on Rick's.

"Perhaps. But Signor Rondini was not universally loved. That fact was not featured at the funeral, as we both know, and I suspect it didn't come up in the events afterward. But he had that reputation." He waited for Rick to respond, and when he didn't, Crispi continued. "So far I have told you a great deal. Did you manage to glean anything from your contacts with the family that you would care to share?"

Rick couldn't decide if he liked Crispi or not. After this initial conversation the jury was still out, and it might stay out for a while.

"There was a neighbor, the man who owns the farm adjoining the Rondini property. Emilio Fiore, if I remember correctly. He freely admitted that he and the deceased did not always get along. He mentioned a plot of land that Rondini owned and was thinking of selling for development, a sale which he strongly opposed, partly because he wanted to buy it himself."

Crispi's eyebrows furrowed, not a radical change in his demeanor, but at least it was something. "I think I remember reading about it in the *Gazzetta*." His eyes strayed to the ceiling as he tried to recall. "A factory, was it? Or a furniture chain store? That kind of development happens frequently around here, and there are always those who oppose it. They want to keep the land pristine, either dotted with cattle or waving with corn."

"That would characterize this man Fiore."

The phone on the desk rang and Crispi leaned over to answer it. Rick gestured to ask if he should step out, but the inspector shook his head. While the policeman talked, Rick got to his feet and walked to the window. The office looked out over a rectangular courtyard that under previous owners may have been filled with grass and flowers, but now was paved and stuffed with police vehicles. The rest of the room was what Rick had seen before in the offices of other police stations, though more orderly than most. Crispi's desk was a model of neatness: a shelf behind it held books in a straight row, and a healthy potted plant was perfectly centered on the windowsill. Quite a contrast with the man's appearance. As Rick began studying the still-threatening sky, Crispi hung up the phone.

"Where were we? You were telling me about Rondini's neighbor?"

"Right," said Rick. "Fiore also mentioned that the deceased had been spending very little time on his dairy farm. Mostly he was here in town, where he had an apartment. The farm manager, Carlo Zucari, said the same thing."

"I spoke to Zucari."

"Fiore made an off-hand comment which I took to mean that Rondini had a lady friend of some sort here in town, which was why he was always here."

Inspector Crispi leaned forward and pulled a folder from the neat stack. "I know about her. Letizia Bentivoglio is her name. Younger than Rondini, as one might expect. I'm going to interview her this afternoon."

"So the word on her was already around."

"This is not Rome, Signor Montoya—there are few secrets here." He paused to let his bit of wisdom sink in. "What about the daughter, Signora Guarino?"

"I only exchanged pleasantries with her. But I spoke briefly with her husband."

"Yes, Francesco Guarino. I met him only in passing, but I got the sense that it is his wife who makes the decisions in that family. She will inherit the farm, of course."

"But Guarino could take over running it, I would assume. He's now a cheese inspector, so I would imagine he has the expertise."

Crispi declined to comment on Rick's assumption. "You said you met the manager. Any words of interest from him? He couldn't tell me much. It was he who took me to the dock where Rondini met his fate."

"If you've talked to all these people, Inspector, why have you asked me to help you?"

Crispi was unfazed. "A valid point. I thought your proximity to the family could yield some valuable information that they would be reluctant to pass to the authorities. They may let their guard down when around you and your employer. Already you have discovered the issue of the possible land sale. There may be nothing there, but it is worth exploring." He didn't try to hide a glance at his watch. "Signor Montoya, as I told you, I have made an appointment to interview Signora Bentivoglio. Thank you again for coming in." He rose and extended his hand. His face had not changed.

Later, as Rick walked back to the hotel, he tried to analyze his mixed feelings about the policeman. *Simpatico*, Crispi was not, but more importantly, did he know what he was doing? Did he even have enough evidence to warrant a police investigation? Maybe the guy just had a hunch, or someone had put a bug in his ear.

Rick had a little time before meeting Rondini, and when he got to the bridge over the canal he stopped to enjoy the view. Water ran happily under the bridge on its way to the lake, oblivious to the dark skies above, that could soon swell the flow into a torrent. All along it, the backs of stone houses were in a colorful competition for how many red and white geraniums could be packed into their window boxes. He pulled out his phone to take a picture, but decided against it. Instead, he hit some buttons and held it to his ear. It was answered after two rings.

"I thought you'd be calling," said Commissario Piero Fontana. "You have met Crispi?"

"Just got out of a meeting with him at the *questura*."

"And you are puzzled. That is the usual reaction people have when they first meet him. It was mine. But let me tell you a bit about the inspector."

"Please do, Zio." Rick leaned on the stone railing and spotted some tiny fish working against the current. "I have a few minutes before I must go back to work for my employer."

"Crispi doesn't look it at first, Riccardo, but he is one of the more brilliant police minds I have encountered. I was his supervisor when he was on a case here in Rome several years ago, and while it took me a good while to understand him, I came away impressed. I won't go into the particulars of the case now, I'll save that for some time when we dine together, but suffice to say it was a complicated one. He sorted out all the details and brought it to a successful conclusion."

"If he is so brilliant, Zio, how is it that he's only an inspector in Mantova?"

"It is always charming, dear nephew, when you drop the Italian subtlety and take on your American directness. But surely you have already discovered the answer to your question. It's very simple, really. Crispi does not interact well with his colleagues, and, something unusual in us Italians, he is not adept at office politics. In a word, he drives his co-workers and supervisors *pazzo*. And that is not the way to advance in any Italian bureaucracy, including the *Polizia dello Stato*."

Since Piero said he had supervised the inspector, Rick assumed that his uncle was one of those driven crazy. "But he's competent, Uncle?"

"More than competent."

"And honest."

"In my experience, yes."

"That's good enough for me. And I have an advantage over his fellow policemen: I don't have to work with him permanently."

"Indeed."

"Perhaps I can get him to smile."

"I wouldn't bet on it."

Chapter Four

Inspector Crispi paused on the street and looked up at the windows of the building. Letizia Bentivoglio lived in a walk-up apartment at the eastern edge of the city's ancient center. At one time it had been the residence of one well-to-do family, but today the building was divided into three rentals, hers being the one on the top floor. The advantage was that she had an unencumbered view of the lake from her back windows, since only a parking lot and some grass separated the building from the water. The disadvantage was the stair climb to reach it, but when her door opened, Crispi could see that this was not an issue for the woman, who looked to be the picture of health. She was about forty-five, her hair color appeared natural, and the figure under the jeans and sweater was slim. He assumed that the initial attraction to her for the deceased Roberto Rondini was the obvious one, but wondered if there might be something else. That could come out in the interview, but at the moment, Crispi's main interest was what happened in the period before the death.

"I'm glad you called on my day off. I wouldn't have wanted a policeman showing up at the office."

She led the way into the small living room and took a seat in one of its two chairs. An empty cup perched on the side table next to it, made him wonder if she would offer him something. He hoped not, since it would only waste time. He made a fast assessment of the surroundings to confirm what he already assumed. The wear on the furniture and the type of decorations in the room indicated that she had been living alone for some time, perhaps her entire adult life. There were no masculine touches to be seen; everything had an aura of neatness and regularity. What would have caused a woman like this to take up with an older man? There could be a dozen reasons, but likely none had any bearing on the case. He had no cause to include her as a suspect, at least up to this point.

"Where do you work?" He knew the answer, and she knew he knew, but it was an easy way to begin the interview.

"The large farm equipment company just south of the city. That's how I met Roberto. He came in one day with his farm manager because they needed a new cattle truck and some other machinery. I do the paperwork for our sales. I'd expected that once he'd made the decision on what he wanted he'd send Carlo—that's his manager—to deal with the details, but instead he came back himself. We became friends. It turned out that he had an apartment in town very close to mine, so we used to have dinner a few times a week. Sometimes I'd make dinner here, but mostly he'd take me out. He liked to go to nice places."

It was more information than the question deserved. She was ready to talk, so he decided to let her do so.

"Tell me about Signor Rondini."

Her sigh was close to a shudder. "He was not what most people thought of him. Oh, I know you're wondering how I know what people thought of him, but it's because he told me. He laughed about it. But to me he was kind and generous, always. He was lonely after his wife died several years ago, and I could see it when I met him that day. I could sense it. He needed companionship, which is something he didn't get from his family, and he could talk to me."

"When did you see him last?"

She looked out the window at the darkening sky, thinking

about an answer, but he knew she had to have been ready for the question.

"The night before the…" Her lips trembled almost imperceptibly. "The night before, we had dinner here."

"Did he seem any different from your previous meetings?"

She looked at the cup next to her, and he thought she might get up to fill it. Instead she pondered the question while Crispi waited.

"Not different from how he'd been for the last few weeks. About a month ago, when he began considering the sale of some property, he was surprised to find that people were against it. Not just his manager, he'd expected that, but people he'd never met. He thought it was none of their business and brushed it off as nothing, but I could tell he was bothered by it. I was the only one who could see this side of him. To everyone else he was just someone who had money and wanted to make more of it. He wasn't like that, Inspector."

She got up, walked stiffly to the window, and stared out across the water. Her hands were clasped tightly and pressed against her chest.

"Also in the last few months," she continued, "he did a lot of thinking about his father."

"I don't understand."

She continued looking at the lake. Did she know that the body was discovered on the shore almost within view of her window?

"I suspect it had something to do with the anniversary of his father's death. Twenty years ago the man had died when he was the age Roberto was about to reach. I suppose it's natural to think about those things. He talked about what his father had done in his lifetime and compared it to his own accomplishments."

"Did he tell you what were his conclusions?"

She didn't answer immediately. "No. No, he didn't. Perhaps he didn't come to any. Contemplating one's mortality is never easy, I suppose. And just a few weeks before his own death, Roberto went to a funeral, which made him even more depressed. Apparently, the family either didn't know who Roberto was, or if they did, they didn't think he should have appeared at the funeral. It's difficult enough when friends your own age start dying...."

Crispi looked at his watch and decided it was time to wrap up the interview.

"Signora Bentivoglio, is there anything that would lead you to believe that his death was not an accident?"

She turned quickly. "It was not an accident, Inspector."

"You seem very sure."

"Roberto had been going fishing in the same place for years, even decades. As he often told me, he had his routine, it was a comfort to him. Always arriving at the same time, no matter the weather, always with the same fishing pole; he even fished in the same place along the river. Some spot only he knew, where he claimed the big fish hid. It was a joke with us. He said he couldn't tell me where it was, since I might sell the secret to someone." A smile appeared on her face for the first time, but it disappeared quickly. "No, Inspector, he didn't have an accident."

Crispi didn't point out that accidents could happen to anyone, especially at Rondini's age. He had seen this reaction before in people close to victims—denial that fate could have simply done its work.

"If it wasn't an accident, who could be responsible? Did he ever talk about enemies he had? Someone who could want him dead?"

She didn't try to hide her agitation. "As you already know, Inspector, he was not well liked. If such dislike could reach the point of murder, I have no way of knowing. I sensed that he and Carlo had reached an understanding. Neither liked the other, but Roberto trusted Carlo and let him run things. There was a neighbor he didn't get along with. I think the man wanted to buy that piece of land. The price might have been right, but Roberto had no intention of selling it to the man. As far as his daughter, I think their relationship was normal, but he said a few times how her husband was weak."

"Weak?"

"Well, you know, not a strong personality like Roberto. He looked down on people he thought had no backbone. How his son-in-law felt about him, I have no idea. I never met him. Nor his daughter, for that matter."

Crispi rubbed a hand across the stubble of his chin, trying to decide whether to ask Signora Bentivoglio an obvious question: Why had Rondini, a widower many years removed from the mourning period, not carried on openly with the woman? He needed female companionship and she was certainly respectable, so why treat her like a mistress? That was the way the family viewed her, it seemed, since she was not at any of the events connected with the funeral. No, better to get an answer from someone else; the question would be too painful for her right now. He could pose it to her later, if needed, but likely would not. It was simply not important to the investigation. He got to his feet.

"You are back at work tomorrow, Signora?"

"Yes." She turned from the window. "We open at seven, and often our clientele is outside waiting. Farmers keep early hours."

Just like fisherman, Crispi thought.

"There is some debate," said Marco, "as to whether Andrea Mantegna in fact designed his own palazzo, but regardless of who did, it remains a spectacular structure. The combination of the circle and the square, which you see so much in the positioning of figures in Renaissance painting, is utilized here in a simple but powerful way."

The driver, along with Rick, Rondini, and Lexi, stood on the damp stones of the Casa Mantegna's open courtyard looking upward. The four sides of the building's outer shell framed the circular opening to a clouded sky. From it, an almost invisible mist of rain fell on their faces. The walls surrounding the open space were an austere brick, broken by doors leading to the inner rooms. Everything about the building, from the drab outside to the floor plan, was rigidly geometric.

"Not exactly warm and inviting," said Rondini, "but it might be better on a sunny day. The circle in the square is intriguing, I have to admit."

Lexi pointed at the curved walls. "My image of Italian Renaissance architecture was always ornate marble and rounded columns, in the classical tradition. This is not like that at all. The four doors are framed classically, and the sun design on the stone floor adds something, but the rest is quite plain."

"Perhaps Mantegna himself was a rather plain guy," said Rick. He looked through one of the open doors into one of the rooms of the gallery. "The exhibit inside doesn't look very plain."

Swaths of bright color filled a large canvas on the wall opposite the door. Angelo scowled. "I can find better abstract works in Chicago; that's not what I came to Italy to see. Lexi, you and Marco go in and check it out. I need to talk to Language Man here."

Lexi and the driver exchanged looks and walked through the door.

"Tell me what happened with the cop," Angelo said, once the other two were inside. "He really thinks my cousin was murdered?"

"Yes, he does." Rick explained the head injury that preceded the drowning, and Crispi's suspicion that it was not caused by a fall.

"Who does he think could have done it?"

"I know you want me to be frank. Am I correct?"

"You better be."

"Well, Mr. Rondini, it appears that your cousin was not universally loved. Whether that was enough for someone to do him in remains to be seen, but there is no lack of people who could be considered suspects. It might be better to begin with who could have gained from not having your cousin around. And that starts, unfortunately, with his daughter and her husband. They inherit the farm."

Rondini's expression remained the same. "Makes sense. Go on."

"The manager of the farm, Zucari, could be out of a job if Livia's husband takes over running the operation and wants to be more hands-on than your cousin was. Zucari didn't agree with selling the plot, as Livia told you, but that doesn't appear to be a big deal. Then there is that neighbor, Emilio Fiore."

"The drunk."

"The one who had too much wine, yes. He even admitted to us that he didn't get along with Roberto Rondini, and was very much against him selling that property for development. In my mind, he's the strongest suspect."

"It all seems a touch weak to build a murder case, don't you think? But if he was killed, maybe Roberto was just mugged by someone who knew he went fishing every morning. It happens all the time in Chicago."

"The inspector didn't mention if his wallet was missing, and I think he would have."

Rondini squinted at Rick. "You think this guy knows what he's doing?"

"I would have had my doubts if I hadn't spoken to my uncle afterward. He told me Crispi is a first-class policeman, and I can assure you my uncle would have said so if it were the other way around."

They looked upward at the same time. The small drops were beginning to get bigger, but the rain felt good on their faces.

"Montoya, after hearing all this I feel like I don't know enough about my cousin and the rest of the family. We need to find out more, but the kind of questions I have now I wouldn't want to ask Livia. See what you can get from the cop. By the way, what about Roberto's friend in town? Did he mention her?"

"He was on his way to interview her."

The thought of his cousin's extra-curricular activities made Rondini smile. He looked over to see Lexi and the driver come back through the doorway into the courtyard.

"A local artist on her way up," she said, "or trying to. Nothing very original."

Rondini was not paying attention. "Marco, I need to find out more about my family. Is there some kind of genealogical society here that could help?"

The question startled the driver.

"I don't know about such societies, Mr. Rondini. If I were you, I would start at the *Gazzetta*. It is the oldest newspaper in Italy and I think they have…" He turned to Rick for help. "*Un archivio?*"

"Archives," Rick said.

"Yes, that's it. Perhaps you could go there, Mr. Rondini."

"You mean perhaps Language Man could go there." He looked up. "Is the car parked nearby? It's starting to rain harder."

"I found a place near the door. I'll get it unlocked so you don't get wet." Marco walked briskly toward the entrance.

"I'm surprised he didn't know about genealogy stuff," Rondini said as the driver disappeared out the door. "Don't a lot of Americans come here in search of their roots? I would think it would be something a guy who works with tourists would know. Am I right, Language Man?"

"Yes and no. The vast majority of Americans of Italian descent trace their roots to the south, people who left to escape poverty in what has always been the least developed area of Italy. During the time of the great migrations, at the end of the nineteenth and the beginning of the twentieth centuries, the boats left from Naples and Palermo. Here in the north it was relatively prosperous, certainly relative to the *mezzogiorno*, as they call the south. So there was less emigration from around the northeast. It's still one of the richest areas of Italy—actually of Europe."

"It makes me wonder why my parents left here. They never talked much about it, and by the time I was curious about it, they were gone and I couldn't ask them." He looked at Rick and then back at Lexi. "Today's advice to both of you from an old man: ask questions now, while you can."

Lexi's expression gave Rick the idea that Rondini was acting out of character.

"We will be sure to take that advice, Mr. Rondini. But perhaps Rick can find out something at this newspaper Marco mentioned. And if needed I can get on one of those ancestry websites and find out what I can there."

When they emerged onto the sidewalk the Mercedes was waiting, Marco holding open the rear passenger door for Rondini and Lexi. Rick put his hand on the handle of the front door and noticed a paper folded under the wiper in front of his seat. He reached over to take it out.

"Were you parked illegally, Marco?" he said. "You may have a ticket."

The driver's head jerked up to look at the signs along the sidewalk. "That's impossible."

As Angelo and Lexi got settled into the back seat Rick unfolded what was more of a card than a piece of paper. The message on it, written in a crude hand with red ink and slightly blurred from the rain, was brief and to the point. He passed it to Marco, who stiffened when he read it.

"What's it say?"

Rick turned to face the back seat. "Short and sweet, Mr. Rondini. The simple translation is 'Go back to America or face the consequences.' Someone is not happy with our presence in Mantova."

Marco stared at the paper, still gripped in his hand. "What shall we do, Mr. Rondini?"

"Drive back to the hotel, of course."

Five minutes later Marco had been dismissed and the three stood in the lobby of the hotel. No words had been exchanged on the way back from the museum, making Rick suspect that Rondini did not want to say anything in the presence of the driver. That was the case.

"Does this happen often, Language Man?"

"Threatening notes?"

"Yeah. 'Yankee go home,' that kind of thing? Is this a hotbed of Communism?"

Lexi stood silently next to her boss and waited for Rick's reply. She maintained her usual stone composure.

"I'd like to say it is, but it doesn't seem likely at all. The only reason I can think of is that someone saw you out in the field and put two and two together to think you wanted to buy it."

Had Lexi not been there, he would have brought up what Inspector Crispi had said about opposition to the sale. Rick had to assume that Rondini was keeping the police involvement between him and Rick. Her next words confirmed it.

"That's the piece of property Ms. Guarino asked you to look at?"

"Yeah. But who would have known that I was going out there to see it?"

"Her husband," said Rick. "The manager of the farm. Probably other people who were there. Someone may have overheard her asking you. I don't think she was trying to keep it a secret, do you?"

"I suppose not. This reminds me of the time outside St. Louis when that group protested one of our developments, and it got ugly. Some kind of bird migration issue."

"The police took care of that without much trouble," said Lexi. "Should the local police be notified now?"

Rondini held his room keycard between two fingers and snapped it with his thumb. "Some scribbled note? I don't think so. What about you, Language Man? You're our authority on local customs, including the police."

"If it happens again, perhaps. But I'd let it go for now."

"Okay, done. I am going to my room and stay there for the night. The spread at Livia's should hold me until breakfast, but if I get hungry I'll get room service. Language Man, I want you to take Lexi to a nice restaurant and get her to talk about something other than business, if that's possible." He laughed and shuffled toward the elevator.

Rick rubbed his eyes. *That will be about as easy as teaching her to speak Italian.*

"All right," Rick said, "let's have the truth. Who are you, and what have you done with Alexis Coleman?"

Lexi's giggle was not the first of the evening, though the first since the second bottle of wine had arrived at the table. The restaurant, in the heart of Mantova, was almost full. The clientele was local and affluent, which reflected the prosperity of this part of Italy. Tables in the middle of the large dining room were each discreetly lit by a single shaded fixture which hung from the ceiling. Thanks to the reservation called in by the hotel, Rick and Lexi were ensconced in a corner booth with a view of the other diners. The atmosphere was low-key and elegant, broken only by table conversation and a barely audible classical CD.

"I like to unwind when I get off work, Rick. Don't you? I love working for Angelo, but I have to clear my mind. You must have the same thing after spending hours doing a translation, or interpreting for someone. I can't even begin to imagine how exhausting that must be. Poor dear." She reached across the small table and patted his hand.

"A translator's lot is not an easy one." He furrowed and then raised his brow. "But every so often someone like you brings a few rays of sunshine into a life of drudgery."

This night's rays included a glimmering gold pendant just visible above the top button of a silk blouse which clung perfectly to Lexi's body. As she laughed, gold hoop earrings quivered as if trying to distract him. He was not distracted. At that moment the waiter cleared away the pasta dishes and carefully placed the menu in front of each of them. She thanked him while trying unsuccessfully to wipe the smile from her face.

"You mean we're going to eat more? I have to say that the idea of ravioli filled with pumpkin sounded very strange, but I'm sure glad you talked me into it. With the butter sauce and sage, that ravioli was amazing, but it was a meal in itself."

"*Those* ravioli, my dear. I believe we each got three. If you'd had only one it would be a *raviolo*."

"I love it when you talk in tongues, Rick. This wine is also amazing, by the way."

"All the better to loosen your tongue, Lexi. I'm waiting for you to tell me more about your boss."

She pulled a face. "Okay, but first, what will we have next to eat?"

The hotel concierge had told him that one of the restaurant's specialties was a warm capon salad. Lexi admitted she'd never eaten capon, and only recalled hearing about it in Shakespearean plays—which seemed a good enough reason to try it. The waiter left with the order and Rick filled her wineglass.

"You were about to tell me more about Angelo, which you seem to call him now, when he's out of earshot. But how did you come to be working for him?"

She sipped her wine and gazed at him over the rim of the glass before setting it back down.

"Angelo Rondini is a complicated man, but I will try to simplify. Only child in an immigrant family very much committed to the American dream. He grew up in the Bronx, went to Fordham on scholarship, started at a construction firm and slowly worked his way up until getting into an argument with his boss and starting his own business. He's been burned enough times in business deals that he's very wary of people's motives. Made his money by doing things his way and making his own decisions. And you can't argue with success."

Rick held up a hand. "You don't need to return to your daytime self, Lexi. You can do this without going all serious on me."

Another giggle. "Sorry." She took more than a small sip of wine. "Angelo is difficult to work for because he has trouble trusting his staff to do the right thing, the right thing being the way he would have wanted to do it. He doesn't micromanage, he second-guesses. It drives people nuts. Some quit every few months, a few are fired."

"He seems to trust you, Lexi. He told me when he got off the plane that he never goes anywhere without you."

The grin showed a perfect row of white teeth. "He said that? How sweet. Well, Rick, we have a special relationship, thanks to Nikki."

"Nikki?"

"Nikki Rondini, his daughter."

The second courses arrived and were placed carefully in front of them on bone white plates. The dishes were as simple as the plates: a few leaves of lettuce topped by white slices of capon breast and drizzled with a vinaigrette sauce that included red raisins. Before departing, the waiter filled their glasses.

"He hasn't asked me yet if everything is tasting all right," said Lexi as she gazed at the plate.

"They don't need to do that here in Italy." Rick waited for her to pick up her fork before taking his in hand.

"This looks fantastic, Rick. Remind me again what capon is. It looks like chicken."

"It is. So what about Rondini's daughter?"

She waited to finish her first bite. "Wow. That is something. Just the right light tang in the sauce, doesn't overpower the pure taste of the capon. And it goes perfectly with this white wine. What is it again?"

He pulled it out of the bucket and checked the label. "*Oltrepó Pavese pinot grigio*. It comes from west of here, near Pavia. *Oltrepó* means the other side of the River Po. So you know his daughter?"

"Rick, you keep plying me with exotic food and drink. How can you expect me to stay on topic?"

"No one has ever accused me of plying."

"Someone should have, you're very adept at it." She took another small bite of the capon and savored it before continuing. "All right, Nikki Rondini. We were roommates our first year at Northwestern and became best of friends. Still are. She took me home one weekend, since she lived right in Chicago, and I became almost a member of the family. The summer before my senior year Angelo took me on as an intern at Rondini Enterprises. That led to a job offer when I graduated, and I ended up as his special assistant. Now let me get back to this chicken."

"Capon. You were a business major?"

"No," she said through a mouthful. "Chemistry. But Angelo said I had a knack for business, whatever that means."

"Plus he trusts you, being a member of the family and all. And Mrs. Rondini?

"She died about five years ago. Wonderful woman of Irish ancestry, so she was able to give as well as she got from Angelo. It took him more than a year to get over her passing, if one ever truly gets over that kind of loss."

"Do you have much time for a personal life, what with having to jet around the country all the time?"

She tilted her head at Rick and smiled. "That sounds like a leading question, Mr. Montoya, and one I will decline to answer. It is also not one you will hear me asking you."

His mind churned in an unsuccessful attempt to interpret her comment; he'd had too much wine.

"Fair enough. And now, since you have almost finished your *secondo*, it is time to return to the business at hand, which is the possibility of ordering something else. I understand they make an excellent banana split here."

"Rick, that's not even funny. Pour us the rest of that bottle and let's take our leave."

A few minutes later Rick was helping her on with her coat inside the door of the restaurant. They agreed that after the warmth of the restaurant the chill night air would feel good on their faces, but they did not expect what they saw on stepping outside. While they had dined, a windless cold front had parked over the city, coating everything with a light layer of snow. The flakes were still coming down softly, glimmering as they caught the rays of the streetlights and dropping silently to the ground. The street, always quiet at this late hour, was made more silent by the insulating whiteness.

"I can call a taxi," Rick said.

"Absolutely not. Look how pristine the snow is. In Chicago it turns to dirty slush even before it reaches the ground. No, we walked here and we'll walk back." She looked down to check out their footwear. "We're both dressed for it."

She took his arm and they started down the street, their boots leaving the only marks in the snow until a single car slowly passed. After two corners they emerged onto the piazza where Rick had been earlier in the day. Two police cars sat empty in front of the *questura* and a young armed policeman stood next to the door trying his best not to look cold. Many public buildings in Italy had guards; would Lexi know that it was the police station? Rick opted not to point it out.

"Rick, do you think that note on the car is really nothing to worry about?"

Perhaps she did recognize the building.

"Like I said to Mr. Rondini, I suspect it was just some silly prank, perhaps tied to the possible land sale, perhaps totally unrelated. If it happens again we'll rethink it."

"How would they know about Angelo being a developer?"

"After that sparkling phone conversation I had with you, I got online and found out all sorts of things about your boss. Anyone who has even minimal English could have done the same."

"I suppose you're right. Angelo doesn't get upset about these things. I'm sure he's sleeping like a baby now."

"And you will too, Lexi."

They had left the piazza and reached a block of covered sidewalk, its shops shuttered and dark. At the end of the street Lexi clutched Rick's arm as they stepped back into the open, noticing that the flakes were now smaller and fewer. By the time they reached the hotel the snowfall had stopped. They stamped their feet on the mat outside and pushed through the doors.

"I am in the habit of taking a run every morning." Rick brushed the snow from his hair and coat while Lexi did the same. "But I don't think the streets will be cleared by tomorrow. I doubt if the city of Mantova has much snow-removal infrastructure."

Lexi brushed a final bit of snow from his shoulder. "Don't be a wuss, Rick. I run every day in Chicago, no matter what the weather."

A picture of Lexi Coleman in running tights formed in his head. "How about a nightcap in the bar to warm us after the long march across the Lombard tundra?"

"I'd love to, but I have to go up and check the messages that piled up while we were enjoying our capon. Oh, I remembered where I'd read about capon. Jaques' monologue in *As You Like It* about all the world being a stage. One of the ages of man is…" She closed her eyes tightly as she thought. "The justice, wasn't it? 'In fair round belly, with a good capon lined.' That's us tonight, even the round belly part."

"I'm impressed that a chemistry major would remember that."

"My minor was English Lit." She kissed two fingers and touched them to Rick's lips. "Thank you for a wonderful dinner, Rick." She walked to the elevator while he watched.

He hadn't thought about Betta the entire evening.

Chapter Five

Rick chose his steps with care, trying to avoid the few ice patches left on the sidewalk from the previous evening. He could see his breath, but in the last hour the temperature had climbed enough to begin to melt the snow. With no clouds, the sunshine would make quick work of it. It was turning into a pleasant morning, but he was annoyed nonetheless. If he'd not been on a job, he would have taken his morning run, snow and ice or not, but the risk of twisting an ankle or worse was not worth taking when he was on Rondini's payroll. He tried not to think what Lexi would say when she found out he'd skipped the run. At least the newspaper office was close to the hotel. Some of the sidewalks had been cleared and others were in the process. Either the Mantovani were fastidious about the walkways in front of their homes or there was a city ordinance that required them to be. He reached the corner, crossed a busy street at the light, and came to the entrance to *La Gazzetta di Mantova*.

The building was not what he expected—the oldest newspaper in Italy was housed in what had to be the city's most modern building. Steel, glass, and sharp edges caught the rays of the morning sun and bounced them off dripping tree branches and the cars driving by. The glass door of the main entrance was marked with the newspaper name. Underneath, in a smaller font, was a simple *Fondata nel 1664*. No big deal.

He pushed the door and entered an open space, its only furniture a tall dark desk behind which a woman sat on a stool. A telephone and laptop were lined up neatly in front of her on the wood surface. She looked up from her screen and smiled at Rick.

"*Desidera?*"

In this context the word meant, simply, "Can I help you?" But since it was a form of the verb "to desire," Rick always found it a wonderfully Italian way to say something so mundane.

"*Buon giorno.* I am doing some family genealogical research. Is it possible to have access to your archives?"

"Of course. Just sign in here." She turned a clipboard in his direction and slid it across. "And if you could give me your identification, please?" She pulled a badge from beneath the table and put it next to the clipboard as Rick wrote. He finished writing, passed his ID to her, and clipped the badge to his coat collar.

"Take the elevator to the basement and follow the signs. Dottor da Feltre will help you."

When he got to the basement, signs for the *archivio* took him down a long corridor to a set of glass doors. The ceiling was low, giving it the feeling of a crypt, which would be appropriate for a place where ancient texts were kept. The lighting was dim, in contrast with the brightness of the atrium just one story above. Rick pushed open the door and once again was surprised. He'd expected rows of shelves, extending deeply into the basement, on which editions of the *Gazzetta* would be bound and stacked, their browned pages reaching back centuries. Instead, two cubicles, each with a chair and computer, were positioned against one wall. Ahead, three imposing doors were marked with the warning: No admittance to unauthorized persons. Unlike the corridor, the room was bright with the light of fixtures set into the ceiling. On the side opposite the cubicles a man sat hunched over the morning's edition. The newspaper was the only item on his desk except for a nameplate, its letters carved from a wood block: VITTORINO DA FELTRE.

The man looked up from his paper when Rick pushed open the glass door. Only a green eyeshade was lacking to give him the central casting image of an archivist: thinning gray hair, thick glasses, and a wrinkled shirt and tie. Rick was disappointed to find that the fingers were not stained with newsprint.

"You lost?"

"Not if these are the archives," Rick answered.

The eyes widened, their outlines blurred through the glasses. "Really?" He closed the newspaper and pushed it to one side of the desk. "I haven't had anyone in here in a week. And he was looking for the boiler room. What are you searching for?" He took off his glasses, pulled a dirty handkerchief from a jacket pocket, and began to clean them while squinting at Rick.

"Background on the Rondini family."

The glasses were replaced. "The guy who just died." He tapped the newspaper in front of him. "I read the paper pretty closely every day. You a reporter? You don't look familiar. Not that the reporters come down here much. They do their research online." He raised his eyes and pointed to the upper floors.

"I'm not a reporter. Is everything you have online?"

"No, not everything, only back to 1875. The older stuff is in there." He pointed his chin toward the doors along the back wall. "You need anything before 1875?"

"I wouldn't think so," said Rick.

"If you do, let me know. Just turn on one of those computers and you're into our system. There's an instruction sheet in each cubicle on how to get in and do a search. By word, dates, whatever. It's pretty easy. There's a printer if you need to make copies, but if you do a lot of them, I'll need to charge you. There's paper if you want to make notes." It was an instructional speech recited by rote. When he finished, the man studied Rick for a few moments, decided that this visitor would not be a problem, and returned to his newspaper.

Rick followed the instructions and quickly found the obituary of Roberto Rondini. It had nothing unexpected, but he took notes on the basics anyway. Son of Enzo and Pina Rondini, long deceased, husband of Berta Rondini, who died four years earlier. Daughter Livia Rondini Guarino. A cousin, Angelo Rondini, lived in America. Owner of the Rondini dairy farm and cheese producer. Italian obituaries, he noted, were considerably shorter than the ones he remembered reading in the *Albuquerque Journal*. There was a photograph which showed more than a strong resemblance to Cousin Angelo. Further searches brought up passing mentions of Roberto Rondini buried inside news stories, mostly related to the dairy industry or the associations of cheese producers. Rick got the sense that his participation in such groups was minimal. Not so with the local fishing club, of which the deceased was active to the point of serving as an officer. The man knew his priorities. Fishing was apparently considered a sport by the newspaper, since a story about the fishing association election appeared in the back pages of the sports section, after all the soccer news. In the same election in which Rondini had been voted onto the board, the previous president resigned from it. Probably not much there, Rick concluded, but worth mentioning to Crispi. He copied down the name of the disgruntled fisherman: Sandro Bastoncini.

Next, he searched Livia and Francesco Guarino. Of Roberto's daughter there was almost no mention, other than her marriage to Francesco. For the husband, Rick found numerous articles in connection with the Parmigiano-Reggiano Consortium, mostly participation in industry meetings or boards involved with production standards. Francesco was a bureaucrat.

It was in a previous Rondini generation that things got interesting.

Enzo Rondini, the father of the deceased, had been a prominent politician in his day, but his prominence had been gained without the support of the *Gazzetta*. From the selection of stories and the tone of the reporting, it was clear that the newspaper had it in for the man. First mention was of Enzo as a student activist, in what the paper considered the wrong political party. His initial foray into politics was on the campaign of a city councilman, then as part of the man's staff when the election was successful. Enzo steadily moved up and eventually gained elective office himself. Rick scrolled quickly through the pages, finding one article after another which insinuated shady dealings, or out-and-out corruption. If the stories were to be believed, Enzo Rondini had used his political clout to go from being a small-time farmer to owning large tracts of land. One of the losers had been a farmer who'd fallen on bad times, been unable to pay his taxes, and had his land confiscated. When it was put up for sale, it was Rondini who managed to put in the winning bid, something the paper did not believe was by chance. On another occasion, posters of a political opponent had disappeared from the walls of the city, with suspicion placed on Rondini's campaign workers. No one was ever charged. The newspaper finally was successful in thwarting his political career when he lost an attempt to get into the national parliament. At that point Enzo Rondini retired from politics and concentrated his efforts on making money from cheese. The paper, still showing animosity, covered allegations that Rondini had bribed dairy inspectors, but Rick could find nothing to show he was ever charged.

Rick looked at the clock on the wall and pushed back his chair. One thing was sure, the *Gazzetta di Mantova* and Enzo Rondini did not get along. But was it something personal between an editor and Rondini? Or could it simply have been a tiny local skirmish in the national political war of that time between the Christian Democrats and the Communists? Hard to know. He reluctantly turned off the computer and got to his feet.

The archivist looked up from the sports pages. "Find what you needed?"

"I found quite a bit. But I'll have to come back."

"You don't need a reservation."

The horse showed impatience, its face lowered and the hoof of one muscular leg raised slightly from the ground. The groom had a hand on the saddle, his expression showing no concern as he chatted with a friend standing next to him. Two large dogs stood next to the horse, tense and ready to jump if the huge white animal next to them showed any more signs of aggression. The animals were more excited than their human masters; they knew they would soon be bounding over the flat fields of Lombardy, the wind in their faces and the smell of the countryside surging into their lungs. It was what they enjoyed most. It was the day of the hunt.

"Bottom line," Rick said, "if what I read is to be believed, your Uncle Enzo was no angel."

Angelo kept his eyes on Mantegna's hunting party for a few more seconds, then craned his neck to study the work on the ceiling. A peacock and several winged *putti*, framed by blue sky and clouds, looked down with curiosity at the group standing in the center of the square room. The uniformed museum guard stood to one side. He worked in the most famous collection of art in the city, but he kept his eyes on the visitors, not the walls.

"It sounds like he might have broken a few rules, Language Man. Sometimes you have to do that to make it in this world. I wonder if any of that was passed on to my cousin, either through the genes or in the upbringing. I've often thought about that with my parents. They were simple, hard-working people, your classic immigrants. I wouldn't call them overly ambitious; they just wanted the best for me. And look how I turned out. I couldn't have been more different."

"You turned out well, Mr. Rondini," said Lexi.

"I bent the rules a few times, Lexi, and as you well know, I've made a good number of enemies." Angelo was looking now at the court scene, the seated Ludovico Gonzaga surrounded by family and courtiers. A trusted aide was whispering something in the duke's ear. "Look at this guy. You don't think he stayed in power by following all the rules, do you? My Uncle Enzo was just following the local customs."

"We should be on our way if you want to go back to the hotel before meeting your niece for lunch, Mr. Rondini."

The Lexi of business hours had returned, without so much as an acknowledgment to Rick that she'd ever been away. On the way to the museum she had sat in the back seat and continued briefing her boss on issues from the home office in Chicago uncovered during the night. Rick wondered if she'd gotten any sleep, not that her appearance indicated it. Quite the contrary.

A few minutes later they had descended into the courtyard where Marco and the car were waiting.

"You enjoyed the castle, Signor Rondini?"

"Immensely, Marco, and they saved the best for last."

"I never tire of seeing those walls."

"I should have asked you to come in with us. Next time." He looked up at the castle stone. "I wonder if the Gonzagas felt cooped up in this place."

"Mr. Rondini, we really must—"

"I know, Lexi. We'll drop you at the hotel so you can get back to work. That's really why you're in such a hurry, isn't it? You can get to your computer and work while Language Man and I go off to have a leisurely lunch, Italian-style."

They all got into the car. Marco drove them back through the winding streets to the hotel where Rick jumped out and opened the back door for Lexi. She unfolded her long legs, stood at the curb, and bent down to look through the open door. As always, she was clutching her briefcase.

"Have a nice lunch, Mr. Rondini."

Her boss waved.

Rick said, "Lexi, don't work so hard that you forget to have something sent up to your room for lunch. You need your sustenance."

She frowned, saw that Rondini could not see her face, and gave him a wink before walking to the door of the hotel. Rick watched her go in and took her place in the back seat.

"I worry about that girl," said Rondini when the car turned onto the street that ran along the water. A few patches of snow clung to the grass where the trees provided shade, but most of it had long melted away, soaking into the ground or trickling down to the lake. "She's all business, which is one reason I have her as my assistant, but I wonder if she has any kind of social life. It's something she never talks to me about, not that it's any of my affair."

"Maybe she just wants to keep business and her private life separate."

"Could be. I've asked my daughter—they're good friends—and she tells me not to worry. Did you get bored to death having dinner with her last night?"

"Not at all. We had a nice conversation."

"Good. Perhaps there's hope for Lexi."

Angelo looked out the window as the car drove under the shadow of the castle and along the city wall before turning onto the causeway separating the Lago Superiore from the Lago di Mezzo. Once across the water, the view was of flat fields, their lines broken only by an occasional farm structure, all the way to the horizon. The restaurant was in Goito, about a dozen kilometers from Mantova. The town and the restaurant itself sat on the western side of the same river which downstream spread into the lake at Mantova. At this stretch it was less than a hundred feet wide and crossed by a two-lane bridge that gave the restaurant its name, Il Ponte. Marco dropped them at the door.

The main dining room was half full, mostly with men in casual but elegant clothing whom Rick took to be businessmen or owners of the farms and dairies in the area. The soil around Goito and Mantova was the most fertile in Italy, producing some of the finest crops in Europe and making the locals wealthy. From looking at the people sitting at the tables, and what they were dining on, one would think that Italy had no economic woes. But this was not representative of the country as a whole, not even close.

They spotted Livia Guarino at a table near the wide window that looked out over the river. Her face showed the same fatigue as the day before, as if she still had not been blessed with a good night's sleep. Her dress was dark and plain, not quite mourning attire, but close to it. She looked up and waved.

"I thought her husband was going to be here," muttered Anglo. "That's why I wanted you along to interpret."

They reached the table and Angelo, now well into the local routine, bent over to kiss his niece on both cheeks. Rick shook her hand and took the seat between them, with Angelo directly across from Livia. As soon as they were seated a waiter appeared and placed menus before them.

"I hope we aren't late, Livia," said Angelo.

"No, not at all. I just arrived."

Angelo opened the menu. "I was expecting to see Francesco."

Livia's smile tightened. "Something…*imprevisto*." She turned to Rick for help.

"Unforeseen."

"Yes, unforeseen. Thank you, Riccardo. An important meeting. When he dropped me here he asked me to send his regrets. And could you give me a ride home after lunch?"

"Of course, Livia. I'm sorry we won't see him."

She took a drink from her water glass. "He's been working too much these last few weeks. Late hours. I haven't seen enough of him." She seemed to be deciding whether to say more. Her eyes did not meet Angelo's, and now they moved to the window. "I hope you enjoy this restaurant. It was a favorite of my father. He loved the river, of course, and this being directly on it…"

And it was in its waters where he found his end, Rick thought. The Mincio would be a constant reminder to her of her father's death, but she was doing her best to associate the river with pleasant aspects of his life. Would she ever succeed?

"It is a beautiful setting, Livia," said Angelo, perhaps with the same thought in his mind. "And I'm sure the food will live up to the setting. You both will have to help me with the menu. What do you suggest, Livia?"

"It is cold outside, a good day for a risotto." She pointed to a line on Angelo's menu. "*Risotto mantecato alla salsiccia tipico goitese*. That's what I'd like. Riccardo, can you translate?"

"Risotto with the local sausage. *Mantecato*, I think, means that butter and cheese are added to make it creamy. I'll have it, too. Shall we make it three?"

Angelo agreed, and the waiter was pleased to take the order. A dry *Lambrusco Mantovano* to go with your risotto? The suggestion was accepted without hesitation.

"Uncle, I have to tell you that the police think my father was murdered." Rick and Angelo exchanged glances but said nothing. She continued, "At first I thought it was absurd. My father was not universally liked, but who would want him dead? But ever since I talked to the police it has been in my thoughts. It is not something I can talk to Francesco about, he would think I was *pazza*. I hope you don't mind that I tell you. I have nobody else I can trust."

"I'm glad you feel that way, Livia." Angelo reached across and squeezed his niece's hand. He glanced at Rick and then turned his attention back to her. "Why are you having second thoughts?"

"Just...the way he died. That he fell into the water at a place where he had been fishing for so many years. His physical condition was good for a man of his age. He would not have, uh, *scivolato*."

"Slipped," said Rick. "But do you suspect anyone?"

"I told the policeman that I could think of no one. I still can't. Unless—"

They were interrupted by the arrival of the wine. The waiter filled their glasses, set the bottle in an ice bucket on the table, and retired. After a toast, the three took sips, though Livia's was more of a gulp.

"Unless," she continued, "it had something to do with that terrible piece of land."

"The one you asked me to look at."

"Yes. What did you think, Uncle?"

Angelo took a deep breath before answering. "If it were located in America I would know exactly what to recommend, Livia, but it is more difficult here. If someone wanted to develop it they would need water, sewerage, electricity, paved roads—all those things. I don't know what the cost would be here, but I assume it could be done. If you really want to sell it, a good real estate agent…" He noticed the look on her face and let Rick translate the term. "A good real estate agent who deals in commercial properties would know if it is feasible and be able to put a market price on the land. Unless you're thinking of developing it yourself."

"I hadn't thought of that, Uncle. My inclination is to keep it and expand the farm." She took another drink of her wine. "Francesco thinks I should sell."

Rick noticed the use of "I" instead of "we." Was that significant? "Since your father died," he said, "has anyone talked to you about buying the land?"

"My husband takes care of the mail, and Francesco said that a letter came from someone who my father must have been dealing with on the possible sale of the land. I didn't read it, but Francesco said it was a note of condolences. Other people don't need to talk to me about it, I know their opinions already."

"Such as the manager?"

"Yes. Carlo thinks we could use it to expand our storage capacity, that it would pay for itself in a few years, but my father didn't want to take on the expense. My father worried that the prices of milk and cheese would drop and he would end up with a loss. That was the kind of thing they would argue about."

"It appears that my cousin was not a risk taker."

"Not just that. He didn't want to upset his routine. The dairy ran itself, under Carlo's management of course, and the money flowed in from the cheese, so why make any changes? Life was good enough for him, and of course he had his fishing. Perhaps he was right."

The risotto arrived, creamy yellow rice in low bowls, a small stack of sausage pieces in its center. A sprig of rosemary stuck out of the sausage like a feather. Strong, earthy aromas rose from each plate with tufts of steam. The waiter warned that the dishes were hot and sprinkled grated Parmigiano-Reggiano over each plate. After an exchange of the traditional *buon appetito*, they took up their forks and tasted.

"*Buon appetito* was one of the few Italian phrases my parents taught me," Angelo said. "By the time I was old enough to talk, they spoke enough English to insist it be the language of the house, though I heard them speaking Italian between themselves. Now I wish they had taught me Italian."

"It's not too late to learn, Uncle."

Angelo shook his head. "An old brain like mine? I don't think so."

Conversation paused while they ate their risotto.

The restaurant had filled, but the elegant surroundings put the diners on their best behavior and kept the noise level to a low murmur. A large truck carrying hay passed over the bridge, silently to them, thanks to the thick glass of the picture window. The color of the massive bales matched the mud that caked the wheels and mud flaps. Had it not been for the freshness of the food, the people eating their lunch might not have known they were in the heart of a gritty agricultural zone, with all the dirt and odors that go along with it.

Rick put down his fork on the now empty dish. "Is there anyone else you might suspect, assuming your father was murdered?"

"He and our neighbor—Emilio Fiore—argued frequently, but I always had the sense that it was normal since they were competitors to a certain extent. Each thought their cheese was better than the other's, kind of like two men who argued over soccer teams. And they both could be...*stizzosi?*"

Rick stepped in. "Cranky, irascible."

"I got that impression when we met him yesterday," said Angelo. "But I thought it was partly due to the wine."

"Emilio does enjoy his wine. But I can't imagine him and my father fighting. Arguing, yes, but not to the point of physically attacking each other."

As much as Rick wanted to run other suspects past her, such as her farm manager, or mention her father's lady friend, he knew he couldn't. And it was time to order a second course, since the *primi* had not been as filling as they feared, given the small portions. The waiter cleared the dishes and again set menus before them. Fortunately, the list was not long, so Rick was able to translate it quickly for Angelo, who settled on the perch with *polenta*. Livia ordered the *fiori di zucca ripieni di ricotta di bufala, menta e erba cipolina su passata di pomodoro e basilico*. Rick told Angelo that the name of the dish—zucchini flowers stuffed with ricotta, mint and spring onions over a tomato and basil puree—could prove more of a mouthful than the dish itself. Rick was last, requesting *carpaccio* with *grana padana*, and black truffles. The waiter checked the wine bottle, saw that it was still half full, and left. No hard sell.

"I don't know what to do about the land, Uncle. Francesco is anxious to sell it, but I'm not sure." Her eyes fixed on Angelo.

"There is no urgency, I assume? If I understand correctly it has stood idle for years, and could continue idle for a few years more. This is not a time, when you are grieving, to make a decision like this. Take your time."

"I'm so pleased you're saying that, it makes me feel much more tranquil. When I talk with you it's almost like talking to Babbo. That's what I called him." Again her eyes moved to the water flowing outside the window. "This would have been a good fishing day for him. He always told me that after a storm the fish were anxious to be caught."

"Did you ever go fishing with him?" Angelo asked.

She shook her head. "No, for him it was a solitary activity. He was a member of a fishing association, but when it came time to fish, he preferred to be alone. I asked him once, had I been a boy rather than a girl, if he would he have taken me out on the boat. He swore that he would have treated a son the same, but his answer was slow in coming."

"So you've never been to the dock?" After he said it, Rick worried that he'd made a mistake, but she was not bothered by the question.

"I know where it is, and I used to walk down there in the summer when I was a girl and dip my toes into the river. It is a beautiful spot. I understand why my father loved to go there."

"I'd like to see it," said Angelo.

"It's hard to find. If you continue past the lot you visited yesterday, look for a turn to the left to a narrow road. After a few bends it goes through some trees and comes out to the river."

"I'll do that before I leave." He pulled the bottle out of the ice bucket and, starting with Livia's, filled up the three glasses. Then he held up his. "We have not toasted your father, Livia. It seems a good place to do it, in one of his favorite restaurants, next to his beloved river."

Her eyes misted as she raised her glass. "To Babbo."

They tapped crystal and drank. When they had finished, the main courses arrived at the table.

Portions once again were small but elegantly presented. Livia's plate displayed three closed zucchini flowers that had been dipped in a light batter and quickly fried, giving parts of it a brown color to contrast with the yellow. A bit of the cheese filling oozed out of the green ends, flowing into the thin layer of tomato sauce under it. Angelo's perch filets had been steamed and placed on a layer of creamy, yellow *polenta* and topped with capers and herbs. The simplest of the three dishes was Rick's carpaccio, its paper-thin raw beef covering the plate. Equally thin slices of the hard cheese dotted the meat along with the occasional shred of dark truffle that gave off its distinctive aroma. Olive oil crisscrossed it all. After taking in the artistic qualities of their own plates, each of them studied the other two before silently picking up their forks. The first sound was the crunch of Livia's first zucchini flower.

"I can see why my cousin enjoyed coming here," said Angelo before taking a taste of perch. "And I can taste why."

"Babbo did love to eat, but never cooked himself. Fortunately, my mother was an excellent cook." She finished another bite of the zucchini flower. "She passed away several years ago, before I met Francesco. I thought for a long time that my father would never recover from her death, but eventually he did."

Rick expected something about her father's woman friend. She had to have known about Letizia Bentivoglio, but something kept her from saying anything to Angelo. Perhaps if Rick had not been present, Livia would have opened up more. Or Rick was an easy way to justify, in her own mind, avoiding any mention of the other woman. He turned his attention to the *carpaccio*, one of his favorite dishes, and wondered why the chef had decided to use *grana padana*, the cheaper and less-renowned cousin of Parmigiano-Reggiano. The difference of taste between the two cheeses was difficult to pinpoint. If anything, the *grana* was a touch sweeter, which might be a reason to combine it with the sharp flavor of the raw beef. Just as likely the reason was more mundane, such as that the chef had a friend who produced *grana padana*.

Angelo patted his lips with his napkin and looked down at his dish where only a few specks of yellow *polenta* remained. "Excellent fish, and it goes perfectly with the *polenta*. I will have to recommend it to the owner of my favorite Italian restaurant at home, but since it doesn't have some kind of red sauce, he won't want to put it on the menu." He gestured toward their plates, also empty. "Just this lunch alone has opened my eyes to what Italian food really is."

"There is still *dolce* or *frutta*, Uncle."

"That sounds like dessert. I will, if you will."

As the waiter cleared the dishes Livia asked if they had *frutti di bosco*. When he said they did, she got a nod from Rick and ordered three, con *zucchero e limone*. As the waiter exited, his place was taken at the table by a large man whom Rick recognized as Livia's neighbor. Emilio Fiore wore a corduroy jacket that barely covered his girth. Under it was a plaid shirt open at the collar, exposing the thin line of a gold chain. He looked down at the two men as if they had sneaked into his private club.

Rick and Angelo got to their feet as Fiore bent over, took Livia's hand in his, and extended further condolences. Then he shook hands with the two men.

"Mr. Rondini," said Rick, "you remember Signor Fiore?"

"I do—Livia's neighbor."

"I hope you are enjoying our region, Mr. Rondini." Fiore had decided to try out his English, perhaps because he hadn't had as much wine as the day before. It was passable but highly accented. "You have seen our, um, *bellezze*?"

"Sights, beautiful things," Rick interpreted. Remembering the truck in the distance during the previous day's visit to the empty plot, he wondered if Fiore meant the artwork or the land. Angelo understood it to be the former.

"We were at the castle this morning to see Mantegna's masterpiece, among other art."

"Yes, his *capolavoro*. We are proud to have it in our city. Will you be staying long in Italy?"

It would have been an innocent question, but his emphasis on the word "long" made it sound otherwise.

"Not nearly long enough, Mr. Fiore. I have to get back to my work."

"You construct things, I am told."

"That is one way to describe my work."

"Here we grow food. Some of the best in the world. Is that not so, Livia?"

"The very best, Emilio."

The man smiled and inclined his head toward the corner. "I must return to my guests. Germans. They love our Italian cheeses. Livia, I will be seeing you tomorrow evening. I look forward to it. Good day." He bowed slightly and walked away. Rick and Angelo sat back down.

"Thank goodness he mentioned tomorrow, with all that's going on, I'd forgotten to tell you. The local cheese consortium is holding an event at seven at the Palazzo Te, in honor of my father. Of course you are invited."

"It will be an honor to attend," answered Angelo. He looked back at Fiore who was at his table with the Germans. "I think I like him better when he's had more wine," he said, eliciting a laugh from his niece.

"Emilio is traditional in all ways. He sees the land as our…" She struggled to find the word and did without Rick's help. "Our heritage, as well as our future. And he is very good at what he does, which is produce Parmigiano-Reggiano cheese. That was the main part of the rivalry with my father, if that is the correct term for their relationship. But what I think annoyed Emilio more was that my father, in the years after my mother's death, didn't care about keeping up the rivalry. Our dairy made good cheese, and Babbo knew it was good, but he wasn't obsessive about it."

"Fiore is obsessive."

"Most definitely, Uncle. And he enjoys a good argument."

The waiter arrived and placed small glass bowls of berries before each of them. Tiny wild strawberries, blueberries, and raspberries were coated with lemon juice and sprinkled with sugar. A small cookie sat on the plate under each bowl.

"I can picture local children with baskets picking these a few hours ago in the forest," Angelo said after tasting his first spoonful. "The lemon and the sugar, I never would have thought of that. Wonderful."

"This is the only time of year you can get them," she said. "And with the snow last night, these may be the last."

"I will have to come back next year."

"I hope you'll come many times before then, Uncle."

Twenty minutes later, after they had accepted *espressos* and declined *grappas*, they walked to the parking lot where the driver was waiting. Marco looked puzzled when he saw Livia Guarino walking with them.

"We will be giving my niece a lift back to her home, Marco."

The driver nodded silently and went to the other side to open the door for her. When she and Rondini were seated in the rear, Rick took his place in the front passenger seat. The engine roared to life and the Mercedes pulled out of the lot into the road.

Chapter Six

"Thank you for the lunch, Uncle."

"You're welcome, Livia." His eyes moved out across the fields where a midafternoon breeze kicked up a brown cloud behind a small tractor making its way along a dirt road. "That guy, Fiore, is right, you do make some great food around here. And you really know how to cook it." He settled back into the seat, but continued enjoying the view. Trees and bushes intermittently blocked it, but when they cleared, more fertile land spread out on either side of the road. "What does that say, Language Man?"

Rick turned his head to see a hand-lettered cardboard sign. "*Vendita Miele*. Honey for sale. Do you want to stop?"

"No. I have to bring something back for my daughter, but a jar of honey wouldn't cut it. She'd prefer something made of leather or gold."

"You must tell me about your daughter, Uncle."

"Nikki is wonderful young woman, Livia, and you two would get along famously. She was raised well, thanks to her mother, since I didn't spend as much time on it as I should have. But I'm trying to make up for it now. You will have to come to America to meet her.

"Or she could come here."

Something caught Rondini's eye and he tapped the driver on the shoulder. "What's that, Marco? I didn't notice it on the way to lunch."

The car rose gently as it went over a bridge. Blue water flowed under it along a cement canal that reminded Rick of the storm channels in Albuquerque built for the monsoon rains. "The river is diverted at several places, Mr. Rondini. The water is used on the crops."

Rondini was now noticing new vegetation on his side of the car, low plants with dark leaves hanging from wires strung above them. "Those are grapes, aren't they?"

"That's right, Uncle."

"Is there anything that doesn't grow here?"

The car slowed to make a turn at an intersection marked by two arrowed signs, both black and yellow, indicating an industry or other business. The top one read *Latteria Agricola Rondini*, and below it was *Latteria Agricola Mincio*, which Rick guessed to be the dairy farm across the road, owned by Emilio Fiore. The other two signs on the post were pointed ahead, one blue and white for Mantova, the other with the distinctive green, meaning that an *autostrada* entrance was to be found in that direction. Cows grazed on either side, unfazed by the passing car. It was dairy country.

Rick noticed that Marco had pushed lightly on the brake. He looked up to see a crowd of people milling around on the road ahead. Cars, and a few mopeds, were parked along the side. The Mercedes passed the entrance to Fiore's property and slowed more as the people got closer.

"*O Dio*," said Livia. "They have returned."

Angelo leaned forward for a better view. "What's going on?"

"Several weeks ago, when the news got out that my father was going to sell out to a developer to build a shopping center, they appeared. Some kind of environmental group. They want to keep the land natural, but of course, only they can decide what is natural."

"What should I do, Signora?" Concern was evident in the driver's voice.

"Drive in, of course."

The reply earned her a smile from Rondini. "They won't dare touch your car, Marco. If they do, we'll call the police." He leaned back in the leather seat. "Try not to hit any of them."

The crowd had now noticed the car and all their faces were turned toward it. When Marco put on his turn signal, there was a visible change in the group dynamic, led by one man who pushed himself forward, brandishing his sign above his head. He wore his gray hair long, matching an unkempt beard. The group began to chant, but Rick had trouble making out the words. Something *si*, something *no*. They needed more practice in their chanting, and also weren't clear on what to do about a car turning onto the property. Everyone except the leader moved aside to allow the Mercedes to enter the open gate. He stood defiantly in front of the car's circular hood ornament as Marco crept forward, but finally moved to the passenger side. As the car slid past, the man stared at Rick with wild eyes, leaving the shouting to his colleagues. The car picked up speed and drove to the front of the house. Marco and Rick got out and opened the doors for the rear passengers.

"I'm sorry you had to witness that, Uncle."

"Not a problem, Livia. It made me feel at home."

"There is a path you can take through the fields that we use for trucks that will get you back to the road so you can avoid them."

Marco perked up with the comment, but was disappointed by his boss' reply.

"Not a chance. We don't want them to think we're taking them seriously."

"And you will come back tomorrow to visit the farm? I think you will find the cheese-making fascinating."

"I would like that very much," answered Rondini.

They said their good-byes and the men waited until Livia got to the door before getting back in the Mercedes. Rick sat in the rear with Rondini.

"Marco," said Rondini, "turn left when you get out to the

road, drive past the field we stopped at yesterday, I want to see the place where Roberto Rondini used to go fishing."

The driver looked in the mirror. "It may start raining, Mr. Rondini. Are you sure you'd like to go there?"

"I just told you, didn't I?"

"Yes, sir." He started the engine.

The crowd came to life again as the car approached the gate. Their leader may have given them a pep talk, since their chant—NATURE YES, CEMENT NO—was clear and loud. They were also more reluctant to give way to the car as it approached, but did move to the side after Marco tapped his horn twice and edged slowly ahead. Once again the bearded leader was in the forefront.

The car turned back onto the road that formed a straight line between the Rondini dairy and the property of Emilio Fiore. Cows on both sides faced toward the road, checking each other out between bites of browned vegetation.

"At least the assholes took a break for the funeral," Angelo said. "I hope Livia doesn't have to get caught up in that every time she goes out. But that's the way you have to deal with these people—ignore them and go about your business. That's what we did that time in St. Louis, which just pissed them off and they got violent, so we had an excuse to bring in the police. That group back there didn't look like they'd get violent, but that old guy better be careful he doesn't get run over." Rondini looked out at where they had walked the day before. "All because of that plot of land, which isn't even very large by American standards."

Rick leaned forward and looked as they passed the field. "It was interesting that she said her husband wanted to sell it. Do you think Francesco can talk her into it?"

"Livia has her head on straight, Rick. She will eventually make the right decision on that land. Whatever it might be."

The comment didn't require a reply. Rondini, as he had done most of the time spent in the car, settled into silent contemplation while staring out the window at the fields. Just before the road bent to the right to go parallel to the river, the car turned onto a narrow dirt path. It ran along a thick line of trees that bordered the river, then turned where there was a break between them. Branches brushed against the car as it made its way through the passage to the riverbank before stopping in a circular clearing. Between the parking area and the river spread open ground. It was carpeted with short grass and dropped gradually to the water, its descent broken only by a few small mounds and scruffy bushes on one side. The Mincio at this point had expanded beyond the width it had been held to at the restaurant, getting ready to spread into a lake on the east side of Mantova. The only sign of human activity on either bank was the dock at the end of a path running from the clearing to the water. Rick and Angelo got out and walked down the path while the driver leaned against the car, his eyes on the darkening sky. A cold gust of wind blew toward them from a black cloud that formed in the distance.

The dock was only a few meters longer than the boat floating next to it on the upstream side. Lines from both ends of it were tied to the dock posts, but the steady current of the river also kept it in place. Angelo walked ahead of Rick, stepping out onto the planks and surveying the scene. His coat flapped open in the wind and he buttoned it while looking out over the choppy water. Rick stood back on the path watching his boss. Rondini had become increasingly contemplative since arriving in Italy. It would make sense; returning to one's roots had to make a profound impression on even the most cynical of people, and Angelo, at least outwardly, played the part of the cynical businessman. This trip was giving Rondini a lot to contemplate, not only because it was Italy, but the Italy of his parents. The likely murder of his closest Italian relative had added another layer to the experience. He'd wanted to visit this site to see where his cousin had spent many happy hours, but also because it was the site of the murder. Rick could almost hear the man's mind processing it all.

"It's beautiful here. I can understand why my cousin loved coming to this spot. There's something to be said for getting close to nature." He walked back to the shore, bent down, and touched the surface of the water. Ripples ran around his fingers and continued downstream. He stood and stared across the river in silence before turning.

"What do you think, Montoya? Could it have happened like the cop said?"

Rick descended to the dock and squatted at the edge, rubbing his hand over the wood. "This surface doesn't seem that slippery now, but it could have been that day, enough to make him fall and hit his head. Either an accident or a homicide is plausible."

Angelo stared down at the eddies formed by the water passing around the dock supports. "Your uncle the cop, he ever talk to you about his cases?"

"Often."

"What would he think of this?"

"Hard to say. But I know he has confidence in the opinion of Inspector Crispi."

"It's time for you to see this Crispi again to find out what's going on."

"I was going to make another visit to the newspaper archive, but I'll call him when we get to the hotel."

"Do it."

Out on the water's surface a dark line pushed toward them, the front edge of a gust bringing not just a chill but rain. A few small drops began to fall, followed immediately by larger ones. Rick heard footsteps and turned to see Marco rushing down the path, holding an open umbrella. Angelo met him halfway and took it, gesturing for Rick to join him underneath while the driver ran ahead. By the time they got to the car and jumped inside it was a full-blown storm.

"You'd better get us onto the pavement quickly," shouted Angelo over the noise of the downpour on the metal roof.

Marco needed no urging. He started the engine, made a quick turn, and got back onto a road that was rapidly turning from dirt to mud. By the time they bumped onto the blacktop a few minutes later, the Mercedes had fishtailed twice on the slick surface. He drove slowly through the storm while his passengers sat silently. The only sound beside the rain itself was the whomp-whomp of the wipers trying to keep up with it. When they passed the gate to the Rondini dairy, there was no sign of the demonstrators. The storm had driven them away. Halfway back to the city, the clouds disappeared as quickly as they had formed, allowing rays of sunlight to play on the lake as they drove into Mantova.

The archive room had not changed since the morning, even down to the newspaper that da Feltre was reading, though it appeared he was on the final pages. Rick wondered if the man paced his reading to make it last the entire day, in conformity with Parkinson's Law. Did he ever leave? He scanned the desk for a telltale crumb indicating a bag lunch, and finding none decided that the man might in fact go somewhere else for his midday meal. There was no sign on the glass door giving hours, but perhaps da Feltre taped a "back in an hour" note when he took his lunch break. He squinted through the thick lenses and a trace of a grin appeared when he recognized Rick.

"My most loyal customer," he said.

"I just can't stay away," Rick answered, and gestured at the work station. "May I?"

"Be my guest." Rather than return to the newspaper, the man kept looking at his visitor.

"Is there something else, Signor da Feltre?"

The man rubbed his finger over his nose, slightly dislodging the glasses. "Yes. Yes, there was. After you left I recalled that someone was here about a month ago, also looking for information about the Rondini family. Strange, isn't it?" After the rhetorical question, his eyes dropped to the paper and Rick walked to his cubicle.

Strange, indeed. But of any significance? Rick tucked the information into the back of his mind and turned on the computer, thinking that he had not yet read the recent stories about the death of Roberto Rondini. Calculating when the murder must have taken place, he quickly found the edition which broke the story. It ran an interview with the jogger who had found the body, including a staged photograph of him pointing to the water's edge near the castle, grotesquely enjoying his fifteen minutes of fame. The next day's paper mentioned Inspector Crispi, who refused to be specific about the cause of death, though that did not stop the reporter from assuming it was a fishing accident since the victim was known to be active in a local sport fishing association. No mention was made by the policeman, nor the reporter, of the fishing dock. Both stories mentioned the Rondini dairy operation and that Livia Guarino was the next of kin to the deceased. Other than the formal death notice, which Rick had read that morning, those were the only stories he could find in the paper about Roberto Rondini's death. He scrolled back to check if he'd missed something in earlier editions about the man before the death, but the same stories caught his eye.

With one exception.

Ten days before the body was found, a report on the inside pages covered a water pollution protest staged in a park area beside the lake. A photo showed a small group of protesters holding signs and shouting for the camera. They were concerned, wrote the reporter, about any development which could dump bad things into the Mincio, and they wanted the government to prevent it. From its size and signs, the group could have been the same one that Marco's Mercedes had squeezed past in and out of the Rondini dairy. It also had the same leader, identified as Domenico Folengo, the man who had glared through the car windows as his compatriots yelled.

Rick took notes and set the search to a couple decades earlier. He wanted to get more information for his boss on the elder Rondini, the man who started the dairy operation that Roberto Rondini had inherited and would now pass to Livia Guarino.

The paper had no lack of stories about Enzo Rondini and again showed the paper's dislike for the man. Rick skimmed over those he'd read on his first visit but found enough new ones to occupy him. The one that jumped out immediately told of the family that had been displaced when Enzo had worked the deal to have their property taken over for lack of tax payments. The head of the family was forced to pack up his family and head north to Verona where a dreary factory job would be his only chance of employment. The paper described him and his bitter wife driving off in a battered car, children squeezed into the back seat with the family belongings. The account made Enzo Rondini into a modern Italian Simon Legree, but Rick assumed much of it to be journalistic license until he saw the photo of a child staring blankly from the rear window of a car.

He was searching for another Rondini story when he heard the muffled sound of the Lobo Fight Song coming from his coat pocket. He pulled out the cell phone and saw that it was an 0376 area code number for Mantova. Signor da Feltre didn't look up.

"Montoya."

"Montoya, this is Crispi."

"Yes, Inspector. I was just going to call about coming to see you again."

"I hope you have something to tell me."

Rick looked at the ancient archivist, who seemed oblivious to the conversation. "Probably nothing of any consequence, but a few details." In truth he had nothing but hunches and conjecture, but he didn't want to say that he'd promised Rondini to get anything new on the case from the policeman. "Shall I come to the *questura* now?"

"Where are you at the moment?"

"In the archives of the *Gazzetta*."

If Crispi was intrigued by Rick's location, it didn't show in his voice. "I am not at the *questura*. I will send a car for you. It will be there in five minutes." He hung up.

Inspector Crispi as his usual loquacious self.

The police car arrived four minutes later, just as Rick was coming through the glass doors of the building. He got in the front seat, and after a short exchange of greetings, the car made a sharp U turn and drove away from the center of the city. He considered asking the driver where they were going, but the policeman didn't appear to be the chatty type. What would be the reason to meet at someplace other than the police station? The car took them quickly to the edge of the city where even a decade or two earlier there would have been fields rather than structures. The houses they passed were cement boxes devoid of personality, despite attempts to add color and life through window boxes and shrubbery. They were almost into exclusively agricultural land when the car slowed down. Rick could see a police vehicle parked in front of a house that looked like it had originally been part of a farm rather than new construction. Age was difficult to judge in farmhouses, but this one looked to date from early in the twentieth century, or even the late nineteenth. In a few more years it would be surrounded by newer construction, even a housing development, as the city seeped outward. The house consisted of two stories, like a square two-layer wedding cake, with a balcony running around the entire second floor. Separate from the house sat a garage, which could have originally been a storage shed, and behind that, rose a tall metal windmill like the old ones Rick had seen in New Mexico. A quarter of its blades were missing, the vane was rusted, and it looked like it hadn't turned in years. Three people stood at the base of the windmill: a woman, a uniformed policeman, and Inspector Crispi. They were looking up at a man sitting on the small platform next to the blades, his legs dangling over the edge.

"What's going on?" Rick asked when he reached Crispi.

The inspector turned his attention from the man above to the new arrival. "Afternoon, Montoya. He won't come down."

The sitter stared back toward the city, oblivious to the group below. He was dressed in canvas work overalls, the knees wrapped with orange strips that caught the sun as the legs swung back and forth. Heavy boots, a dark blue sweat shirt, and a knit cap completed the outfit of a highway construction worker.

"Excuse me, Inspector," Rick said, "but what does this have to do with the murder of Roberto Rondini?"

In reply he got a puzzled look from Crispi. "Rondini? Nothing, of course. Do you think I have the luxury of dealing with only one case at a time? I needed to talk to you and this is where I happen to be at the moment." He jerked his thumb upward. "Here with Lando."

"Why is he up there?"

He glanced at the woman. "Let's go over to the house and I'll tell you." They had started to walk when Crispi stopped and turned back to the windmill. "You've made your point, Lando," he shouted up at the man who continued to stare at the horizon. When they were out of earshot of the group, Crispi stopped and took a deep breath which spoke more than words about the present situation.

"He came home early from work because of a water main break and found his wife with the neighbor."

Rick looked around, wondering in which of the few houses he saw the neighbor might have resided. "*In flagrante?*"

"They were having coffee in the kitchen. Both fully clothed."

"But Lando is the jealous type."

"It appears so."

Rick dug his hands into his coat pocket. The temperature was noticeably lower out in the country than in town. Perhaps the cold would get Lando off his perch. "Do you have some news on the Rondini investigation, Inspector?"

"We were contacted by your hotel about an hour ago. Someone called and left a threatening message for your *capo*. 'Tell the American that he should leave immediately or he will be in grave danger,' was what the desk clerk remembers. It was a man's voice. Of course the American could be you, but I doubt it. There are no other Americans registered in the hotel at the moment except you, Rondini, and his secretary. I wanted to talk to you before we speak with Mr. Rondini."

"There was a similar message yesterday, written on a note and left under the wiper of the car."

For an instant Crispi's normally bland expression changed almost imperceptibly to a frown. "And you didn't tell me?"

"It didn't appear serious enough to waste your time. It could have just been a prank."

"My time will now be wasted on it. Did you keep the note?"

"I think the driver threw it away."

Crispi nodded his head slowly. "And now the prankster has returned, likely annoyed that his first message wasn't taken seriously."

They were interrupted by the shrill voice of Lando's wife. Rick couldn't make out what she'd said, but from the tone and the way she was shaking her fist he concluded that her words did not convey much tenderness.

"So you will talk with Rondini?"

The reply was another nod. "With your help. My English is minimal. This threat is just another small detail added to an already murky case, making it messier but no more conclusive. I am not in the good graces of my superior for pursuing it, since he preferred Roberto Rondini dying in a tragic accident. I'm not sure how he will react to this development."

Rick recalled what his uncle had said about Inspector Crispi's relationships with the rest of the police force. It was impossible to read anything into the inspector's comment, to know if he was concerned about his boss, or with anything else. The words were said as if he was describing what he'd had for breakfast.

"What else have you found since we last spoke?"

Rick looked back at the windmill before answering. All the players were still in their places, looking up at Lando. "Rondini had lunch today with Livia Guarino, and I was present. She is coming around to the possibility that her father was murdered."

"Which would argue for taking her off the list of suspects. Go on."

"The lunch was mostly about family and how her father loved the river, but she did talk about that plot of land. She doesn't know what to do about it, and asked Rondini's advice. Their neighbor, Fiore, was against any kind of development, and the two men used to argue about it. By coincidence, Fiore was having lunch at the restaurant and came to our table."

"And?"

"The normal exchange of pleasantries, as you would expect. He asked Rondini if he'd seen the sights. He knows that Rondini is a developer, and I'm guessing he made a connection in his mind between Rondini's appearance and the possible sale of the land to build a shopping center or factory."

"Is there a connection?"

"Pure coincidence, as far as I can see, but I'm still not Italian enough to see plots behind everything."

"Just give yourself time, you'll come around to it. What else of interest?"

"After the lunch there was something. We gave Signora Guarino a ride home, since her husband didn't make it because of an appointment, and had dropped her at the restaurant. When we got to her farm there were demonstrators at the gate."

"I heard they were back. Any problems?"

"We got in without incident, dropped off the *signora*, and got out without a problem, though they squeezed in close to the car. By coincidence, when I was looking up Rondini family stories in the *Gazzetta* just now, I came across a photo of the man who appeared to be the leader of the demonstrators. The caption with the photo said his name is Domenico Folengo."

"Yes, Folengo. He is, as the saying goes, known to the police. We have never actually arrested him, but he has been detained temporarily for getting too boisterous in his demonstrations. The issue is always the same, what he sees as environmental destruction in any and all forms. We had a case of vandalism early this year, some construction equipment had tires slashed and windows broken, and we suspected it was Folengo's doing, but couldn't find evidence to justify bringing him in."

"What does he do when he's not demonstrating?"

"Not much. He lives off an inheritance from a wife who died a few years ago. He spends all his time saving the world. It would be nice to have family money, wouldn't it?"

Rick assumed that Crispi's question didn't require an answer. "Something else I found in the archives was interesting, regarding the fishing association that Roberto Rondini was active in."

"I knew that he was a fisherman, of course. What did you find?"

"When Rondini was elected to the board, the former president resigned. The man's name is Sandro Bastoncini." Rick passed him the piece of paper with the name. "I couldn't tell if it was in protest to Rondini's election, or something totally unrelated, but he might be someone you'd want to talk to. If nothing else, he can tell you about Rondini's activities in the fishing group."

Crispi studied the name and then slipped the paper into his pocket. "Another person who likely won't be of any help. But you are correct, it may at least give me some more insight into the fascinating private life of Roberto Rondini."

"In that regard, how did the interview with the woman go?"

"As expected. Add Letizia Bentivoglio to the list of those who think it couldn't be an accident. She said Rondini was getting moody in weeks before, set off, she thinks, by the anniversary of his own father's death. Concerned with his own mortality. Going to some funeral a few weeks before he died didn't help his mind-set. He was also bothered by the uproar when people found out he was thinking of selling that plot of land."

"The demonstrators? This guy, Folengo?"

"Must have been." Crispi looked over at the scene around the windmill. Nothing had changed. "I did a background check on Signora Bentivoglio and didn't find anything out of the ordinary. She's never done anything to bring her to the attention of the authorities. I also checked on Roberto Rondini's farm manager, Carlo Zucari, but that was different."

"How so?"

"About twenty years ago he was arrested for assault and did prison time after an argument in a bar that led to violence. He almost killed a man in a rage. He somehow got himself a job at the Rondini farm after he was released, and he worked his way up to the manager position. We don't often find instances of an ex-convict turning himself around, but that was the case with Zucari. I can't help but wonder if he really is a changed man, or if the violence was simmering below the surface."

"What would be his motive?"

Crispi looked at his watch and up at the man on the windmill. "That's what puzzles me. Rondini gave him a chance after prison, so why would he want to do in his benefactor? It also puzzles me why Rondini gave him the job in the first place, but we'll likely never know. Maybe he's ready to jump."

The last sentence was uttered after they heard some commotion coming from the windmill. Lando had taken his eyes from the horizon and was now engaged in an animated conversation with his wife. At one point he waved his arms wildly, almost losing his balance, and she screamed. Their voices lowered and the uniformed policeman, who had been joined by Rick's driver, edged away from the metal ladder that extended up to the platform, to give them privacy. Slowly, as Rick and Crispi watched, the man began climbing down the ladder. When his feet were about ten feet off the ground, the woman said something that Rick couldn't make out, and Lando's head jerked around, causing him to lose his balance and start to fall head-first toward the ground. His wife screamed again as the nearby policemen rushed toward the base of the windmill. Crispi stood and watched. It was Lando's turn to scream as his left ankle caught in a rung, keeping him from falling all the way to the ground but causing great pain. Grunting and struggling, the two policemen managed to extract the foot from the ladder and get him down without further complications. It was a toss-up as to which was now louder, Lando's groans or his wife's admonitions. Crispi walked to the small group, gave orders to the two policemen, and returned to Rick.

"They'll get him into one of our cars and take him to the hospital. They should examine his head as well as his ankle, when he gets there."

The two policemen got Lando to his feet, put his arms over their shoulders, and he hobbled on one foot between them toward one of the cars. The scene reminded Rick of an injured linebacker being taken off the gridiron with a torn ACL, his wife following behind in the part of the team doctor. After Lando was squeezed into the back seat of one of the police cars, his wife got in the front and they were driven off toward the city.

"I'm not sure if that was a good outcome or a bad one," said Rick.

Crispi watched the car disappear down the road. "She may break his other leg before the night's over." He pointed at the other car where the second policeman awaited them. "Get in, we'll go talk to your *capo*."

● ● ● ● ●

"I'm the one to get the threat, and the hotel calls the cops? What am I, chopped liver?"

Rick interpreted Rondini's second question as "I should have been told first"—not a direct translation, but it got his boss's point across. They sat on white leather chairs in a corner of the hotel lobby with Rick taking the interpreter position between the two of them. The policeman, who had little experience with Americans and even less with those raised on the East Coast, appeared intrigued by Rondini's manner. At least that's the way Rick interpreted the slight squint in Crispi's eyes.

The inspector did not attempt to justify the hotel management's decision. "Would you like me to assign a policeman to the hotel, Signor Rondini?"

Rick sensed that Crispi's offer was *pro forma*. He also expected Rondini to turn it down.

"Montoya will keep his eye on me. And my assistant is trained in the martial arts."

Another facet of the multifaceted Lexi Coleman, Rick thought as he interpreted.

"In addition, Inspector, I would not want to keep any manpower from helping you to solve my cousin's murder. Can I assume you believe these threats are connected to the crime?"

Crispi rubbed his stubble before replying. "You have declined my offer for protection, Mr. Rondini. Would you change your mind if I told you there is a connection? The fact is, I don't know. But if there are any other threats, no matter how they are delivered, you must promise to contact me immediately. Signor Montoya has my number."

"I will do that," said Rondini after getting it in English from Rick. "And you must promise to inform me if there are any developments in the investigation. You have Mr. Montoya's number."

In a battle of wills, Rick was certain that Rondini would come out on top. Inspector Crispi was good, but out of his league.

"Signor Rondini, I have just told Signor Montoya what I know, he will be pleased to inform you and we won't have to go through the translation. I really must return to the *questura*. Please be careful." Crispi didn't wait for Rick, but got to his feet, bowed stiffly, and walked to the door, leaving Rick and Angelo seated.

"Is he pissed off?" Rondini asked after the policeman had left.

"His manner is always the same, so it's difficult to tell. Are you sure you don't want police protection? It might be a good idea since someone appears to be unhappy with your presence in Mantova."

"We don't need a cop getting underfoot. If you have to take down some kook who attacks me, I'll pay you extra. You look like you could handle it."

"Is bodyguard part of Lexi's job description?"

"It could be, Language Man, it could be. Which reminds me that she should be made aware of what is going on. I didn't want to say anything, since she has enough to do, but you'd better tell her all about it."

"Me?"

"Yes, you. After that big lunch, I'm staying in tonight, so you are again assigned to take her to dinner. Tell her everything." He removed his glasses, took out a handkerchief, and started to clean the lenses carefully. "Now what does that cop know about the murder of my cousin?"

• • ● • •

Rick was initially surprised by what got Lexi's attention, but when he thought about it, it made sense. She was, after all, Angelo's assistant, and her main focus would be on the business, not on possible murder suspects.

"Do you think Angelo's niece asked him to come here because he develops shopping centers?" she asked.

"I really don't know. She knows what his business is, but she could have found that out after she decided to track him down and invite him to the funeral. But the same thought crossed his mind."

"That doesn't surprise me. I told you he's very suspicious of people's motives."

"Or perhaps it's just his Italian genes," Rick said.

She had requested a less formal restaurant than the previous night, wanting to see "the real Italy," as if affluent people eating in an upscale ambiance wasn't really Italian. It was something about many American tourists that intrigued Rick, their idea that rustic meant genuine. The place this evening was brightly lit, noisy, and small, its wooden tables squeezed into a long, rectangular room that ended in the door to the kitchen. A few shelves built into niches were lined with dusty wine bottles, and the rest of the bright red walls were covered with art by local amateurs. No tablecloths this time, only brown paper place mats stamped with the restaurant logo, a plump goose. The menus were hand-written and stained. Strong aromas, which would have stayed in the kitchen in most restaurants, floated through the air. Lexi loved it.

"So the two threats could be connected to the possible murder of Roberto Rondini."

"I don't see how, Lexi, but it's too much of a coincidence to discount. And Inspector Crispi did offer your boss police protection, so the cops are taking it seriously."

The waiter arrived at the table with a bottle of mineral water in one hand and a basket of crusty bread in the other. He set both on the table and deftly popped the cap off the water with an opener he had in his pocket.

"*Un litro del vostro rosso,*" Rick said to him, and the man walked away.

"What was that?" Lexi asked.

"I ordered a bottle of the house red. You want to eat like the locals, you have to drink like them, too. Do you want me to order for you tonight?"

She pushed away her menu. "I can't read this anyway. Go for it. Just don't order anything that comes from inside the animal."

"I'm with you on that. You know, when I first saw you I feared that you might be a vegetarian. You looked like the type."

"I was a vegan for a while in college, but it didn't last long."

"What made you change your mind?"

"Bacon."

"Ah."

The wine, dark and crimson, arrived in a decorated ceramic pitcher. Rick filled their glasses and they toasted their absent host and looked around the room, which was beginning to fill with a clientele distinctly different from the previous evening. Most of the diners chatted with the waitstaff like they ate there often. Many only gave the menu a cursory glance before ordering. Greetings were exchanged between tables. This was a neighborhood hangout.

"Tell me, Rick," Lexi began after taking a long pull on her wine, "is it Richard or Riccardo? I heard the driver calling you Riccardo."

"It's Rick. But for the full name, it depends on which side of the Atlantic I find myself. By chance my two grandfathers shared the name—Riccardo Fontana and Richard Montoya—so when I was born, the decision was easy for my parents. In both countries kids are often named after grandparents, of course. My American passport has Richard, and my Italian one Riccardo. What about Alexis?"

"I think it was an aunt. But maybe some TV star. My mother watched a lot of soap operas when she was carrying me."

The waiter appeared and Rick made a quick study of the menu before giving their order. "Be surprised," he said to Lexi. "Good peasant food, all."

"I'm for that. You wouldn't think that working on a computer and a telephone would give me such an appetite, but it does." She pulled a piece of bread from the basket. It was mostly holes and had a thick crust darkened by the oven. "Do you think Angelo is really in danger, Rick?"

"I think that if someone wanted to do him harm it would

have already happened. But there's no doubt in my mind of a connection between the demise of his cousin and those threats, and that connection is probably the infamous plot of land. That's what draws in your boss."

Lexi bit down on the bread with a crunch and chewed. "There must be somewhere in Chicago where I can get bread like this." She swallowed and took another drink of wine. "I'm worried. Tell me I shouldn't worry, Rick."

"Wish I could."

"You said you have an uncle who's a cop. What did he think of the threats?"

"I haven't talked to him since the first one, but he'll probably just tell me to be careful. That's what he's always said in such situations."

"Did you?"

"Most of the time."

A large platter of sliced *salumi* came to the table along with two plates that the waiter put in front of them. He pointed out *culatello*, *coppa*, and *bresaola* before wishing them *buon appetito* and retiring.

"This looks great," said Lexi as she picked up her fork. "Which should I try first?"

"The *culatello* is the king of local cured meats, but you shouldn't choke on the other two either."

They speared slices on their forks and transferred them to their own plates before cutting and eating. The bread served as a palate clearer between tastes of the three types, along with sips of the red wine. When the plate was empty they agreed that the *culatello* was the best, but the other two were in a tie for second place.

Conversation returned to the murder and Rick told her about the possible suspects: Livia's husband, Francesco; the farm manager, Carlo Zucari; Emilio Fiore, the gruff neighbor; and now perhaps one of the protesters outside the farm gate.

"Not just random, or a mugging gone bad, or a nutcase?

That's what many of the Chicago murders turn out to be."

"Mantova isn't Chicago, Lexi. There's something behind this one. My uncle always tells me that there are very few motives when it comes to murder. Revenge, sex, and money are the big three. Vendetta is an Italian word, of course, so revenge could be the motive, but revenge for what? And sex? A widower with a girlfriend a few years younger? Doesn't seem that that one flies either. Money is what I would bet on at this point, and that plot of land is worth a lot of it. Ah, the *pasta* has arrived."

The *salumi* plates had been cleared, and in their place the waiter set a large bowl filled halfway with thin ribbons of pasta coated by a dark sauce. Next to it was a single dish. The waiter took a fork and spoon, stirred the pasta a few times, and transferred half of it to the dish before saying something to Rick. Rick inclined his head toward Lexi.

"He seems to have forgotten the other plate, Rick."

The waiter picked up the serving bowl and placed it in front of Lexi. Rick got the plate.

"There was a restaurant in Rome near the embassy that used to serve *spaghetti alla carbonara* this way," he said. "My sister and I would order it and argue over who got the bowl. Used to drive my parents crazy. This is *papardelle al sugo d'anatra*, ribbon pasta with duck sauce." He peered at her portion. "I think he gave you more."

"You're not getting my bowl." She took a bite and her eyes widened. "I think I'll just let you order for me from now on."

Talking was put on pause to allow enjoyment of the *papardelle*, but then it returned to less pleasant issues than food. Rick was regretting he'd had to tell Lexi about the murder. It was causing her daytime personality to creep into her evening breeziness. It showed a protective side in her as well. Angelo had told Rick he was concerned about Lexi's social life, and now she was worried about her boss's safety. Like father and daughter, these two.

After a simple green salad to help digest the earlier two courses, they decided to call it an evening, with a stop for coffee on the way back to the hotel. Once again the chill of the air greeted them as they stepped into the street, but instead of snow, the stones were coated with the moisture of the evening fog. It was a cold, penetrating fog that went deep into their lungs with every breath. Its invisible droplets were bent on cleansing the city, pushing against doors and windows and wafting through the leafless branches of trees. Halfway to the hotel they spotted the defused yellow light of a bar still open despite the hour. Rick opened the door and Lexi hurried in.

It must have been one of the few establishments in the city that was both open and serving warm drinks, since the small room was almost filled to capacity. He guessed that a movie had just let out nearby, and a controversial one, since most of the customers were in animated conversations. Many of them sipped from small glasses, but cups were the container of choice, and the one man behind the bar banged away at his coffee machine to keep up with demand. Customers stood two deep at the bar, and around small tables that stood on one side of the room.

"What would you like, Lexi? An Italian would never order a *cappuccino* at this hour, but you're a tourist, so you are allowed. With the chill it might be just what you need."

"It does sound perfect."

"Go over and guard that last table while I get it." Rick worked his way through the people and got the attention of the barman. "*Un cappuccio e un caffè macchiato.*" The man was pouring two shots of *grappa* but nodded to confirm that he'd gotten the order. Rick looked back to see Lexi standing patiently next to the table, ready to repel any interlopers.

The barman was fast, despite the volume of orders. After leaving a good tip, Rick picked up the two cups and saucers and squeezed back through the people to get to their table. A bowl of sugar awaited their coffee. Rick set the *cappuccino* in front of Lexi and spooned sugar into his coffee. She picked up her cup, held it in both hands to absorb the warmth, and took a sip. No sugar for her.

"Excellent, Rick." She looked around after a second swallow. "I feel like I'm really in Italy on this trip." She glanced back at him. "I know. Where else would I be? But you know what I mean."

He finished his coffee in one swig. "I know exactly what you mean. It is the advantage of getting off the tourist track, coming in the off season, and most importantly, seeing someplace other than the big cities."

"Speaking Italian helps. Or traveling with someone who does."

He shrugged. "I'm sure you could learn it easily. Do you speak another language?"

"College French."

"Better than nothing."

She finished her coffee and rubbed her fingers over the window, wiping away the moisture caused by the heat of the room. The street was narrow, but the building on the other side was barely visible through the fog. "We'd better get back, Rick. There will be e-mails waiting for me to answer and reports to read."

"Let me get rid of these so they can use the table."

Lexi watched as he picked up their cups and saucers and carefully worked his way through the crowd. After placing them at one corner of the bar he turned and found himself hemmed in by a man who was carrying on an animated conversation with the woman next to him. Rick tapped the man on the shoulder to get by. The man turned, said something to Rick and shook his hand. The man introduced Rick to the woman and they shook hands. After a minute of conversation, Rick gestured toward Lexi, tapped his finger on his wrist where a watch would be, and took his leave. Lexi was waiting for him at the door.

"Someone you know?" she asked.

Rick pushed open the door and they stepped back into the cold arms of Mantova's fog. They both pulled their coats tighter around them as they started in the direction of the hotel.

"One of them. Carlo Zucari, the manager of the Rondini dairy. He reiterated the invitation to tour the operation. You are invited, too, of course."

"I'd enjoy that. Is that his wife?"

They turned the corner and Lexi tucked her arm under Rick's. The street was deserted save for a line of cars parked along one side. Fog and cold had scared away any cats which normally might have prowled at this hour. They were indoors, on something warmer than the dark cobblestones.

"That's the interesting part. He introduced me to her. I don't know if he's married or not, but that's not his wife."

"Why is that interesting?"

"Her name is Letizia Bentivoglio. If I remember correctly, she is the one Inspector Crispi said is the lady friend of the recently deceased Roberto Rondini."

"Hmm. As they say in mystery novels, the plot thickens."

"Lexi, no mystery author worth his salt would ever write that." From deep inside his coat pocket he felt the vibration of his phone. He unhooked his arm from Lexi's and extracted it with some difficulty, squinting to read the number. "I'll call them back." He quickly returned it to his pocket.

● ● ● ● ●

Despite the chill, he was perspiring. The evening had not gone well, continuing a pattern of the last few weeks. He knew he should have concentrated on the business at hand and not be distracted, but for him that seemed impossible. Where had he left his car? He took in a breath of the night air and coughed when the cold exploded in his lungs. Damn this fog. He looked up and down the street, trying to remember where he'd parked, and decided it had to be just ahead. His footsteps echoed along the narrow street as he searched the line of cars. Darkness took away the features of everything on the street. All the buildings looked the same: flat, two-storied fronts, silent and shuttered.

The cars, no matter what their daytime color had been, were black. A few streetlamps, unable to penetrate the heavy fog, left weak circles on the stone pavement or on the roofs of vehicles. Finally, he spotted his Alfa three cars ahead and increased his pace, pulling out his keys as he went.

Just as he reached the car the attacker struck.

He screamed in pain and fell forward toward the curb, his hands instinctively extended to stop the fall. The palms slid off the wet metal of the car's hood and his forehead slammed into the glass of the windshield. As he slid into the gutter he reached for the back of his head where he had been struck. Warm blood covered his hand and seeped into the cuff of his shirt. He was on his knees now, grasping the fender of the car parked behind his. A second blow hit him, but the thick collar of his overcoat rendered it harmless. His body stiffened in preparation for a third, but instead he heard a voice and the rattle of a shutter opening above them. Thank God, someone had heard him cry out. The weapon clattered to the ground and his assailant took off running. Running fast. He got to his feet and peered through the fog at the sound, but could see nothing. On the ground next to him was a thick piece of wood. An axe handle? Whatever it was he didn't care, his only thought now was escape. He pulled out a handkerchief and pressed it to his neck before opening his car door and dropping into the seat behind the steering wheel.

When the old man looked down from the open window, all he saw was fog and a pair of red tail lights disappearing into the darkness.

Chapter Seven

After a final pandiculation, Rick was ready to go. He was never one for extensive warm-up, even on cold days like this one, but Lexi apparently felt differently. She placed her left heel on the rim of the tall flowerpot in front of the hotel and bent her head down to touch her extended leg. She repeated the stretch with the other leg, then did several knee bends. Rick bounced in place and watched her, trying to remember the word for "tights" in Italian. It wasn't something that came up often in translating articles for academic journals.

"Lead the way." She made a few jumps on the balls of her feet.

The streetlamps had just clicked off when they came out of the hotel, but one car that passed them still had its headlights lit, though more for the fog than the darkness. They ran shoulder to shoulder along the narrow sidewalk, keeping to the curb so as not to knock down anyone who might emerge from one of the buildings. There was not much chance of that; the city was just beginning to wake up and this section of town was mostly residential. Only the bars would be open at this hour, dispensing strong coffee to those who couldn't sleep or had the bad fortune of working an early shift. Stores and other businesses would not open for three hours, and most of their clients would arrive well after that.

They crossed the small canal that cut across the southern

part of the town center and turned east toward the lake. A wide path ran above the water's edge, a promenade where the families of Mantova strolled on Sundays and holidays. Without saying anything to Rick, Lexi took the lead. This morning the fog wafted in off the lake, cutting the visibility of both path and water, and bringing with it a humid chill. They didn't feel the cold; if anything, it added to the pleasure of the run. Rick took in gulps of the air and noted its difference from what he was used to breathing on his morning runs in downtown Rome. Perhaps Lexi was noticing the same contrast with Chicago, though, like Mantova, it had its own lake. She ran like she was by herself, and thanks to a long stride, that was just what was happening. Rick watched as she steadily lengthened the distance between them.

The castle loomed up on the left. Floodlights which lit the walls each night had been shut off, and there was not yet enough natural light to bring out the texture of the stone, leaving the walls a uniform dark gray. The path dropped lower, closer to the surface of the lake, running along the initial section of the causeway before looping down beneath it. A truck rumbled overhead as Rick turned under the roadway and continued along the path which now rose back to its former level. A male runner, dressed for the cold, passed him going in the opposite direction, nodding a silent greeting. Lexi was now about twenty yards ahead, and the path was flat and straight. The grassy area between it and the street widened, and the occasional wood table and benches appeared, waiting for good weather to bring picnickers. On the other side of the street, the city's northern wall stretched for a few hundred yards before being replaced by the side of a more modern building. Lexi, then Rick, passed three fishermen seated on metal lawn chairs and bundled against the morning chill. They kept their eyes on the lake, seemingly oblivious to the runners as well as to each other. Rick looked up and saw that Lexi was running in place in front of a tunnel that went under the road.

"Time to turn back?" she asked when he reached her side.

"Good idea," Rick said while breathing heavily. "I've studied the map and I'm pretty sure this doesn't go anywhere except up to a busy street." As they turned, his phone rang.

Lexi raised her eyebrows. "You better get that, it could be your policeman."

After pulling the cell phone from the small pocket with difficulty, he saw the number and realized he hadn't called back last night. "I'd better take this, Lexi. It'll only be a minute."

She gestured that it was fine, and wandered toward the water, pulling her knees up as she went so they wouldn't stiffen up in the cold. Rick switched to Italian.

"*Ciao*, Betta. Sorry I didn't get back to you last night."

"You sound out of breath."

"Out for a morning run along the lake. It's beautiful. How is your, uh, case going?"

"We're going to be wrapping it up this morning. I thought I might take a couple days off, catch a train up to Mantova this afternoon. I'd love to see the Mantegnas again."

So the draw for a trip to Mantova would be the art. Very typical of the Betta of late. He glanced at Lexi, who was still pulling her knees up to her chest to stay loose. "Betta, this is a fascinating job, but the guy is keeping me busy day and night, I wouldn't have any time to spend with you."

There was hesitation before she replied. "*Va bene.* I understand. Have you been to the castle?"

"Yes, it turns out Signor Rondini is an art collector, so we went yesterday and saw the Mantegna masterpiece. Today we're going to learn about cheese production. It's nonstop with him."

"I'll be anxious to hear all about it when you get back to Rome."

"And you can tell me about your case."

"Yes. Yes, I'll do that. Call me when you're back."

"Will do. *Ciao*, Betta."

He took a deep breath and squeezed the phone back into the pocket.

"We'd better get going or you're going to stiffen up from the cold." Lexi was running in place. "Everything all right?"

"Yes, everything's fine. It was a friend from Rome checking up on me." He wondered if she could hear that it was a female voice on the other end of the call.

"It's good having friends who care about you, Rick. Same way back?"

Before he could answer, she was off, quickly up to regular speed, making long, smooth strides. He started running, maintaining the same distance behind her as before, moving his eyes between the grassy scenery, the lake, and her figure. The runner they had passed earlier was on his return loop, and smiled again at Rick. Three others came behind him and also waved, indicating that this was a popular morning route for the locals, despite the fog which was again wafting off the water, occasionally obscuring Lexi's form just ahead of him. They passed the castle and turned into the small square that would take them to the hotel's street. He was almost even with her now.

As Lexi approached the corner, a male figure with gray facial hair appeared around it, looked at Rick, and raised his arm. The man was close to Lexi, and she took the gesture as menacing. After a quick lash with her leg and a chop of her arm, he was on the ground looking up with a dazed expression on his face. She stood over him, arms raised and body tense. Rick reached them a moment later.

"Easy, Lexi, I know who this guy is."

"You do?" She was taking in short breaths. "I'm from Chicago, Rick. It was a reflex reaction. Hope I haven't caused an international incident."

"Probably not." He switched to Italian. "You can get up, Signor Folengo. I'll protect you against her. You shouldn't go around making threatening moves at people, especially those who know how to defend themselves."

The man got slowly to his feet, pushing back the long gray

hair that had fallen across his face. He looked like he had not bathed since snarling through the window of the car at the Rondini farm gate. He tried to brush off a patch of mud from his knee, but only succeeded in spreading it over his already dirty jeans and hand. "I recognized you and was calling for you to stop. She could have hurt me, and then you both would have been in great trouble with the police. But how do you know my name?" He was standing now, and edging back from Lexi, who continued to stand her ground.

"Somehow, I don't think the police would take your side." Rick purposely did not answer his question.

"Who is this creep, Rick?"

He told her, then returned to Italian and Folengo. "Why would you want to talk to me?"

"It was your employer I wanted to talk to. I assumed that the rich relative from America would be staying at the most expensive hotel in the city, and I was on my way there."

"Do you really think, after that scene at the farm, that Mr. Rondini would want to talk to you?"

"Perhaps not, but I also have a petition to leave with him. We are a large group, and we want to have our voices heard. The very well-being of the Po Valley depends on our message getting through."

"Rick?" She had her hands on her hips.

"Oh, sorry Lexi. The guy wants to give your boss a petition."

"For that he had to attack me? Take it and we'll see what it says." A touch of her businesswoman persona had crept into her voice.

He turned to Folengo, who, from his expression, did not appear to understand English. "Give me the petition, and I'll see that he knows about it. I can't promise he'll read it. I assume this is about the sale of the land, like your protests?"

"You assume correctly." He pulled an envelope out of his pocket and passed it to Rick. He was about to speak when Lexi raised a hand.

"*Basta*," she said, to which the man froze, then turned and hurried off. They watched him disappear around the corner.

"*Basta?* So you do speak Italian, Lexi."

"Really? I thought it was Spanish. That makes me bilingual."

"Let's get back to the hotel before we catch a chill."

Angelo was in a more talkative mood. Instead of staring out of the car windows, as he'd done on previous drives into the Lombard countryside, he grilled Rick and Lexi about their encounter with the "ecofreak," as he characterized Folengo. Not that there was much to see from the Mercedes; the fog that had obscured the views of the lake for the morning runners had settled over the fields. As soon as the car emerged into some sunshine, it would be engulfed again. Marco kept the speed low, and he had turned on the car's penetrating, red fog light on the rear to make it visible to any traffic approaching from behind. As everyone living in the Po Valley knew, pileups caused by low visibility could happen at any time, but especially on the autostrada where too many drivers insisted on high speeds, despite the conditions. There was little traffic this morning on the two-lane road from Mantova to the Rondini dairy, but Marco took no chances.

Angelo was laughing. "Lexi, you did well to take that creep down. I wish I could have been there to see it. I hope he's there when we get to the gate so I can catch the look on his face when he sees you sitting in the back seat." He chuckled. "What a bunch of garbage in that letter. I think I'll tell Livia to sell the farm to a developer, just to piss off the guy."

There were no protesters at the gate. Marco slowed and turned in before pulling up to the house. The driver hopped out to open Angelo's door, and Rick did the same for Lexi. They walked up the steps to the house, but before reaching the door, Livia opened it and gave Angelo a welcoming hug. She greeted Rick and shook hands with Lexi.

"It's good to see you again."

"Thank you for inviting me along, Mrs. Guarino," said Lexi.

"Please call me Livia. Come in, everyone. Can I offer you coffee before you take the tour?"

"We just had some at the hotel with breakfast," answered Angelo. "Whenever you're ready, we are."

Livia's fingers brushed her face. "I won't be going with you on the tour. Francesco had an accident last night on the way home from the office. Nothing serious, but he's upstairs and I want to keep an eye on him. I've asked Carlo to show you around."

"I'm sorry to hear that," said Angelo. "Is there something I can do?"

"No, no. We'll be fine. I hope you'll enjoy seeing how the cheese is made." She opened the door and walked out to the porch with them. "Carlo will be there at the office." She pointed at a low structure a hundred yards away, visible behind the row of trees. The fog had lifted enough to see it and the other buildings of the dairy. "Come back when you're finished, and I'll offer you that coffee again."

"We'll do that."

They descended from the porch to the car and the driver got out to open the rear door.

"Over to that building, Marco," said Angelo as he stuffed himself into the back. Rick and Lexi took their assigned seats.

They drove slowly along the gravel road between two fenced fields, cows in one, open grass in the other, to reach the connected buildings. They were made with prefabricated cement, the lines of the ribbed walls interrupted only by small, high, windows, or by doors that rolled up to open. A shiny steel tank, which Rick assumed held milk, towered over the parking area, next to machinery that looked to be for cooling, something not needed on a day like this one. This outside view gave Rick the impression of a fanatical cleanliness. The cement walls were scrubbed and the stainless steel storage tank looked like it had been polished that morning. He could imagine what it was going to be like inside.

The car drove onto the pavement that surrounded the building and up to the door which Livia had pointed to from the house. Parked in front was a pickup truck which looked vaguely familiar to Rick. He remembered where he'd seen it when Zucari came out of the office with Emilio Fiore, the neighbor from across the road. The manager noticed the arriving Mercedes and said something quickly to Fiore, who nodded and walked toward the far end of the building. By the time Rick was opening the passenger-side door, Fiore had disappeared around the corner of the building and Zucari was walking toward the arriving car.

Knowing that the manager spoke no English, Rick prepared to earn his pay. After greetings were exchanged and Lexi introduced, they moved inside, leaving Marco leaning against his car. The entrance door brought them into a small waiting room outside the office of the Rondini dairy. Through glass partitions they could see two women working at computers in cubicles that took up half the room, the rest of it filled with files and office machines. As in the office itself, decoration in the waiting area was minimal; on the wall behind three chairs hung a company calendar, a map of northern Italy, and two posters from the Parmigiano-Reggiano Consortium. While they stood in the outer room, Zucari began his explanation of the process. He spoke in short sentences, which made it easier for Rick to interpret, but also gave Angelo and Lexi the impression the man was annoyed that he was taking time away from his real work.

He began by pointing to the map and explaining that Parmigiano-Reggiano cheese, by law, was produced only in certain geographical areas within the regions of Emilia Romagna and Lombardy, a system similar to the geographic designations for wines. Within those areas, thanks to the climate and soil, the quality of the milk was unique, and milk was, of course, the most important factor in making the end product. The diet of their cows was strictly controlled, never included silage or fermented feed, and the milk was always fresh from the previous evening. No additives or preservatives were ever used to make the cheese. The process followed a strict procedure beginning with the milking of the cows and ending more than a year later when the cheese was ready to be tested, certified, and finally put on the market.

"Follow me, please, and I'll show you how it all begins." He opened a heavy door with a small window, and motioned them to follow him.

The change from a small, drab, office of paper and computers to a bright, spacious workroom of milk and cheese was overwhelming to the senses, beginning with a strong odor of fermentation. The room held a dozen copper cauldrons, each the size of a large, round bathtub. They were filled with a white mixture and watched over by men dressed completely in white, including their caps. Everything was immaculate: white tiled floor, steel pipes, cauldrons, and workers.

"The milk from the late afternoon has been resting through the night," Zucari explained, with Rick interpreting, "and in the morning it is put into these cauldrons and mixed with other natural ingredients to curdle and ferment it. With the heat of the cauldron it begins to coagulate almost immediately. As it cooks, it is stirred with mixers." He pointed to machines that looked like small outboard motors, clamped to the side of each cauldron. "During the process he tests the mixture using a *spino*, a tool that goes back centuries."

Rick did not attempt to translate the word, but simply pointed to what the man at the cauldron closest to them was using. It looked like a small, round, birdcage on the end of a thick wooden pole. The worker stirred it slowly in the milky mixture that was thickening into cheese as they watched.

"With the price of copper, these kettles must have cost a fortune," said Angelo. He walked to one of the cauldrons and peered into the glutinous mixture, with Lexi at his side.

Rick stood back with the manager. "Wasn't that Emilio Fiore who just left?"

Zucari looked at him with a penetrating frown. "You met him after the funeral, Signor Montoya, and you know his farm is across the road."

"I did meet him, and he told me himself that he and Roberto Rondini didn't get along well at all."

"I've never had a quarrel with the man. He's here to look at some equipment we have which he's thinking about purchasing for himself. When he asked to see it, I was glad to help."

New management. Rick tried to figure out a way to ask about the woman Zucari was with the previous evening, without revealing that he knew she had been the mistress of his deceased boss. Before he could come up with something, Angelo and Lexi walked back to join them.

"Quite an operation," Angelo said, and Rick translated for the manager, who appeared glad to leave aside talk of the neighbor and continue his description of the process.

"Once the milk has coagulated enough, two of the men dip into the cauldron using those cloths." He nodded toward a shiny table loosely piled with large rectangles of white material. "A ball of the cheese mixture is lifted out and hung over the cauldron to drip out excess liquid, then wrapped in its cloth to be fitted in those molds." He pointed to another table with a row of ring-shaped pieces of plastic that looked like huge cookie cutters. "With experience they can tell just how much will fit into the molds. They wrap the cheese in the cloth, squeeze it inside the molds, and label them with the month and year." He walked to a long metal table on wheels where another row of molds was lined up. The rings enclosed the newly formed cheeses, wrapped inside their white cloths and marked with small, round stickers. "They will rest here for several days and harden into the wheels whose shape and size are the hallmarks of Parmigiano-Reggiano."

"It's not cheese yet?" said Angelo, tapping on the plastic ring.

"It's not the finished product yet," Zucari answered.

"How much milk does it take to make a wheel of the cheese, and how much will it weigh?"

Rick translated the answer, then made the conversions from liters to gallons, and kilos to pounds. "So about a hundred-fifty gallons of milk, and each wheel weighs about eighty-five pounds."

"This way, please," said Zucari when Rick was finished.

The three visitors followed him to the far end of the room under the eyes of a half dozen white-clad workers. He pushed through a set of swinging metal doors, once again polished to a glossy sheen. The room they entered now was equally large, but in contrast to the bright light of the cauldron room, it was dimly lit. Most of its space was taken up by long rectangular troughs filled with bobbing wheels of cheese. At the far end of the room, a man dressed in the standard white outfit walked along, slowly turning them in the liquid. Unlike the other room where the air was filled with the noise of pumps and other machines, here the only sound was the sloshing of the white wheels in the water.

"The cheese stays in this salt solution for several weeks, continuing the maturation process and absorbing the salt. The forms are regularly turned by hand to give the surfaces a uniform consistency."

Once again Angelo and Lexi wandered off to get a closer look.

"How long have you been working here, Signor Zucari?"

The manager watched Angelo as he answered. "About twenty years."

"How did you get the job? If you don't mind me asking."

"Why should I? My father knew Roberto Rondini and asked him to take me on, as a favor. That's the way things work here in Italy, Signor Montoya. I worked my way up to become manager."

"Things work that way in America, as well, Signor Zucari.

Clearly you had an aptitude for the work, or you wouldn't have ended up where you are."

"I'd like to think that."

The floating wheels of cheese were too much for Angelo to resist. He pushed one below the surface and watched it bob up and down, earning a smile from Lexi but an annoyed look from the room's lone worker. The two visitors rejoined Rick and Zucari.

"What's next?" Angelo asked.

"From here the wheels go into the aging room for the final step in the process. The rooms are kept at a precise temperature and humidity, and the wheels are periodically turned to assure that the aging is uniform throughout. They will be on the shelves for a minimum of twelve months, but up to and exceeding twenty-four. They are then tested by specialists from the consortium, first by tapping on them with a small, steel hammer, and then, if necessary with a needle, and at last resort a sampling dowel. When the quality of the cheese is confirmed, then, and only then, is it branded with the seal of Parmigiano-Reggiano and can be sold as such."

Zucari's eyes darted to a large metal clock on the wall and then to his own watch. He turned to Rick. "I'm afraid I forgot that I must deal with an issue of importance. It should take only a moment. Please tell Signor Rondini that I regret the interruption. You can go through those doors to the aging rooms."

He nodded at Rondini, walked quickly back toward the first room, pushing through the swinging doors. Rick told them what he'd said.

"I guess he didn't find out until this morning about having to show us around," said Rondini. He leaned over the pool and pushed another cheese wheel. "I saw that you were talking to him while Lexi and I were wandering about."

"I asked him what Emilio Fiore was doing here."

"Ah, Fiore. Lexi, that was the guy getting into the pickup.

He has the farm across the road and did not exactly get along with my cousin."

Lexi nodded. "I see. And now that your cousin is gone, the neighbor and the foreman are on friendly terms. Curious."

"Zucari told me that he's always gotten along with the neighbor," said Rick. "I also asked him how he got his job, and he said Roberto Rondini was a friend of his father."

"It's not what you know, but who you know," said Rondini. "It's the same everywhere. But in order to keep the job, and move up, you have to be good at it. Having an in with the owner only gets you so far. Isn't that right, Lexi?"

She smiled. "If you say so, Mr. Rondini."

Rick pointed to the doors at the opposite end of the room. "Shall we go into the aging room?"

"Lead the way, Language Man."

They walked between the troughs under the gaze of the worker, and past a row of steel trolleys ready to transport the cheese to its next location. Rick pushed through the doors and they found themselves in a room with a ceiling three times as high as the one they'd just left. Rows of shelves, separated by narrow aisles, towered above them. It was like the inner sanctum of some huge library, dimly lit and musty. But instead of ancient books, the shelves held wheels of light brown cheese, and the mustiness was the pungent odor of aging Parmigiano-Reggiano.

"Wow," said Lexi. "This is impressive. There are thousands of these wheels in here. It must be worth a fortune." She pulled out her smartphone and ran her thumbs quickly over the screen. "Nine dollars a pound in the States." She looked up at the rows. "It's like being in Fort Knox."

"*Grana* is a slang word for money in Italian," Rick said. "Which is the same word used for this kind of hard cheese."

"I can see why," said Angelo. He walked to the end of one of the rows and touched a wheel of cheese. "It's like an assembly line printing money. Every time you put a new row of cheese up to age you pull off another row and sell it. With a capable manager keeping an eye on things, my cousin could just let the process take care of itself and spend his time fishing. Not bad at all."

"What about marketing and sales?" Lexi said.

"Sales must be easy," answered Rick, "when only a relatively few producers, by Italian and European law, can make Parmigiano-Reggiano cheese. The consortium, which was created by the dairies, protects the geographic monopoly and does a lot of the marketing and public relations, so that helps too." He ran his hand along the shelf. "But it wouldn't work if they didn't have a good product."

They started up one of the narrow aisles, Rick first, followed by Angelo and Lexi. Hundreds of round sides peered down at them from the shelves, the top rows barely visible from below. The silence was broken only by their footsteps, and then by the faint opening and closing of a door somewhere behind them. Zucari must have returned, Rick thought, but after ten seconds the manager had not appeared. Rick listened for footsteps and decided that the sound of the door must have carried from a different part of the factory. Then he heard another noise.

It sounded like scraping or sliding, and it coincided with the slightest movement of the shelf on the right side of the aisle. He looked up and noticed a slight teetering of the cheese stacked five feet above them. One of the wheels began to slide slowly forward. From the next aisle over he thought he heard a low grunt just as another of the wheels started creeping toward the edge of its shelf. Then another began to move.

Rick spun around. "Go back! They're going to come down!"

Angelo's head shot upward, but he was mesmerized by the moving cheese and his body froze. Three of the wheels at the very top were almost halfway to the edge and the entire shelf rocked slowly and steadily. Fortunately, Lexi understood immediately.

"Get his left arm," she yelled.

They picked up Angelo and dragged him backward just as the first wheel of cheese hit the floor and smashed into pieces behind them. It was followed by another, and another, until most of the top shelf's contents was crashing to the floor. Rick and Lexi had almost gotten Angelo to the end of the aisle when one of the wheels glanced off the shelf on the other side and struck Rick just above his right knee. He let go of Angelo and dropped to the ground while Lexi kept pulling her boss until the two were safely against the wall near the door. Rick looked up to see another eighty-five pounds of cheese starting to tip off a top shelf above. He rolled over and it exploded next to him. On his hands and knees, he scrambled to the end of the row and out of harm's way.

"Somebody was pushing the shelf from the next row," he said to Lexi and Angelo, who were huddled against the wall. "Stay there, I'll get him." Rick pulled himself to his feet but immediately crashed back to the ground, holding his knee. "I guess I won't get him."

At that moment Carlo Zucari appeared, followed by a slew of white-clad workers. Rick looked up at the manager.

"Too late. You missed all the excitement."

Chapter Eight

The broken shards of cheese that covered the floor added new pungency to the air of the curing room. Only by counting the empty spaces on the shelves could Zucari calculate how many wheels had been lost. He was overseeing the salvage operation under the eyes of Rick, Angelo, and Lexi. The three of them stood back against the wall and watched two workers put chunks of cheese on wheeled trolleys. A third worker, raised up by a narrow forklift, was checking the shelving and adjusting cheeses that were still on it.

"I told Signor Rondini that we needed to replace these shelves," Zucari muttered to nobody in particular. Only Rick, among the three standing against the wall, understood him. He translated for Angelo and Lexi.

"Don't say anything about it being pushed," Angelo ordered. "Livia has enough to worry about; she doesn't need to think someone is trying to bump off her uncle."

"It could have been Rick they were after," said Lexi as she poked him without Angelo noticing.

Rick poked back. "Perhaps Folengo wanted to get back at Lexi for attacking him this morning, and he sneaked onto the farm under the cover of fog. But another possibility is that it could have been meant for our friend here." He inclined his head toward Zucari, who was directing the man working on the top shelf. "Don't forget that he slipped off just before it happened, and the person who did it may have been expecting him to be with us."

"The other scenario is that Zucari himself pushed the shelves," Angelo said. "Or it was done by his friend, Fiore, who was here looking at equipment he wants to buy."

"Mr. Rondini, Rick should report this to the police."

Angelo took in a deep breath and let it out slowly. "I suppose so. You're due to talk to him anyway, aren't you, Language Man? He may have some news about the investigation. Do you think you can make it out to the car?"

Rick rubbed his knee. "I'll be fine. It's just a flesh wound."

"Then let's get that coffee from Livia. It's going to taste good after this. And I have something important to tell her."

Inspector Crispi glanced at the array of food behind the *vetrina* before pushing open the glass door and entering the shop. A mixture of smells coming from all manner of fresh delicacies assaulted his senses, causing his thoughts about homicide to be momentarily pushed aside. The *salumaio* was laid out in typical Italian fashion: a refrigerated display case ran the length of the space, and behind it shelves were crowded with less perishable food. *Mortadella* and other meats and cheeses hung from hooks above the shelves, waiting their turn to be taken down and sliced. Bottles of wine, in twos and threes, were squeezed in everywhere. To the right was a small counter that held a cash register. Behind it stood the man Crispi assumed was Sandro Bastoncini. He looked up when the policeman entered.

Bastoncini wore the white coat that was standard for his profession, one which could have been that of a druggist, had it not been for traces of food near one of the buttons. Thanks to sprinkles of salt that had crept into the pepper of the man's well-trimmed hair, Crispi calculated him to be in his early fifties. The face was ruddy, no doubt due to his hours catching fish rather than those spent slicing salami. He squinted down his nose over a pair of reading glasses, not happy to see his visitor yet curious as to the reason for the visit. When he'd called, Crispi had purposely not told Bastoncini why he needed to see him.

"Inspector Crispi?"

"Yes. Thank you for seeing me, Signor Bastoncini." He didn't feel the need to show his identification, and it wasn't requested. "I only have a few questions. It shouldn't take very long."

"I hope not. My assistant called in sick today so I'm by myself until my son comes in after school to help. What's this about?" He folded his arms across his chest.

"I'll be brief. We're doing a routine investigation into the death of Roberto Rondini, and—"

"Rondini? I wouldn't be surprised if someone did him in, having known the man. But from what I read in the paper it was an accidental death."

Crispi's expression stayed the same. "Every indication points to an accident, yes. You knew Signor Rondini through your fishing association, I understand?"

"That's correct."

"From what you just said, can I conclude that you did not get along well with the deceased?"

"You can well conclude that, Inspector, though that was years ago. It was not a secret that we had some disagreements, but I was not the only one, I can assure you. It all came to a head when I was running for re-election on the board of the association, and Rondini spread false rumors about me to the members."

The door opened and a woman entered carrying a cloth shopping bag that was partially filled. She looked at Bastoncini and smiled. A regular.

"*Ciao*, Sandro."

"*Buon giorno*, Signora. I'll be with you in a moment."

Crispi made a gesture to indicate he should take care of the customer and Bastoncini walked behind the counter in front of where the woman was now standing. She ordered four *etti* of sliced *prosciutto*, but with as little fat as possible, unlike the last time she was in. With two hands he pulled out a leg of the ham and held up the end that would be sliced. He said something that Crispi couldn't hear, which made her giggle, and dropped it in the slicer. He turned the blade on and cut off several paper-thin slices, which he carried to the scale. It was a bit more than the four hundred grams she'd requested but she didn't mind. She then asked for a ball of *mozzarella* and a portion of the Russian salad, and chatted while he got them for her. That was all for today. He brought the three items to the cash register where he totaled them up and carefully put them into the bag she held open for him. After paying, she looked Crispi up and down and departed.

"What kind of rumors?" asked Crispi.

"I beg your pardon?"

"You said Rondini spread rumors about you."

"Oh, yes, of course." He wiped his hands on a cloth from under the counter. "Things which would seem unimportant to non-fishermen, but are very significant for us. Like what kinds of lures I used to win our competitions or even whether I was the one who actually caught the fish. Unfortunately, there were those gullible enough to believe his nonsense." He again folded his arms across his chest. "But, as I said, Inspector, the incident was years ago. I have gone beyond it and am involved in the association. I can't say I'd forgiven Roberto, but it just stopped being an issue. I was even in attendance a few days ago at his funeral."

Crispi tried to recall the face of Bastoncini among the mourners, but since he had sat at the rear of the church, he'd seen mostly the backs of people's heads. "I am not a fisherman, Signor Bastoncini, so I can ask you a basic question. Was it strange that he was fishing at that hour of the day?"

"Not at all, Inspector. The early morning hours are usually the best time to catch fish. They are ready for their breakfast, you might say. Those of us who work don't have the luxury of being able to fish every morning, like Rondini could."

"Everyone knew he was usually on the river at that hour?"

"He enjoyed telling all of us in the association how often he was on the river, and I'm sure he said the same to his non-fishing acquaintances. Being seen as a wealthy man of leisure was extremely important to Roberto Rondini, especially by those of us who have to work most days."

"What mornings do you fish?"

"You know the days the shops are open in this province, Inspector."

Crispi made a mental note to check the day of the week Rondini's body was found.

●●●●●

The coffee Livia served was dark *espresso* in small cups. A dish of cookies sat on the tray, decorated with colored icing and sugar, but she appeared not to have noticed them. She talked in short sentences as she poured each cup, interrupting herself to ask each of her three visitors how much sugar or cream they wished.

"I'm mortified that you were in there when the shelf broke. Carlo says that only a dozen wheels were damaged. It could have been much worse. When we had the earthquake a few years ago, it was terrible. Some dairies were almost put out of business. The worst damage was well south of here. Carlo will have to check all the shelving now. Oh, the cookies. Alexis, please try one."

Lexi took one of the cookies from the tray and stirred her *espresso*. "Touring the dairy was fascinating, Mrs. Guarino. I will appreciate the cheese even more now that I've seen how it's made."

"Lexi is right," said Angelo. He stirred his coffee and sat back into the cushions of the sofa where he and Lexi sat. The other three people sensed that he was not finished, and waited in silence for him to arrange his thoughts.

"I want you to know, Livia, that coming to Mantova, and especially to this farm, has made me more appreciative of my own roots. Meeting you, of course, is a great part of it, but just being in the land of my parents, where I was born, has opened my eyes to so much. Breathing the air here, seeing the fields, watching the river flow past…" He stopped to take a sip from his cup. "My great regret is that I did not come here sooner in my life."

At first Rick thought his boss was simply trying to get Livia's mind off the accident, since she was already upset about her husband and the falling cheese hadn't helped. A kind gesture, of the type Rondini was not likely to be known for in the competitive world of business. He hadn't gotten this far with kindness. Yet Rick sensed that Angelo's little speech was more than an attempt to comfort his niece. He'd spent relatively few total hours with the man since picking him up at the airport, but somehow Rick thought that something new was going on. It was a different side of Angelo Rondini, or perhaps a side that hadn't existed before. A quick glance at the puzzled expression on Lexi's face convinced Rick that he was correct.

Angelo continued.

"I'd like to make a gesture, Livia, to honor the memory of my cousin. In his death he did me a great favor by pulling me back to the land of my birth. I will be forever indebted to him for that, and want to do something to honor his memory." He saw that Livia was about to speak, and held up his hand. "I would like to have a small memorial made, something in stone. It would be placed near the dock, overlooking the river. With your permission, of course. When I visited it yesterday I was impressed by the beauty and tranquility of the spot. I understood why your father spent so much time there—I could almost feel his presence."

"Uncle, that would be wonderful. Of course you have my permission." The smile on her face disappeared as she looked past Angelo toward the hallway behind him. "Francesco, are you feeling better?" She spoke in Italian.

The others turned to see her husband standing in the hallway. Unlike the day of the funeral, he was dressed informally and was in need of a shave. An ugly, red bruise covered half his forehead, and he brought up a hand to cover it while his eyes squinted at the visitors.

"I didn't know they were here."

"I told you this morning, dear. You must not have heard."

"I'm sorry, Livia. The pain pills I took are making me groggy."

Angelo glanced at Rick, as if silently reminding him to remember what was being said so he could tell him later. The two men stood as Francesco approached them unsteadily.

"You will forgive me, I hope," he said. "An unfortunate accident last evening. I am in no condition to be sociable, I'm afraid, but Livia is capable of extending the hospitality for both of us."

Rick interpreted his words for Angelo and Lexi, and transmitted the answer in return.

"Mr. Rondini hopes you feel better soon."

Francesco nodded and shuffled off. A small bandage was visible on the back of his head. Whether he was coming into or about to leave the house was unclear. Had the farm manager called him about the falling cheese? Rick decided there was no way to know, and certainly no way to find out. The group in the living room settled back into their chairs, and Livia was anxious to move the subject away from her husband.

"Uncle, you are very kind to think of a memorial to my father. I know just the place you are thinking of, an open area overlooking the river and the dock. When I was a girl I used to sit there and watch the Mincio flow past."

He placed his empty cup on the tray. "Then it's done. Montoya will help me find someplace that can do the work quickly. There is something else I'd like to do, Livia, and perhaps you can help."

"Of course, Uncle."

Angelo leaned back against the cushions and adjusted his tie. Since the day of the arrival, except for the funeral, he had worn the same light-gray wool suit, but always with a different tie. Today it had a red-and-blue-stripe pattern.

"Where would I find records of my own birth? I know that my parents emigrated to America when I was an infant, but there must be something written somewhere. My birthplace was Voglia, which I think is just south of here."

"It is. It's in the area called Virgilio, named for Mantova's most famous native son. Voglia is where my grandfather Enzo lived when he was young."

"Probably the whole Rondini family lived there, including my parents. Your father wasn't born in Voglia, was he?"

"No, in Mantova at the same hospital where I was born. I've driven through Voglia a few times, and I can tell you there isn't much to it. You should try the *municipio*, where births and deaths are recorded, but also the parish church, where you'd find records of baptisms."

Later Rick, Angelo, and Lexi stopped halfway down the path in front of the Rondini home. They had said their good-byes to Livia, who reminded them of the event in honor of her father that evening. The early fog had disappeared, leaving a sparkle on the ground from the rays of the late-morning sun. Along the fence next to the road, a worker perched on a mower was making his final turn in the direction of the dairy build-ings. Ragged lines of grass-cuttings left by the machine sent off a rich smell that enveloped the three people standing on the path.

"We have enough things to keep us busy until that event this evening," said Angelo, talking like the CEO in a staff meet-ing. "Language Man, can you find someplace where I can order a monument? If we pay them enough, they should be able to do it on a rush basis. And you have to talk to your cop friend to find out what's going on with his investigation. You should also tell him about the falling cheese, though I don't want him pushing me again to have police protection. And let's see if we can get to that town of Voglia to look up my birth record. I think it would be fascinating to see."

"Lexi," said Rick, "if you can lend me your tablet, I'll look up some stone places and also find where Voglia is."

Lexi fished out the tablet from her bag, hit a button to turn it on, and passed it to Rick. "It automatically reset from Chicago to Italy when we got here, so any search you do will be based on this location."

Rick checked the screen and started tapping in letters.

Angelo took her elbow. "Lexi, while he's doing that, I need to talk to you about the Hawaii project. I read the notes you put on my breakfast tray, and I think I know what I want to do." They strolled down the path toward the car where the driver was waiting. Angelo talked and gestured as he walked, while Lexi made notes on the small pad she'd taken from her purse. A few minutes later Rick was walking toward them, holding up the tablet.

"This thing works great, Lexi. If I can ever afford it, I'll get one for myself." The two had paused next to the Mercedes, where Marco stood holding the door open. They watched Rick reach them. "I found what looks like the perfect place to buy stonework, including grave markers and other memorials. It's just south of Mantova. Marco, do you know where this place is?" He held the screen close to the driver.

"Yes, of course. It's in the *zona industriale* near the river."

Rick passed the tablet back to Lexi, who turned it off and stowed it in her purse. "Shall we go there now?" he asked.

"Yes," answered Angelo, "but we'll drop Lexi at the hotel first. She has to get on the phone and spoil the breakfast of a few people back in Chicago."

He dropped himself into the back seat of the car. Lexi flashed Rick a quick grin and took her place next to her boss.

Rick extended his leg onto the floor of the front seat but pulled it back slowly and eased into the seat from a different angle. Perhaps the flying cheeses had done more damage than he'd realized.

● ● ● ● ●

The industrial zone just south of the city was not on any of the tourist itineraries. Not that it was especially unsightly; it had its own style of orderliness, one which marked a prosperous local economy. But rather than the tranquility of history and art found in the center of Mantova, the atmosphere here was movement and noise caused by metal and machinery. Small factories, service businesses, depots, and warehouses lined both sides of the street, its surface showing the wear that came from the traffic of large vehicles. Save for the license plates on the trucks and the gauge of the railroad tracks that cut across the street, it could have been an industrial park outside any small American city.

The Mercedes turned through the iron gate of the monument business and drove past stones of various sizes and shapes before coming to a stop in front of the low metal building that served as the office. When Rick and Angelo emerged from the sealed-in silence of the car they could hear the sound of metal against stone coming from a shed to one side. The door to the office opened and a young woman dressed in jeans and a sweater came out. A gust of wind caught her long hair and blew it in front of her face.

"Can I help you?" she asked in Italian while brushing the hair aside.

Rick stepped forward and got right to the point. "This is Signor Angelo Rondini, visiting from America. He is looking for a small stone memorial for his deceased cousin Roberto Rondini. My name is Montoya, I'm his interpreter."

She shook Rick's hand and then Angelo's. "I'm sorry I don't

speak English. We'll be glad to help, but there is something I
don't understand. We did the gravestone for Roberto Rondini,
so what is it this gentleman needs?"

Angelo listened without understanding, but knew from her
body language that she had asked a question. "You know what
I want, Language Man. Explain it to her." He walked off and
began looking at the stone pieces that sat in the open air.

"He must be upset by the death of his cousin," she said
when Angelo was some distance away.

Or something else is bothering him, Rick thought. Perhaps
the Hawaii project, whatever that might be.

"Mr. Rondini would like to put up a small memorial along
the river, near the place where his cousin loved to go fishing.
Unfortunately, it is a rush job, since he would like it installed
tomorrow. He will of course pay you extra to get it finished
expeditiously. There would be some words carved into it, but a
minimum. 'In Memory of Roberto Rondini,' is all."

"I think we can do it. People usually die suddenly, so we are
used to working on short deadlines, and right now business is
slow. If he can choose the stone, we can do the wording in a few
hours and have it put in place in the morning."

They looked at Angelo, who had stopped in front of an
ionic column about four feet high, its top broken off leaving a
jagged surface.

"That one is very popular," she said. "The broken stone sym-
bolizes a life cut short."

"Let's see what he thinks." They walked to Angelo, who continued to study the column, his hands deep in the pockets of
his overcoat. "She can do it, Mr. Rondini. Is this column what
you had in mind?"

"What? Oh, yeah. I think this would be fine. They can do it
all by tomorrow morning, including the inscription?"

"Yes, sir."

Angelo nodded and waved his hand weakly to indicate it
was a deal. The woman went inside to prepare the paperwork,

leaving the two men standing next to the column. They watched a truck loaded with stone blocks drive in past the Mercedes where Marco was standing, smoking a cigarette. With a loud grinding of gears the truck shifted into reverse and backed toward the shed. Two men in overalls came out, brushed gray dust off themselves, and surveyed the shipment.

"They're going to need some equipment to unload those pieces," said Angelo. He spoke the words but his mind was elsewhere.

"You okay, Mr. Rondini?"

"Huh? Sure, I'm fine, Language Man. Got a lot on my plate."

"Business issues?"

He shook his head. "No, that will work itself out. It's this whole deal with my cousin. His death. A possible murder. And then someone pushes the cheese on us. Add to that the whole trip here, bringing me back for the first time to where I was born. There's a lot for me to absorb. I'm glad you're here to help."

"I haven't really done anything, Mr. Rondini."

"Yeah, you have." They watched as a small forklift came out of the shed and pulled up behind the truck. The two workers argued about what should come next in the process. "I suppose you know all about your Italian family."

"My aunt and uncle have told me a bit. I probably should pick their brains more about the Fontanas, and ask my mother when I see her next. I was pretty young when my Italian grandparents died, but I remember the funerals. Every once in a while I think that I should make a visit to their graves, outside of Rome, but I haven't yet."

The forklift driver had taken charge, slipping the metal prongs under the pallet that held the stone. The hydraulic motor groaned as it lifted its load from the bed of the truck.

"Do it," said Angelo. "Life is short." As if to make his point, he checked his watch. "I had wanted to visit Voglia now, but

I'll tell Marco we'll do it tomorrow morning, since I have to get back to confer with Lexi on that project. We'll get lunch at the hotel. I want you to go to the newspaper again to find out more about the various Rondinis, including yours truly." He pulled a piece of paper from his pocket and passed it to Rick. "These are my parents' names. See if there's anything there about them. And I want you to go see your friend the cop and get an update from him. That should keep you busy until it's time to go to the event at the—what's the name of the place?"

"Palazzo Te."

"Kind of a strange name."

"I looked it up. Comes from the local word for huts, since apparently there were many of them on the acreage when the Gonzagas decided to build the *palazzo* there. Perhaps a bit of ironic humor on their part."

"So it's not a hut?"

"We'll see this evening."

Crispi had suggested they meet over lunch, which sounded good to Rick. There was something about being attacked by cheese that gave one an appetite. As would be expected for a restaurant only a few blocks from the *questura*, police sat at many of the tables, and the caste system of their profession was evident. Uniforms dined together. Plainclothes—many with pistols on their belts—sat separately. The clientele was mostly male, with a few women mixed in with the uniformed cops. The noise level was high, another indication that the place was filled with regulars, and the plain walls and stone floor did little to dampen the decibels. One of the waiters, who was clearly aware of Crispi's status, led the inspector and Rick to a quieter table in the corner and placed menus in front of them. He took their order for wine and mineral water and departed.

Rick had glanced at the tables as they'd walked to theirs, and most of the choices were what he had expected policemen to eat in cold weather: hearty, stick-to-the-ribs fare. He barely had time to study the choices when the waiter returned with a bottle of water and a liter of the house red. Crispi, who had made a cursory glance at the menu, passed it to the waiter and ordered *agnoli in brodo* followed by the *stracotto di manzo*. Rick listened and told the waiter he'd have the same. Stuffed pasta in broth was the perfect way to start a meal when there was a chill in the air. Then pot roast on a bed of *polenta*, likely enough food to last him through the rest of the day. He snapped off a crust of bread and took a sip of the wine.

"You have some information for me, Montoya? This investigation, such as it is, appears to be going nowhere. No more threats to your employer?"

"No more threats."

Strictly speaking, it was true. An actual attempt to harm someone was not a threat, after all. And Angelo, just before leaving Rick in the hotel lobby, had said that, on second thought, he didn't want Crispi to know about the incident in the cheese-aging room. The inspector would become more adamant about police protection, and Angelo still wanted no part of that. Rick rubbed his sore leg under the table and wondered if it was the right decision.

"We went to the dairy this morning on Livia Guarino's invitation and did a tour of the cheese-making operation."

"Did she say anything that might help with the investigation?"

"No. And in fact she didn't take us on the tour since her husband had an accident last night and she wanted to stay close to him."

Crispi frowned. "What kind of accident?"

"Hard to say. He made a brief appearance and I saw bruises on the front and back of his head, but they didn't elaborate on what actually happened. So the manager, Carlo Zucari, gave us the cheese tour. Something else. The guy who owns the dairy across the road, Emilio Fiore, was coming out of the plant when we drove up, so Zucari doesn't appear to hold the same antagonism toward the man that his late boss did."

The *agnoli* arrived, floating in shallow bowls of almost clear, capon broth. Lexi would be pleased. They sprinkled on Parmigiano-Reggiano, mixing its pungency with the rich flavor of the capon, before picking up their spoons and wishing each other a *buon appetito*.

"Perhaps the two were talking about that plot of land which appears to be the source of so much grief," said Crispi after eating a few *agnoli*. "I had one of my sergeants, who is good at such things, do a title search on that plot. I wondered why it has been left to seed."

"What did he find?"

"She. She found that it was originally owned, decades ago, by a farmer who couldn't pay his taxes. It was taken over by the province and then sold to Roberto Rondini's father."

"I read about that incident in the archives of the *Gazzetta*, but didn't know that it was the same piece of land that now may come up for sale."

"According to tax assessment records, the plot was never developed, even though it is part of the Rondini dairy farm. Neither the recently deceased Roberto Rondini, nor his father, ever did anything with it."

"Until, possibly, now." Rick finished the last of the *agnoli* and started on what was left of the broth with his spoon. "But why wouldn't they have used the plot to grow grass? I don't know anything about farming, but I would assume that it is efficient to rotate your cows among various pastures."

"That was my thought as well."

"Something else curious about Carlo Zucari, the manager. I ran into him last night when Lexi Coleman, Signor Rondini's assistant, and I were having coffee after dinner. He was with a woman, and he introduced me to her."

"And?"

"Letizia Bentivolgio. Isn't she the woman who Roberto Rondini was seeing in town?"

Crispi put his spoon inside the empty bowl. His expression hadn't changed. "Yes, she is, and yes, that is curious. When I interviewed her she told me she'd met Rondini when he and his manager had come to buy equipment where she worked. It should have occurred to me that it was Zucari. I'll have to think about that one for a while."

"Well, I've thought about it, and concluded that it gives Zucari a motive to murder his boss." Rick took Crispi's silent stare as an invitation to continue. "Zucari and Letizia were a couple, and then Roberto Rondini moved in on her. She goes with the rich owner instead of the manager. Motive. Now that Roberto is out of the picture, Zucari moves back into it."

Crispi drummed his fingers on the table. "We have quite a drama."

"Another member of the drama's cast showed up early this morning when I was doing a run with Lexi along the lake."

The bowls were taken away by one waiter seconds before another put down the dishes with their second course. Not exactly fast food, but the staff knew that most of the policemen had a limited time for lunch. Rich vapors wafted up from the pot roast served on a bed of *polenta*, the meat's dark red juices spreading over the yellow edges. Both men studied their plates for a moment before taking forks in hand.

"And which one of the *dramatis personae* would that be?" asked Crispi after his first bite.

Rick recounted the encounter with Domenico Folengo, describing in detail how the activist had confronted Lexi and had paid the price.

To Rick's surprise, Crispi actually smiled. "I wish I had been there to see it. What a shame Folengo didn't come running to my office to bring charges for assault. We could have used some levity this morning." He resumed his deadpan expression and tucked into his main dish. "What did his manifesto say?"

"What you would expect. Keep the environment natural, save the planet by starting with the Mincio River. It did not make much of an impression on Signor Rondini. In fact he said in the car on the way to the dairy that he might tell his niece to sell the land for development just to annoy Folengo." Rick noticed the puzzled look on the policeman's face. "He was joking, of course."

"I never understand your American humor."

Nor Italian humor, Rick decided. He took up a piece of the *stracotto* and dipped it in the *polenta*, recalling the *polenta* under Angelo's perch the day before at the elegant restaurant in Goito. His today had to be just as good. At half the price.

"Inspector, can I interrupt for a moment?" The man who spoke had been walking by the table toward the door when he saw Crispi. Now he noticed Rick and waved his hand. "Never mind, I can talk to you later."

"It's all right, Lanzi. What is it you wanted to say?"

Though not comfortable with a stranger listening, Lanzi continued. "The gambling investigation. As you suspected, it looks like it involves an out-of-town syndicate. Probably from Milan. I've got a call in to the *questura* there this afternoon."

"Good. Let me know the details."

The policeman joined his colleagues waiting for him at the door.

"Should you really be talking other police business with a civilian listening, Inspector?"

"If there's one civilian I'd trust to be discreet it would be the nephew of Commissario Fontana."

Rick suspected his status as a confidant was due more to uncle Piero's position than his own personal qualities, but he was pleased to accept it nonetheless. Now could he get the cop to lighten up a bit, so they might have a normal relationship? Not likely.

"Did you interview the man from the fishing society?"

Crispi finished a mouthful of food and patted his lips with the napkin before answering. "Signor Bastoncini. Yes. The only information I got was another confirmation that Roberto

Rondini was at times a difficult man. He claims that Rondini spread rumors which cast doubts as to the honesty of his fishing practices, something which resulted in Bastoncini leaving the board. Cutthroat politics in a fishing association—can you believe it? But why am I surprised? My mother tells me stories about her lace-making group where two women are always at each others' throats. Once, when one was in the bathroom, the other got into her basket and untwisted all the bobbins. Montoya, these are women in their seventies and eighties." He took a drink of wine. "And they meet in the basement of the church."

Rick had no way to top that story. "There's an event tonight at the Palazzo Te that the cheese consortium has organized to honor Roberto Rondini. I expect most of those in your investigation will be there, certainly the Rondini manager, Carlo Zucari, as well as the neighbor, Fiore."

"I would expect every producer of Parmigiano-Reggiano cheese in Lombardy will be in attendance. A good opportunity to get together and exchange gossip under the pretext of honoring one of their own." Crispi raised an index finger. "You'll let me know if Francesco Guarino appears, despite his injuries."

"Of course. And there's another event. My boss has ordered a small stone memorial to be put up along the river to honor his late cousin. The ceremony will be tomorrow afternoon. I don't know who will be there."

"Near the dock?"

"That's what Angelo wanted, and Livia Guarino agreed."

Crispi shook his head. "That's a bit tasteless, isn't it? Near the place where the man was murdered?"

"She thinks of it as a place where her father spent many pleasant hours."

The detective shrugged and put his fork on the empty plate. "You and your American employer will be busy. How long does he plan to stay in Mantova?"

"I'm not sure. Originally, I was told that he couldn't be away for more than a week, and the inference was that it would be less. So I would expect only a couple days more before he flies back. I don't think I'm betraying any confidences to say that the trip is having an effect on him…apart from the murder investigation, I mean. It has opened his eyes to his Italian past, even though he left this country as an infant. He's got me doing research on his family, but I'm not sure if he's pleased with what I'm finding out."

"You mean about Roberto Rondini's father?"

"Correct. His Uncle Enzo was no angel, and neither was Cousin Roberto. Mr. Rondini has a forceful personality himself, as you have witnessed. It's one reason why he's been such a successful businessman in America. But I sense he has mixed feelings about his family's reputation here."

"I fear that if we solve this murder, that reputation will not be improved."

Other than a small, red carnation in his lapel, Signor da Feltre looked the same. The tie was plain, as was the suit, and the day's newspaper was once again spread out on the desk in front of him. The only sound was a soft hum coming from the florescent lights in the low ceiling which gave everything in the room a faintly ghostlike hue. The archivist looked up and smiled when Rick pushed through the doors. As usual, they were alone.

"What's the occasion?" Rick asked, pointing to the flower. Not that he and da Feltre were now close buddies, but after two previous visits, the question did not seem impertinent. But he added, "If you don't mind me asking."

Signor da Feltre looked down as if noticing it for the first time. "This? I'm meeting a lady friend after work. Coffee. Or perhaps a glass of wine. Who knows what it could lead to?"

Was that a wink? At the very least it was a twinkle in the man's eye. Rick had hoped that the guy had some sort of life outside the crypt where he spent his days, and it now appeared that he did. Da Feltre made an "it's all yours" gesture toward the computers and Rick walked over to take his usual place. He sat down, pulled out the sheet Angelo had given him with his parents' names, and pushed the ON button.

What little information Rick found on Angelo's parents was noticeably different in both tone and quantity from what he'd read earlier about the uncle. Angelo's father was a graduate of the local *liceo* and worked as a clerk after getting his diploma. One story mentioned a scholastic award he had received on graduation. His employment at an insurance office was noted in the wedding announcement, but as would be expected of those times, no mention was made of the work status of the wife. She would become a *casalinga*, a housewife, and take care of the infant Angelo when he came along. The marriage took place in Voglia, where the Rondini clan had apparently lived at the time, and where Angelo was later born. There was one small story about membership in a fishing association, but it wasn't clear if this was the same one that Roberto Rondini would join decades later. Rick concluded that fishing, when Angelo's father was involved, was a relatively inexpensive pastime, and which brought some food to the table. It would be a natural hobby for a clerk on a limited budget. Would he have given it up completely when he emigrated to America? Fishing was not something Angelo had mentioned, even when they had visited the dock and seen Roberto's boat. Not that the man was sharing all his childhood memories with Rick. Far from it.

The only story that mentioned the family's departure for the States was a short piece on the social pages about the annual Christmas party of the insurance office, held at a local restaurant. It listed awards and bonuses handed out, including to Angelo's father, with a mention that he would be leaving the firm to take a position with an Italian export company in New York and would be sorely missed by his colleagues.

Rick let the wheels of the chair roll him back from the monitor. He meshed his fingers together and stretched them in front of him while pondering the information he'd found about Angelo's parents. The picture that formed of the elder Rondini was one of a solid citizen—hard-working and a follower of the rules. Perhaps even a bit dull, but that could be Rick wanting to read something into it that was not there. What was fascinating was the contrast between the two brothers, at least as described on the pages of the Gazzetta. Angelo's father, keeping a low profile, working hard, and always toeing the line. The father of the late Roberto Rondini, brash, highly political, and somewhat shady. This might have been due to the newspaper's political slant, but in addition they had given Enzo Rondini considerably more ink than given to the brother who had slipped off to America, never to be mentioned again. Rick scooted the chair to the keyboard and searched again for Enzo Rondini, Angelo's uncle. He might have missed something on his previous visits to the archive.

What he found was coverage of the man's marriage. It took place four years after the departure of baby Angelo and his parents for New York. Enzo Rondini and his young bride, Pina, were married in the cathedral at Mantova—not, like his brother, in the parish church in Voglia. The man had moved up in the world. Rick cross-checked the names of those in the wedding party and found several to be local political leaders. He found no mention of the brother who had left for America several years earlier. Either Angelo's parents were not invited to the wedding or maybe it was too expensive for the young family to travel back to Italy for it. Either way, it appeared that the two Rondini brothers from the little town of Voglia were living very different lives, and not just because they found themselves on opposite sides of the ocean.

Rick folded his notes and slipped them into his pocket before turning off the computer and getting to his feet.

Signor da Feltre looked up from his paper. "Did you find what you were looking for?"

"I did. Thank you for your help." The man hadn't helped at all, but it seemed like the correct thing to say. He looked at

Chapter Nine

Covered with a greenish hue, the robed figure of the most famous Mantovano looked out over the park, past the bench where Rick and Angelo sat. Virgil held a scroll under his arm, perhaps a copy of his "Aeneid," and extended the other in a dramatic oratorical gesture. Adding to the classical stereotype, the sculptor had given the poet a long, flowing robe and conferred well-earned laureate status with a crown of laurel leaves. Though the metal Virgil was oblivious to the light wind that blew along the paths of the park, causing the stubby topiary to vibrate slightly, the two men on the bench felt it. Angelo adjusted his scarf and Rick buttoned his overcoat. The park was deserted save for an older couple who were walking the rectangular path around its grass center. Their serious faces and lack of conversation gave the impression it was their daily exercise, to be completed, no matter what the weather. Angelo and Rick watched the two pass their bench for the third time.

"What you've found about my father is what I would have expected. He was not the most outgoing of personalities. I'd always thought it was because he remained uncomfortable speaking English, despite reasonable fluency, or that he was ashamed of keeping his Italian accent. But I suppose he was just that kind of person, a bit introverted and more interested in numbers and spreadsheets than people. My mother was more outgoing than he was, but even she was pretty quiet.

When it was just the two of them they spoke Italian, of course. I'd overhear them, and just by a process of osmosis was able to understand a few words. I definitely could tell, from their voices, if it was an argument, even without knowing what they were saying. Not that there were many arguments."

"They must have kept in contact with your uncle. Letters, phone calls?"

Angelo looked up at Virgil and pondered the question before answering. "I knew I had an aunt and uncle in Italy, and a cousin, but it just didn't come up very often. My parents were Americans by then, and proud of it, and it simply wasn't something they dwelt on." He rubbed his chin in thought. "Strange. Talking about this makes me remember one night when I was about ten. I was in bed and heard my parents talking. It wasn't an argument, but they were clearly upset about something. I heard the name Enzo, so I knew they were talking about my uncle. I cracked open the door to my room, and when they saw me my mother rushed over and hugged me and I could see tears in her eyes. Funny the things you remember from your childhood."

"I can see how that would have made an impression on a kid."

Angelo nodded, his eyes still on the statue. "Now that you've told me all this, my guess is that they'd heard about my uncle Enzo's activities and were glad they were in the States and had no part of it."

"And were very relieved that you weren't exposed to it."

"Exactly. That must be why they didn't talk about Italy that much, they were not proud of what my uncle was up to here. And why not say it—the two brothers likely didn't get along very well when they were growing up. That happens in families."

Rick thought of his sister and was thankful that they always had been, and always would be, the best of friends. Moving around frequently as foreign service brats had forged that bond.

There were new cities, sometimes new local languages to learn, and the formidable task of making friends in a new school, but they always knew they had each other to face it with. The idea that they would not have been close was unthinkable.

Rondini tilted his head as he looked up at the statue, past a round fountain that had been drained for the winter. "Did you ever read anything by this guy, Language Man?"

"I had to read some of "The Aeneid" for a course in college."

"You read it in the original Italian?"

"The original was Latin, but no, I read an English translation."

Rondini didn't appear to mind being corrected. Even though he was looking at Virgil, his mind was elsewhere. "So your buddy the cop didn't tell you much of anything new when you had lunch with him. He seems to be ready to move this murder to the cold case file."

"I don't think I'd go that far, Mr. Rondini, though he is frustrated that not much new has surfaced. It's difficult to read the guy, if I might understate."

Rondini grunted. "I'm starting to think that this investigation won't be resolved before I fly back to Chicago. You think something might come up at this event we're going to tonight?"

"Hard to say. I expect that it will be attended by the usual suspects, along with lots of others."

"I want you to poke around as much as you can. I should be able to find enough people who speak English to talk with. Put on your detective hat and detect. Did your uncle the cop issue you a badge?"

"No, just a building pass to get into his office."

"That would get you a job on the police force in Chicago." He rose from the bench, and a gust of wind off the lake pushed open his overcoat. "Let's get back to the hotel, I need to have a shower before we go. I probably smell like cheese, though that would make me fit right in with this crowd."

Rick didn't need to be reminded of the encounter with the cheese wheels. The cold air was making his sore leg worse.

• ● ● ● ●

As he drove, Marco gave his three passengers an introduction to what they were going to see. He spoke quickly, since the Palazzo Te was not far from the hotel. Nothing in a town this size was very far from anything else, even a building that had been built as a country villa and was, at that time, outside the walls of Mantova.

"Palazzo Te is considered Giulio Romano's masterpiece, one of the gems of the Mannerism movement, not only for its architectural style but for the paintings found on the walls of its many rooms, several done by Romano himself. It was built by the Gonzagas, of course, specifically Federico the Second, between 1525 and 1535. The building has been described as a pleasure palace, which was certainly the case with Federico, since it started as an extension of his stables and was enlarged to include living space for his mistress."

Angelo tapped Rick on the shoulder from his place in the backseat. "Are you familiar with Mannerism, Language Man?"

"I had a friend in Rome who is an art history professor, Mr. Rondini. Her specialty is Mannerism, so she talked about it a lot. Some of it rubbed off, I suppose." Rick looked back at Lexi, who had a slight smile on her face. "She lives in the States, now," he added, and Lexi raised an eyebrow.

Rondini didn't notice the exchange. "Well, you can be my guide when we're inside."

"I'm sure many of the people in attendance will be glad to explain the artwork, and can do a better job than I could," said Rick.

The car had been navigating the narrow streets of the city, but now the lines of buildings had given way to open space, a reminder that Palazzo Te had been built so the Gonzagas could escape to the country. Late afternoon light glistened off flat athletic fields visible through a long row of trees, and in the distance to the left they could barely make out the outline of the city's soccer stadium. After a few turns the car slowed and turned into a parking lot next to their destination. It pulled up to a low stone structure with the classical decoration to be expected for a palazzo of the early sixteenth century in Italy.

Rick helped Lexi out of the back seat, noticing the shapely leg as she stepped to the ground. She wore a simple black dress under her wool coat. Very little wind was getting through the protective line of trees, but overcoats were still needed, even for the short distance between the car and the door. The three walked to the entrance, their shoes crunching on the gravel path.

From the outside, it was unclear if the building was one story or two, which Rick suspected Giulio Romano had done on purpose to confuse. The Mannerists, his art historian friend, Erica, always said, liked to show that they knew the rules but enjoyed bending them. A sign outside the door announced that the museum would be closed to the public for a private event. The Parmigiano-Reggiano Consortium had some pull, as well as the cash to pony up for the rental.

Inside they were met by a young woman who took their coats before pointing them toward a doorway. "The ceremonies will take place in the Sala dei Cavalli," she said.

The spacious, rectangular Hall of the Horses was aptly named. Wide panels set high around walls were painted with images of horses—the pride of the Gonzaga stables—looking sleek and bored as they posed for the artist. Perhaps several centuries earlier sawdust had covered the floor and those very animals had been brought into the room for show, but this evening the only horseflesh lay in the art. The room was set with a long table along one side, and a small podium with a microphone stood against the opposite wall in front of a tall, gaping fireplace, its spotlessness indicating it hadn't been used in centuries. The table, covered with a linen cloth, held platter after platter of food, with the emphasis, not unexpectedly, on cheese. Wheels of Parmigiano-Reggiano sat regally at the ends, a quarter of each one sliced out and arranged on a board with a number of their signature teardrop knives at the ready. The invitees, though mostly dairy operators who saw the stuff every day, were wedging off small chunks and popping them into their mouths. Other hors d'oeuvres were displayed on elegant dishes between the cheese, all against a background of soft-hued flowers. From a distance Rick was able to identify *prosciutto* wrapped around cheese strips, miniature pizzas, rice croquettes, and *crostini* spread with pâté and other toppings. He was beginning to wish he had skipped lunch. White-coated waiters circulated with trays of fluted glassware that had been filled from a bar behind the food table. The gathered friends and colleagues of the late Roberto Rondini, many with their spouses, talked in low voices, as appropriate for the occasion, but Rick had the sense they were talking business rather than sharing recollections of the dearly departed. Livia Guarino stood in the midst of a small group who were taking turns giving her embraces of condolence. She wore a gray dress accented by black lace around the sleeves and neck. Her husband was nowhere to be seen. When she spotted the three new arrivals she excused herself and hurried over. The men in the group looked to see where she was going and when they did, their eyes stayed on Lexi.

"Uncle, so good to see you." They exchanged air kisses and she shook hands with Rick and Lexi. "Thank you for coming. Had you already visited the Palazzo Te?"

Angelo looked around, his eyes raised to the wall paintings and the highly decorated boxes inserted into the ceiling. "No, and this is quite a place."

"The other rooms are open, you will have to see them all. I'm told the program will be short, with very few people speaking, so you'll have time to wander around. Unless you'd prefer to talk about local politics and cheese. That's all these people are interested in." She glanced over Angelo's shoulder. "Some people just arrived I must talk to, Uncle. Please get yourself something to eat and drink, the three of you."

They promised they would. Livia walked over to meet the new arrivals just as a waiter stepped up to them with a tray of glasses. Angelo and Rick waited for Lexi to take one before they served themselves.

"Here's to Federico Gonzaga," said Rick. "He knew how to build them to last."

"Almost five hundred years," said Lexi, as she looked at the wine in her glass. "And still holding parties here." She surveyed the crowd. "There's the farm manager, Zucari. He must have cleaned up the broken cheese by now. Do you recognize anyone else, Rick?"

"I recognize who he's with. It's Letizia Bentivoglio."

Angelo, who had been studying the ornate designs in the ceiling, turned quickly in that direction. "Roberto's lady friend? I wonder if Livia realizes that she's here, or even knows who she is. She looks younger than I expected, given my cousin's age."

"Men at that age don't usually take up with women older than they are," said Lexi.

"That's true," said her boss. "Very cynical on your part, Lexi, but true."

Rick watched the people who were starting to drift toward the food table. One large man stood next to it, deftly balancing a wineglass and plate in one hand while eating with the other. "There's the guy who owns the dairy next to the Rondinis', Emilio Fiore."

Angelo frowned. "The one we met after the funeral who'd had too much wine, and then at the restaurant. It looks like he's at the grape again. Be sure to talk to him, Language Man."

At that point a man in a dark, tailored suit came up to Angelo and introduced himself as the president of the consortium. He spoke fluent English with a slight British accent. Rick realized that the presence in Mantova of the American cousin would have been common knowledge among this group. He took advantage of the situation to excuse himself and head for the food, even though he wasn't hungry.

Rick's father the diplomat was a master at working the crowd at a reception, but unfortunately he'd never schooled his son in the skill. The only time Rick had observed it closely was one time in high school when one of the waiters didn't show for an event in their home. Rick was given a white coat and a tray of food, and while he worked he observed the senior Montoya moving from one group to another, playing the perfect host. Fishing for clues to a murder was not exactly analogous, but it was close enough. He began with two couples standing close to one of the wheels of cheese, and introduced himself.

As he half expected, they knew about Angelo, the American cousin, but were unaware that he'd brought his own staff along on the trip. Rick explained that Angelo's assistant came from Chicago, but he was an interpreter based in Rome. He sensed that the four thought someone who lived in Rome to be even more exotic than an American from Chicago. Did they know the deceased well? The two men did—at least they claimed to, since they were connected in some unspecified way to the cheese business. Their wives shook their heads, though they exchanged looks that Rick read to mean they'd heard about Roberto, and what they'd heard may not have been flattering. He decided he wasn't going to get much out of them, excused himself on the pretext of getting something to eat, and moved on.

As he stood deciding which of the culinary treats to try, a man dressed in a dark suit approached him, his hands clasped against his chest.

"Can I help you?" the man asked, and then noticed Rick's puzzled expression. He held out his hand. "I'm Lorenzo Dini, I cater all the events for the Parmigiano-Reggiano Consortium. You look like you needed some guidance."

Rick shook Dini's hand. "Nice to meet you, Signor Dini. Riccardo Montoya, visiting from Rome. Everything here looks delicious. The consortium does a lot of receptions like this?"

"They keep us busy, not just here in the production area but all over the country. And a few events in other parts of Europe. I was in Munich last week. The Germans love cheese."

"I'm sure they do." It seemed like a good time to pick up a small chunk, which he popped into his mouth. "Did you know the honoree this evening? Signor Rondini?"

"Oh, yes."

Rick swallowed the cheese and paid closer attention. "From these kinds of affairs? I'd never met him, I'm just working here, like you. As an interpreter." He hoped his being an outsider would loosen the man's lips.

Dini looked to one side and then the other. "You can learn a lot about people from how they act in a social setting like this. I should not speak ill of the departed, but Roberto Rondini was the kind of person who would treat people differently depending on what he wanted from them. He was all smiles with foreign cheese buyers, but with others he could be quite different."

"That seems like a lot to conclude just from seeing him at receptions and dinners."

"You'd be surprised, Signor Montoya." Again he looked furtively before continuing. "Do you see that man over there? With the woman?"

Rick followed Dini's eye and came to the manager of the Rondini dairy, who was standing with Letizia Bentivoglio and three men. This could get interesting. "The man with the good tan?"

"Yes, that's the one. I've never seen the woman, but I remember him from a reception several months ago at the chamber of commerce for a group of Arab investors. That man and Rondini were speaking with members of the visiting delegation, all very polite, but a moment later the two of them were in a corner of the room arguing. They weren't raising their voices, but it was clearly an argument. Rondini was poking his finger into that man's chest, and from the look on the man's face I thought he was going react violently. Now what kind of a person would berate someone in public like that?"

Dini was apparently unaware that Zucari had been in Roberto Rondini's employ, and it was not Rick's place to tell him. "Were there other times you saw Rondini like that?"

"That's the one I recall."

So the man—a world-class eavesdropper—was basing his view of Roberto Rondini on one incident. It was better than nothing, and it did involve the manager of the Rondini dairy. What would they have been talking with a group of investors about that would cause such a flare-up? Rick's conjecturing was interrupted by a voice coming over the microphone of the man who had been talking with Angelo and Lexi. Rick walked over to his boss, ready to interpret, and as the crowd quieted, he positioned himself behind Angelo and Lexi so they both could hear his English playback.

The remarks about their departed colleague were bland and neutral, and likely could have been given about most of the people in the room. Roberto Rondini had been, the president said, a prominent member of the consortium, always supportive of its ideals and standards, helping to grow the industry and the reputation of Parmigiano-Reggiano cheese in Italy and abroad. His words were as much about the consortium as they were in praise of its departed member, and they were greeted with polite applause. Someone else, whose title Rick didn't catch, stood up and gave an equally bland discourse.

"These guys are going to put me to sleep," said Angelo after Rick finished his interpreting.

Livia was the last speaker, and the group appeared to pay closer attention to what she said. It may have been because she was Roberto's daughter, and as the grieving daughter she deserved deference, or perhaps they were trying to size up the new owner of the Rondini dairy. She thanked everyone for coming, and said how much the consortium had meant to her father. She recounted an anecdote about her father and Rondini cows that got smiles and warm applause, and ended by saying that the Rondini dairy would continue to be a loyal member of the consortium as it had been when her father was alive. More applause followed, and the president thanked those gathered for their presence and declared the ceremonies ended.

"She did well," said Angelo. "I could see it on everyone's faces. I wonder how many of the dairies are owned and run by women. My guess is very few."

"Very poised," Lexi noted, "given the circumstances. What is it they always say? For most people the two most stressful things in life are funerals and public speaking? She had both of those tonight."

Angelo nodded.

The crowd was moving toward the food table, ready to do it justice after the formalities had been dealt with. Rick scanned the group, looking for someone who might give him something, anything, to help shed some light on the investigation as Angelo had ordered. He spotted Emilio Fiore, the neighboring dairy farmer, still with a glass of wine in hand. He was in a circle of other men which included the Rondini dairy manager, Carlo Zucari. Rick immediately recalled when Fiore had come out of the dairy office just before the curious incident of the falling cheese. And that brought to mind the dull ache he still had in his leg. Something else occurred to him. If Zucari was in that group, where was his date? Rick's eyes moved through the people and spotted Letizia Bentivoglio standing apart, looking up at a dark brown horse depicted on the wall. He excused himself to Angelo and Lexi and walked to her.

"A stunning animal," said Rick when he got to her side. She turned around, and he could see she was trying to remember who he was.

"Yes. I've always loved horses." Her eyes widened slightly. "Now I recall where I saw you, in the bar last night. You're the one who's translating for the visiting American cousin."

"Interpreting," Rick said. He couldn't reveal that he knew about the relationship she had with the deceased Roberto Rondini, but why not ask about her present companion?

"Signor Zucari gave us an interesting tour of the cheese-making operation today. I must thank him again for it." Her face betrayed nothing, so Rick guessed she had not been told of the falling cheese. "Have you known Zucari long?" It was a lame question, but she didn't appear to notice. Her reply was equally lame, or perhaps purposely vague.

"Everyone knows everyone else in this city, either personally or by reputation."

A waiter appeared with a tray of glasses. Letizia's hand moved quickly to take one, and Rick joined her. They exchanged wishes of good health and she took a deep drink. Rick sipped his.

"I was under the assumption," he said, "given his present position, that he was from the country."

"You would think that," she said, wiping her lips with the paper napkin that came with the wine, "him being a manager of a farm. But in fact he grew up in Mantova. His was not an easy childhood." Her eyes darted to where Zucari was standing with the other men.

Rick had the impression that this was not her first glass of wine that evening. It would make sense that she needed to be fortified, attending a memorial for the man with whom she was romantically involved, and in the presence of the dead man's family. He was still unsure if Roberto's daughter knew about Letizia Bentivoglio, or if she did, whether she disapproved. It was something he would likely never know, but he also doubted it could have anything to do with the man's demise. He was trying to decide if he should ask her about Roberto Rondini when she abruptly excused herself and walked away. So that was all he was going to get from Letizia Bentivoglio. This was getting frustrating. Time for a break from investigating. He looked at Angelo, who was in deep conversation with two men. Lexi stood to one side, talking with two much younger men. As he watched, she took a sip from her wineglass and her eyes moved around the room before resting on Rick. He inclined his head in the direction of the far door, and she nodded before saying something to the two and walking off.

"Enjoying yourself, my dear?"

She made a face. "I was standing there trying to think of the last time I'd had this much fun. It's enough to make me swear off cheese."

"Somehow I think those two guys were interested in more than just your views of cheese production. Well, Lexi, while you were enjoying a chat with Mantova's rich bachelors, I pretty much came up dry with the people I've talked to. But I'm not done yet. Let's take a quick break and see what's in this next room. Then I'll get back to doing what Angelo ordered me to do, and you can…well, do what you were doing."

"Sounds good."

The next hall—every room in the Palazzo Te was a hall—formed one corner of the square main building. The decoration on its walls and ceiling was even more ornate than the horse room, but the theme was different. Rather than horseflesh, what covered these walls was just flesh, very pink and either muscular or plump. The note on a stand in the middle of the floor identified the room as the Sala de Psiche, and explained that the decoration recounted the mythological tale of Cupid and Psyche. Those two were featured in one of the panels, but everyone else depicted around the walls paid little attention to them. They were too busy having a good time.

"Well," said Lexi as her eyes moved around the room, "I guess we know what the Gonzagas used this room for. Did you bring me in here on purpose?"

Rick laughed. "I didn't know, I swear."

"Nobody seems to be wearing clothes."

"It's mythology, Lexi. And orgies are clothing-optional affairs. Thankfully, most of them are carefully draped."

"Most, but not all." She pointed at a chubby figure, one arm around a satyr, the other embracing a wine jug. "That guy seems to be enjoying himself the most."

"Bacchus. You can always spot him since he's drinking wine and wears grape leaves on his head. It's quite a banquet. Look at all that food."

"As if they all came for the food."

They were standing in one corner, the better to get the complete sweep of the paintings on the opposite walls. As they studied the art, two men walked resolutely in, crossed the room, and exited through the other doorway. One gestured as he spoke, while the other studied the floor. Neither one paid any attention to the decoration or noticed the two people standing in the corner.

"Wasn't that…?"

"Yes," Rick answered. "Carlo Zucari, our cheese guide, with Emilio Fiore. Fiore was coming out of the dairy this morning when we drove up. They keep getting more and more chummy, those two."

"Why don't we follow them? Maybe you can overhear what they're saying."

"I can follow them and you can stay here and enjoy the artwork."

"I'll come with you, thank you very much."

The two walked into the next highly decorated room, then into the next, still with no sign of the men. Rather than an open doorway at the other side of this room, there was a heavy door. Rick pushed it open and they found themselves enveloped by cold air, causing Rick to whip off his jacket and put it around Lexi's shoulders. They were in a covered portico that connected two open areas on either side, and in keeping with the other rooms, its vault was decorated within an inch of its life. To their right lay the grassy, square courtyard in the center of the building. In the opposite direction, past columns and arches, was a bridge over a pool, and beyond that stretched the Gonzaga formal gardens. Rick looked both ways while Lexi stood shivering, despite the jacket.

"They're not out there, they must have continued into the

next set of rooms." He pushed open another door and once again they were inside an ornate space, but this one with little color. An endless army of ancient warriors marched in two rows along a stucco frieze around the room just below the ceiling. More classical figures adorned the barrel vault, carved like large cameos and set inside the open boxes. It was all shades of white, with the occasional light blue, and after the other rooms the effect was striking. If the symmetry of the palazzo was to be maintained, there would be another room before getting to the one at the corner. In fact they could see a second and third room through the narrow doorways. They could also hear the voices of the two men, coming from the corner room.

Rick held his finger over his mouth and gestured for Lexi to follow him quietly into the next room. She handed back his jacket before they slipped through the doorway and moved to the opposite side, near the opening to the room where Fiore and Zucari were talking. The two kept their voices low, but the words were clear enough for Rick to understand.

"…you can't let her do that."

"What am I supposed to do? She owns it, she can do with it whatever she wants."

"But that's insanity. What does her husband think?"

"He had some kind of accident last night and hasn't made an appearance. You saw that he's not here tonight. So I haven't talked to him and I don't know where he stands, or if he even knows what she's decided to do. Knowing what a weakling he is, it wouldn't surprise me if he isn't even being consulted. I've always thought he married her to get control of the dairy one day, but now I don't think she's going to let that happen. She's changed a lot since Roberto died. Before she was content to stay in the background, but now she's become a different person. She's her father's daughter, Emilio, but we all had to wait until he died to find that out."

Lexi poked Rick in the ribs and put her ear close to his head. He twirled his finger in an "I'll tell you later" gesture.

"You don't think she—"

"No, no, of course not."

"I agree. I think it had to do with something that happened long ago."

A few seconds passed before the manager spoke. "We'd better get back."

Rick froze. He hadn't thought about the two men coming back through the room where they were listening in on the conversation. Lexi apparently realized their dilemma at the same time. She pulled him roughly into the corner. A few seconds later, when Zucari and Fiore stepped through the doorway, what they saw was a couple locked in embrace. The two men chuckled to each other and kept walking into the next room, then through the door out to the portico.

Lexi reached up and rubbed her smudged lipstick from Rick's mouth. "You can take your arms from around my waist now, Rick, they're gone."

"They might come back." He breathed in her perfume and tried to place it. A bit flowery but with a certain powdery aura. One of the Chanels?

"Rick."

"All right, all right." He let his arms drop, but didn't step away from her.

Nor did she from him. "We should return to the other room—Angelo may be wondering what happened to us. But first tell me what they were saying."

"Let's go into the next room to do that. I think it may be the famous Hall of the Giants that I read about. We shouldn't miss it."

As they walked through the doorway Rick told her about the conversation, recalling it as best he could. "They had to be talking about the land," she said when he'd finished. "It sounds like she's leaning toward selling it for development."

"I agree, and neither of those two will be pleased when that happens."

"And they will put two and two together and conclude that the American developer pushed her into the decision, which we know is not the case, at least from the conversations between Angelo and Livia that you and I have heard. Did Angelo ever nudge her toward that decision?"

"Not when the three of us had lunch, Lexi. They might have talked other times when you and I weren't around, or by phone, but I don't have the sense that your boss wanted to influence her one way or the other. I would guess the opposite."

"I agree." She had been concentrating on what Rick had been saying, and now she looked around the room. "This is quite a place, I can understand why it's so famous."

Rick read the panel that was attached to a stand in the center of the square room while Lexi craned her neck in an attempt to take it all in. The paintings recounted the mythological story of the revolt of the giants against the gods of Mount Olympus and the gods' brutal and decisive reaction to the uprising.

The scene was one of total chaos.

Perched on a ring of clouds in the center of the round ceiling, the gods of Olympus looked down in fear and surprise. On one side, Zeus, larger than the others, was about to unleash another string of lightning bolts which had already begun to have their deadly effect on Earth. The columns, arches and walls of stone buildings on the ground had broken into huge pieces, crushing the rebellious giants whose ugly, contorted faces cried out in pain and anguish. The beautiful figures of the gods in the heavens contrasted with the brutish, deformed bodies writhing amidst the rubble on the Earth below.

Rick took his eyes from the panel and looked at the walls. "It says that at the time this work was finished, about 1535, people would surely have been reminded of the sack of Rome a decade earlier." He moved his head slowly to take it all in. "Makes you realize that having a few wheels of cheese fall on you is not that big a deal."

She took his elbow. "Time to get back, Rick, our boss may

be wondering what's become of us. Keep your eyes averted when we go through the cupid room."

Rick did as he was told, and when they emerged back into the Sala dei Cavalli they found that the group had thinned out along with the amount of food on the table. He spotted Angelo talking with two men near the food table. He appeared to be understanding them, so Rick decided his interpreting wasn't needed. Instead he whispered something to Lexi and walked to a man standing almost in the corner, holding a wineglass and staring blankly at the brown horse on the wall above him. Emilio Fiore looked up and focused on Rick's face for a few moments before there was recognition.

"Ah, Signor Montoya. I saw you here earlier with that lovely young lady. She's Angelo Rondini's assistant, I've been told." He chuckled and took a long pull from his wineglass.

Rick was unsure if Fiore was referring to seeing them in this room or the other one, not that it mattered. "Was it you we saw coming out of the dairy this morning, Signor Fiore?"

There was a puzzled frown, but the question finally registered. The wine was having its effect. "Oh, yes, this morning. I had just stopped in to ask Carlo something. He told me you all were going to tour the cheese-making process. You were, I trust, duly impressed?"

Rick thought for an instant that Fiore knew about the falling cheese and the question was intentionally and cleverly double-edged. If he did know, the dairy manager must have told him. Or else he was the one who tried to push over the shelves. But it wouldn't make sense for the perpetrator to make jokes about it, even after a few glasses of wine, when it could bring suspicion on himself. But Fiore could also believe everyone had decided it was a terrible accident and nothing more, and he was not under suspicion. Or, Rick finally concluded, he was reading too much into Fiore's words and the question was posed in total innocence.

"We were fascinated. The aging room was especially interesting."

"Yes. As quiet as a morgue."

A curious analogy. "Is your cheese production similar, Signor Fiore?"

"I don't turn out as much cheese as the Rondini dairy, but we are at full capacity. If I had more pasturage I could increase it, but that doesn't appear to be in the cards." He checked his wineglass, realized it was getting low, and looked around for a waiter.

"Is your dairy a family business, like the Rondini's?"

Fiore thought about the question longer than Rick expected. "Well, I own it, if that's what you mean, but not by inheritance. Unlike with Roberto, it was not handed to me by my father. I bought it about a dozen years ago when it came on the market. Not cheap, but it was worth it to me. Anyone in your family own farm land, Signor Montoya?"

A passing waiter took Fiore's empty glass and gave him one that was full. Rick declined the offer.

"I have an uncle in America who raises chiles. He has a few horses and chickens, but I didn't see any cows the last time I visited him several years ago. So no cheese."

"That is unfortunate. Cheese is one of man's greatest creations, and transforming a simple product like milk into something so delicious is almost like performing magic. You must have felt that when you did the tour with Carlo."

It wasn't the only thing I felt, Rick was tempted to say. Instead, he decided to go right to the point. "Signor Fiore, I've heard that some people think Roberto Rondini's death was not an accident. What is your opinion?"

The glass stopped inches from his lips and slowly lowered. "I have heard the same thing, Signor Montoya, but have no way of knowing. The police investigated it immediately after his body was found, so I assume that their conclusion was that Roberto was the victim of an accident. Unless they are still investigating, of course. Have you heard anything in that regard?" As he took a drink his eyes stayed on Rick.

"You should probably ask the local police, not an outsider like me."

Fiore shrugged, then noticed something over Rick's shoulder. "Your employer is looking this way, so he may be requesting your presence. Perhaps he's heard enough stories about cheese for the evening."

He turned and caught Angelo's eyes before they moved back to the people with him, which Rick took to mean that his boss approved of his conversing with Fiore. "Mr. Rondini seems to be holding his own. Tell me something, Signor Fiore. I trust you know about the acreage that lies between the Rondini dairy and the river. It does not appear to have ever been planted, or if so, it's been many years since. Do you know why the late Roberto Rondini never did anything with it?"

Fiore took the small paper napkin in his hand and passed it roughly over his mouth. "Your employer is curious about that, I suppose. Has he ever seen a plot of land that he didn't want to develop?"

Rick could have pointed out that Angelo had no interest in this plot, but thought it better to keep the man in doubt. He recalled the day of the funeral when they had walked through the field and someone he assumed was Fiore had been watching them from a distance.

"You haven't answered my question."

"No, Signor Montoya I haven't, and it is because I don't know the answer. That piece of land was like that when I bought my farm, and my relationship with Roberto, as I told you, was not the best. I did make it known to him that I would be interested in purchasing the plot, but as a rule we didn't share secrets. So I never found out the reason for leaving such prime real estate purely for the enjoyment of the birds and insects. It is unfortunate that you didn't have time to ask that question of Carlo Zucari when you were touring the dairy."

"From what you said about reaching your full capacity, I take it you could put that land to good use."

Fiore's mouth turned up slightly, as much a sneer as a smile. "That would be the case."

Chapter Ten

The Mercedes pulled slowly out of its parking space and started down the path to the street. Darkness had overtaken the green area around the Palazzo Te, but invisible floodlights spread wide yellow beams along its stone sides, picking up the texture of the design.

"You enjoyed seeing the rooms, Signor Rondini?" The driver kept his eyes on the road as he made the turn onto the pavement. There were no cars on the street except those parked silently along the side.

"Yes we did, Marco," answered Angelo. "I didn't get into any except the horse room where the event took place, but that was very impressive. I believe Lexi and Rick saw more of the place, am I right, Lexi?"

"Yes, we did get into the other rooms. The most interesting was the one with the giants, don't you think so, Rick?"

"I liked the cupid room, and especially the one just before the giants." Rick glanced back at Lexi, who was staring out the window.

"The Sala dei Giganti is the most famous room," the driver said, picking up on Lexi's comment. "The lower figures, the giants, were done by Rinaldo Mantovano, a local artist, but Giulio Romano himself painted the gods on the ceiling and oversaw the whole work."

"Next time we'll take you inside, Marco, and you can explain it all." Angelo tapped Rick on the shoulder. "I hope you were able to find out something, Language Man. I saw you talking to people. Are we closer to solving this mystery?"

"We might be," Rick answered, thinking it wasn't something to discuss with the driver listening. "I'll tell you about it when we get back to the hotel."

Angelo looked out his window but didn't appear to be focusing on the passing building. "I had a couple invitations at the reception to have dinner later, but I told them I needed to have a business meal with my assistant. Lexi, we really have to go over those three new proposals."

"Of course, Mr. Rondini. I'll pull up the files on my tablet when we get to the hotel."

Angelo leaned forward and tapped the driver's shoulder. "Marco, you can take the night off again. We'll go somewhere we can walk to from the hotel. I got some suggestions at the reception."

"Yes, sir," Marco answered, keeping his eyes on the road.

Ten minutes later Angelo, Lexi, and Rick sat around a small round table in the bar of the hotel. In front of Angelo was an empty coffee cup. Rick and Lexi sipped white wine but eschewed the small, marinated *mozzarella* balls the waiter had brought to the table.

"The friendship between Fiore and Zucari does seem curious, given that my cousin wasn't on the best of terms with his neighbor. When you overheard them, the two of them must have been talking about the infamous plot of land, and the manager appears to know what Livia has decided to do with it. We talked at length this evening, but she didn't mention that issue, not that she needs to share her business with the uncle from America. She did appear to be more upbeat, but I thought that she was just starting to come to terms with her father's passing. Perhaps there is something else going on here. Maybe we'll find out tomorrow when we gather at the river." He looked at his empty *espresso* cup as if deciding whether to have another. "She has invited other people to the unveiling of the column tomorrow, if that's the right word for the event. I'm glad I decided to make this gesture, it may help her to get over her grief. The more ceremonies of remembrance the better, in my experience."

Lexi looked at Rick, and her expression told him that Angelo was referring to his own grief in the loss of his wife. He tried to remember from the bio he'd read just how long it had been.

"It doesn't appear that this case is going to be resolved any time soon," Angelo continued. "And we will be flying home the day after tomorrow, when the flight crew's vacation in Verona will end. Maybe your uncle can keep an eye on the investigation, and you can let us know if anything happens."

"Of course, Mr. Rondini."

Angelo raised himself slowly to his feet. Fatigue lined his features. "Let's postpone our business dinner, Lexi. I got enough to eat at the reception. I thought I was getting over the jet lag, but it seems to be hitting me again. You two go out for something."

Rick and Lexi exchanged glances. "Of course, Mr. Rondini," she said. "You can have something sent up to your suite if you get hungry."

"I'll do that." He shuffled toward the elevator as they watched.

"I think it's more than jet lag," said Lexi when her boss was out of earshot. "It's like he's got the weight of the world on him. The only other time I saw him like this was after Mrs. Rondini passed away."

They sat in silence for a few moments before Rick spoke. "The upside is that I get to have another meal with Alexis Coleman. Did you partake too much at the reception or are you up for another restaurant meal in Mantova?"

"I could use something," said Lexi. "Maybe a salad." She looked at Rick. "Is there somewhere we can get a light meal?"

"Light. Heavy. Whatever you want."

• • ● • •

Lexi did order a salad, but it was a second course after a bowl of *stracciatella*, chicken broth swirled with egg and grated Parmigiano-Reggiano, topped with a slice of toast. Rick convinced her that it was a simple peasant dish. The salad was fresh greens lightly coated with oil and vinegar. He explained that Italians are minimalists when it comes to salads. He, too, went with lighter fare, though if pushed, he would have ordered pasta. *Minestrone* was first—fresh vegetables in the same broth as Lexi's—and for *secondo*, asparagus that had been cooked and then topped with Parmigiano-Reggiano and run under the broiler. Lexi's spoon, and then her fork, had darted across the table to sample both. The dishes now were gone, as was an empty wine bottle, and they were sipping *espressi* while nibbling on pieces of *torta sbrisolona*, which the waiter said was a specialty of the city. It turned out to be something between a cookie and a cake—flat, crunchy, and flavored with almonds. It was so perfect with coffee that they ordered second cups after Rick convinced her that *espresso* wouldn't keep her awake.

"I have to get some of this to take back to Chicago. It looks like it would travel well." She picked up and quickly ate the last of the crumbled pieces, one with a whole almond.

"There's a bakery I passed on the way to the police station that will have it for sure. We'll pick some up tomorrow. I'd like to take some back to Rome as well." He took his last sip of coffee. "Italian regional cooking is always full of surprises. I'd never heard of this stuff and I doubt if I can find it in Rome. I'll just have to come up here every few months and stock up."

Lexi inclined her head and smiled. "You can come up with that friend of yours who's an art historian and she can explain the paintings."

"She really is in the States now. And married."

"I'm sure you can find someone else to keep you company, Rick."

"Mantova would never be the same without you, Lexi." He reached across the table and squeezed her hand. "And without Angelo paying for it, of course."

She laughed, pulled her hand away, and slapped his. "You are terrible. But that reminds me who we are both working for, and that I should be getting back to the hotel to go through my e-mails. Angelo will want a complete report at breakfast. And speaking of breakfast, I must check that buffet at the hotel more carefully. Will they have *torta*...?"

"*Sbrisolona.* If they don't, we'll demand it."

"It will taste good after our morning run."

Rick rubbed his leg. "Lexi, I don't know about that. I'm still pretty sore and shouldn't push it."

"First a dusting of snow stops you and now some minor discomfort in your leg? What kind of an athlete are you, Mr. Montoya?"

"A fair weather and injured one, it appears. Have you ever worked as a personal trainer? You sound like it."

"No, but at Northwestern the track team had a trainer. He was tough."

Rick shook his head and signaled for the bill. "The many facets of Alexis Coleman."

A few minutes later they emerged into the Mantova night. The restaurant was a few blocks from the hotel on a quiet side street, though almost all the streets in the city's historic center were silent at that time of night. As they walked they heard only an occasional TV voice muffled by wooden and metal shutters closed tight to keep out the cold. They walked in silence, arm in arm, enjoying the stillness of the medieval surroundings, when Rick's phone rang. He fumbled and brought it from his jacket pocket.

"It's my Uncle Piero, I'd better take it." He pressed the screen. "*Zio, buona sera.*"

"Good evening to you, Riccardo. I hope I am not interrupting dinner."

"No, we're just walking back to the hotel from the restaurant."

"One always eats well in Mantova. I was wondering if there is any news on your investigation. I didn't want to call Inspector Crispi, but I trust you are *aggiornato* on everything."

"As up-to-date as Crispi, unless he's learned something new since the last time we met. At this point we're stuck in a rut, but we're both convinced that the murder was connected to a plot of land."

"Land owned by the dead man?"

"Correct, and now by his daughter. It was acquired decades ago by less-than-honorable means, which probably has nothing to do with it. The issue seems to be whether the victim was going to sell it to someone who would develop it in ways not connected to the traditional agriculture of the area. There is no lack of people who are against such development."

"So, no lack of people with a motive to murder."

"That's right. The deceased was not universally loved, as I've found out, but I doubt his personality was malevolent enough to be the only factor in his murder. There had to be something else, and this land appears to be that something."

Lexi listened without understanding, waving to indicate that he should take his time.

"It wouldn't be the first time someone was killed over a land dispute," said Piero. "You'll remember Romulus and Remus."

Uncle Piero, the true Roman, Rick thought. For them there was nothing new under the sun.

"Was this land acquired recently?"

"No, Uncle. It was decades ago. I think the issue is what should be done with it now."

"People can have long memories, Riccardo."

Though she was trying to hide it, Rick read Lexi's body language, and it was saying that she was anxious to get back to the hotel and get to work. "That's where we stand, *Zio*. I'm not optimistic that a murderer will be found, certainly not before

Mr. Rondini flies back to the States and I return to Rome, the day after tomorrow."

"You're walking with your employer?"

"No, he stayed in. I'm with his assistant. She's standing here but doesn't understand Italian."

There was a pause before Piero replied. "I suppose this assistant is aged and walks with the aid of a cane."

"Not exactly, *Zio*."

"I see. Then I should not be taking your time. Call me if anything comes up, otherwise I'll see you when you get home."

They said their good-byes and Rick returned the phone to his pocket, realizing he hadn't mentioned the threats. "My uncle the cop. He wanted to know if anything was happening in the case." They had come to a corner and he pointed to a very narrow and straight alley. "If I have it right, this should bring us out at the street our hotel is on."

"It doesn't look very inviting, but lead away." Lexi again took his arm.

As they started down the pavement it became obvious that they were walking past the backs of residences and businesses. Doors were metal, some with multiple locks, and bars covered every window at street level. It must have been pick-up day, since metal garbage cans sat empty at intervals, some turned on their sides. The street was so narrow a parked car would have blocked another trying to pass, and signs with P crossed out appeared at intervals on the walls. With this parking prohibition, other than the garbage cans, it was empty. To match the lack of traffic was a lack of lighting; only a few dim lamps attached to buildings lit the way. In Rome at night on a street like this Rick would have at least seen a cat or two creeping under the shadows, but here there were none. About a hundred meters in the distance they could see the bright lights of the hotel's street.

"I could tell by the way you talked that you're very close to your uncle."

"Are you starting to pick up some Italian, Lexi?"

"No, of course not. It was the tone of voice, and your body language."

"You're very perceptive. Piero and I get along very well. He always tells me the truth, without preaching to me, and I'm always honest with him. And he's a pretty impressive guy. I wish you could meet him sometime."

"What kind of preparation do cops in Italy need?"

They moved together to one side in order to avoid a garbage can that had rolled into the center of the alley. Rick pushed it to the side with his foot as they passed.

"My uncle has a degree in law from *La Sapienza*, that's Rome's state university. I think a law degree is a pretty common career path. Then they do their own training, of course."

"*La Sapienza?*"

"It means 'wisdom,' or 'knowledge.' An appropriate name for an institution of higher learning, wouldn't you say? Has a much classier ring to it than the 'University of New Mexico,' where I went."

"Or my Northwestern, which isn't even in the Northwest. Of course it was in the northwest when it was founded in 1851, but then the Northwest moved northwest and Northwestern stayed where it was."

"It's not too late to move it to Washington or Oregon."

"I doubt if the board of trustees is considering that." She stopped and turned back. "What's that?"

Rick looked and saw that a car was slowly turning into the alley behind them. It backed up once and then squeezed through the opening of the buildings on either side of the corner. In the darkness he couldn't tell what kind of a car it was, but from the low pitch of the engine it sounded like an SUV or perhaps a small truck. Just into the alley it stopped.

"He's probably realizing it's too narrow and is now going to back out," Rick said.

They started walking again but were stopped by the sound of the revving engine behind them. Along with hitting the gas pedal, the driver had switched to high beams, sending a blinding light toward them that bounced off the bare walls of the buildings.

"I don't like the looks of this, Lexi." He tried to calculate the distance to the end of the alley and safety. It looked like about fifty yards. At that moment they could hear the car shifting into gear and starting toward them. "Let's go."

Lexi unbuttoned her long wool coat so that she could run more easily, and Rick did the same. Fortunately she wore slacks and low heeled shoes, and was able to get up to a stride quickly. Rick, for one of the first times in his life, cursed his cowboy boots. He also immediately started feeling the pain in his leg from the falling cheese. Lexi might make it, but he was beginning to doubt if he could.

The sound of a garbage can hitting the bumper and bouncing off a wall temporarily cut into the growl of the engine, along with a high squeal of tires. Perhaps the can had slowed down the driver enough to give them enough time to escape. The hope disappeared when Rick heard the car roar back to full power. The light from the high beams was getting stronger, throwing Rick's long shadow ahead of him as he followed Lexi.

"Look for a doorway!" he shouted. Why hadn't he taken her up a wide street?

All the doors they passed were flush with their buildings, and the one garage door was the same. No indoor space would be wasted in an alley, the niched entrance-ways would be on the opposite side of the building, the street address.

The car was fifty yards away and closing.

"Up on the right!" shouted Lexi, pointing ahead. There was a small indentation in the back of the building, but it was filled with two plastic garbage cans. Lexi reached it and grabbed one of the cans, flinging it across the pavement. Rick was right behind her and pushed the other one into the beams of headlights coming at them. Lexi squeezed into the space and pulled him in next to her. They had to bend slightly to get their heads inside, but there was enough room to get them out of the car's path. Lexi put her arms around Rick's waist and squeezed close to him just as the car was about to pass.

It didn't slow down, even when it hit the plastic can that Rick had pushed into its way. The empty can careened off the bumper with a thump and slammed into Rick's leg as the car sped past the two huddled figures. A moment later it was gone and the silence returned.

"You know, Lexi, I love holding you in my arms, but next time, let's pick a more comfortable location." They disentangled. "Are you okay?"

"I'm fine. What about you? Did that thing hit you?"

Emerging from the niche, Rick picked up the two garbage bins and put them back where they had been before the incident. "In the leg. But fortunately it was the other leg."

"So now you have two excuses for skipping our run tomorrow morning." She watched as he pulled out his cell phone. "Who are you calling?"

"Crispi. I got the license plate." He scrolled and pressed the screen. After two rings the call was answered. "Inspector? Can you have someone look something up for me?"

As in any five-star hotel, there was someone on duty at the bar, even at the late hour. In one corner was a gray-haired man with a woman who could have been his daughter, but wasn't. They were working through a bottle of something bubbly that nestled in an ice bucket. Rick and Lexi sat at a small table at the opposite end of the room. Their two small glasses, containing a caramel-brown liquid, were being carefully nursed. Next to the glasses was Rick's cell phone, still warm.

"The car belongs to a man who lives just across the river. When the police called him he said that was ridiculous, his car was parked in front of the house, and started complaining about police inefficiency and getting him out of bed for nothing. Of course when he looked outside, his car wasn't there."

Lexi finished a sip of her brandy. "Stolen vehicle."

"Exactly. They're looking for it now. But more importantly for us, Crispi is not happy that this happened after Angelo turned down police protection."

"But the car tried to run us down. Angelo wasn't the target."

Rick shrugged. "Of that I'm not sure. But the bottom line is that Crispi is insisting we have a police escort for the rest of the time you're in Mantova, and won't take no for an answer. Your boss won't be happy. I'm not happy. Nobody is happy."

"I'm happy the two of us got out of that alley in one piece."

"Between my bad leg and these boots, I almost didn't make it."

"You need a good massage."

He took her hand in both of his. "What a great idea, Lexi."

"The hotel spa opens tomorrow at seven a.m. I'm sure they can get you in."

Rick smiled. "You're good." He leaned closer. "There's something I couldn't help thinking, both when we were outside the giants hall, and later in the alley when we ducked to get away from the car."

"You mean when you had me in your arms?"

"Right."

"I'm afraid to ask."

He leaned closer and sniffed. "I kept thinking, what is that perfume she's wearing?"

Lexi laughed. "What are you, some kind of perfume expert?"

Rick's response was an offended frown. "Well, as a matter of fact, I do know a thing or two about perfume, my dear. When I lived in Albuquerque, I had a friend who worked at the perfume counter at our big department store. While waiting for her to get off work, I used the time to familiarize myself with the various scents."

Lexi stared at him. "You're not joking."

"Certainly not. It's become kind of a hobby."

"I'm impressed. Well, I wear—"

"No. Don't tell me. I'm still trying to place it. I'm narrowing it down."

"I suppose you need more time and more whiffs of it."

"That would be very helpful."

She leaned over and kissed him on the cheek before finishing her brandy and getting to her feet. "There. Hold that memory. Thanks for a wonderful dinner and an exciting walk home, Rick. Sorry we can't go for a run tomorrow. I'll see you at breakfast."

He watched her slacks as she walked to the lobby, remembering how those long legs looked in running tights. Then he rubbed his thigh and cursed the fates.

They could not see the water of the Po River as the car went over the long, double-lane bridge. After reaching the southern bank, visibility improved, but Marco still made his turns with care. The morning fog, which had been heavy since leaving Mantova, was showing signs of lifting, thanks to a tenacious, probing sun. As the car got farther from the bridge, what had been a heavy curtain of gray was turning to wisps of vapor, revealing the drab, flat landscape. On the left side of the road any view of the river was blocked by a thick grove of trees, planted decades earlier for flood control and now leafless in the fall chill. To the right, dark dirt stretched from the pavement to the horizon. At the far edge of the field, at the end of a row of high trees, the white walls and red roofs of houses offered the eye a slight contrast to the brown earth and cloudy sky. The driver slowed and signaled for a turn. Angelo twisted to look out of the rear window at the police car that was keeping a discreet distance behind them.

"Maybe we can get Marco to lose the tail on the way back. It could be fun."

Rick, who sat next to him in the backseat, wasn't sure if his boss was joking, so he decided to ignore the suggestion and change the subject. "We're coming into your place of birth, Mr. Rondini."

They had just passed the sign announcing their entry into Voglia, followed by another sign mandating a reduction in speed, not that they were going at all fast. Tall trees lined both sides of the straight two-lane road. The open field continued to stream by on the right, but a combination of brick wall and tall hedge began along the left, hiding either a residence, farm, or both. They passed a gate but were unable to catch a view of what was inside. When the hedge ended, they were into the town itself. Standing under two pine trees in the center of a square of gravel was a statue of a soldier. A wreath, its white ribbon blowing slightly in the wind, was affixed to the pedestal. The soldier, dressed for the First World War, held a rifle in one hand and saluted the horizon with the other. The memorial indicated they had come upon civic center of town, and the two buildings on the opposite side of the street confirmed it. They had the architecture of the late nineteenth century, as well as the light-yellow color and white trim used so often in government buildings. Each flew the Italian flag from its center balcony and was marked by raised letters: *Scuola* and *Municipio*. There were likely classes going on behind the shutters of the school, but it was not evident from the street. City Hall showed some activity; people were entering the building and the shutters were raised. Most of the movement on this street, however, was in a large parking lot across from the municipal building and next to the church. It was full of canopied vehicles, each in an assigned spot and decked out to sell food, clothing, hardware, and sundries. Locals, bundled against the chill and armed with shopping bags, walked the aisles among them.

"It appears that we're here on market day," said Rick. "They must have planned it that way so you could get some local color."

In fact, the stands and the people were as drab and gray as the weather. This was not a market like Campo dei Fiori, near Rick's apartment in Rome, full of bright flowers, where the clients knew the sellers, traded daily greetings and jibes, and haggled over quality and price. But that was a permanent market. Voglia was this day's stop for the tireless itinerant vendors of the province. By midday they would pack up and drive to another town where they would set up again at dawn, work all morning, only to move again.

"This has to be the most inefficient system for the sale of goods in the western world," said Angelo. He pointed to a bar just down the street. "Can we get a coffee in there?"

The way Angelo said it made Rick wonder if this return to his home village had been a good idea. The man was cranky, which could have been the result of bad business news Lexi had given him in the morning briefing, or simply his annoyance at having a police escort. The other possibility was that he was having second thoughts about visiting Voglia. They parked the car and got out while the police vehicle slipped into the space next to them. The cop driving made a point of not meeting Angelo's eyes. Perhaps Inspector Crispi had told him that the American was not happy to be protected.

Angelo stopped in front of the car, took a deep breath, and looked up and down the street. "Not exactly the kind of place that's going to keep its young people from leaving for the big city, is it?"

They walked to the door of the bar, saw that it was open, and went inside. At one table a man whom Rick guessed to be one of the vendors had his hands around a large cup, absorbing its warmth. Otherwise, despite market day, the place was empty of clientele. They had likely been in earlier and would show up late. A woman stood behind the bar and sized up the two new arrivals. Rick assumed she was the owner, otherwise she would be enjoying her grandchildren in retirement. It was impossible to know how long her gray hair was since it had been tied up in a bun, but likely at least shoulder-length. The skin signaled smoker, and her voice, when she spoke, confirmed it.

"What can I get for you, *Signori?*"

Angelo understood without knowing the words. "Can she make me an American coffee?"

"*Per piacere, un caffè lungo per lui, un espresso per me.*"

She grunted and turned to the silver machine behind her while Angelo looked around the room. Under the glass display case were what was left of the morning pastries and a larger number of *panini* awaiting the lunch crowd. Lined up on the shelves behind the bar was a meager collection of *grappe* and *digestivi*, with one bottle of whiskey, unopened and gathering dust. Rick expected another disparaging comment from Angelo, but the man was silent, staring into the large mirror that ran the length of the back wall. The woman finished her preparations and put a large cup of black coffee in front of Angelo, a small one in front of Rick.

"Is this the rich American?" said the woman, stopping Rick's sugar spoon in mid-air.

"*Scusi?*" Rick asked.

"The American. Our mayor went to the funeral of Roberto Rondini a few days ago and said there was some rich American cousin there who was born here. I hear a lot in this place."

Angelo had caught the name when she spoke and asked Rick to interpret.

"She heard about the funeral, and that an American cousin of Roberto was there." He left out rich. "So she put two and two together and thought you might be him."

"Your cowboy boots blew my cover, Language Man." Rick was surprised to see his boss turn to the woman and extend his hand. "Angelo Rondini, my pleasure."

The woman shook the hand and introduced herself before giving Rick a questioning look.

"And I'm Riccardo Montoya, Signor Rondini's interpreter."

The woman pushed back a bit of hair that had escaped the

bun. "We have something in common. I was born here, too. But I stayed."

Rick went into his interpreting routine.

"Ask her if she knew the Rondini family."

Rick did, and got her answer. While she spoke, Angelo waited patiently, stirring sugar into his coffee and tasting it.

"She was young when Enzo Rondini, your uncle, moved to Mantova. She never knew Roberto, and says neither of them ever came back to visit, despite being so close. She thinks the Rondinis didn't want to be associated with the place, and people here were fine with that."

Angelo looked at the woman while he listened, nodding his head. She stared back.

"Looking at this place, I can understand why my uncle stayed away. Don't translate that, just tell her I found what she said interesting. Then let's get out of here and visit the church."

Rick complied.

A few minutes later they were back on the street. Marco was chatting with the policeman between their two cars when they noticed Rick and Angelo starting to cross the street. The cop watched them cross and then left the driver to follow at a distance. A light wind blew in from the west, taking away any vestige of the morning fog but bringing with it an equally humid chill off the river. It was like a silent signal that the market would soon be packing up, and the sound of metal canopy poles clanging to the ground followed, though a few women still poked around the open stalls for last-minute bargains.

Angelo pushed open the door to the church and was followed in by Rick, who dipped his fingers into the small font just inside and crossed himself. Angelo didn't seem to notice; he stepped in and squinted at the darkened space. Vertical windows were cut high up into the walls, but little light was getting in thanks to the clouds, or perhaps too-long-postponed cleaning. Two small bulbs illuminated a tiered table of votive candles, some lit and adding a fluttering, eerie light to that side of the church. The only decoration on the walls was a set of stations of the cross, hung at intervals on bare nails. Rick counted eight rows of empty wooden pews, a number which likely was enough to accommodate the town's faithful for mass. They fit easily into a single open space that lacked columns and side chapels. The only ornamentation was on the altar, raised by a few steps from the cement floor of the main church. A gold crucifix hung from the ceiling over the cloth-covered altar, flanked by silver candlesticks. Had he not known better, Rick might have thought they'd wandered into a Protestant church.

"So you think this was where I'd have been baptized?"

"There could be another church, but I doubt it. This is the only game in town, and from the exterior, I'd guess it's been here since the nineteenth century. So, unless they took you into Mantova, which was unlikely, you were baptized right there." He pointed to a stone font on a pedestal at one side of the altar area.

Angelo walked along one side past the pews, pausing briefly at the table of candles before coming to the altar and crossing himself. Rick watched, wondering what was going through the man's head. In Rome, he still attended the small church where he'd been baptized—though not with enough frequency to satisfy his mother—and his Roman priest today was the same man who had sprinkled water on his head back then. Between all the diplomatic assignments of his father, the family always made regular trips back to Rome to visit relatives and attend mass in the family church. His mother insisted on it, a continuity in Rick's life that he'd never thought much about, that he took for granted. Angelo Rondini was not as fortunate. Now he was returning to a church he never knew in a town he'd left as an infant, trying to decide what it meant for his life now. Or if it even meant anything.

A door slammed on the right side of the chancel and a bent balding man appeared, dressed in black with a stained apron and carrying a broom and dustpan. When he saw the two men standing below him, his face turned to a puzzled and annoyed frown. After a moment of thought he put down the dustpan, walked to a corner, and began sweeping as if he were the only person in the church.

"Ask him if he can show us the baptism records," said Angelo, his voice lowered as if the man understood English.

Rick walked up the three steps and approached the sweeper. "Excuse me, we're visiting Voglia and would like, if it's possible, to look up a name in the records of baptism. Would that be possible?"

The man stopped and stared, making Rick wonder for a moment if he was one of the many immigrants who had come to Italy from Eastern Europe, whose Italian was not up to the task. Then the man spoke.

"That's impossible. I'm here by myself. You'll have to come back another day."

Rick interpreted for his boss.

"You know the local culture, Language Man. Work some magic."

Rick turned back to the custodian, opened his overcoat, and reached into his pants pocket. From it he pulled his money clip and took two ten-Euro notes from it. "I'm sorry you are so busy, and we don't want to take you from such important work. By the way, is that the donation box over there?"

The man looked at the money and back at Rick before nodding. Rick walked to the box, slipped the two folded notes through the slot, and walked back to Angelo.

The man held up a hand. "Perhaps I can find the time for such a good friend of the church." He scurried over and leaned his broom against the wall. "Come this way, please."

"Well done," said Angelo.

"I'll put it on my expense account."

The door took them from the old church to a more recent addition, though still old by American standards. After passing a kitchen and large meeting hall, they came to a closed door where the man stopped to reach into his apron and pull out a set of keys. He found the one he was looking for, and with some difficulty got the lock open. If there were windows, they were shuttered, since the room was as dark as an ancient closet, with a musty smell to match. He reached inside the doorway and found the light switch. After some buzzing from the ceiling, an uncovered florescent tube came to life, revealing a small rectangular space, not quite a room but more than a cubicle. A wood desk was wedged between rows of stuffed shelves, but no chair. On the desk stood a single lamp with a parchment shade that looked like it had come with the original building. The custodian looked at the floor, perhaps realizing that it had been too long since it had last been swept, and then pointed to the shelves, now bathed in a pale yellow light.

"They're by year," he said. "Turn out the light and close the door when you leave. It locks itself." He disappeared down the hall and Rick wondered if he was on the way to empty the donation box.

"If they really are in chronological order, you should be easy to find," said Rick as he stepped to the shelf. The first book he pulled down was a ledger that had been filled in by hand and dated to the year 1756. So there must have been another church on this site, or somewhere else in Voglia, before the present one. The items listed showed church income from donations and fees for marriages and other services, as well as expenses, everything from fixing the roof to stipends for the priest. Rick found it fascinating, but it wasn't what they were looking for. He replaced the ledger, brushed the dust off his hands, and moved to another section of shelves. Here he found the baptism records. Angelo told him his birth date, and Rick started pulling down books.

In the period just after the war they changed from bound volumes to hole-punched sheets kept in notebooks, but still handwritten. Everything was recorded in the elaborate script of the time, full of curls and loops. He found the year, then the month, and began leafing carefully through the pages, each with columns for the date, name of the child, names of the parents and godparents, and the officiating priest.

"Here you are. It was about three weeks after your birthday." Rick held his finger on the page and Angelo bent closer.

"It's hard to read in this light."

Rick pulled out his phone and activated the flashlight mode. The page came to life.

"There are my parents. Who are the other names?"

"These two are your godparents, the other is the priest." He read the names.

"My mother's sister and her husband, I think. They lived in Milan. I haven't heard those names in years, since I was a kid."

What would have made more sense would be that the brother from right there in Voglia, Enzo Rondini, had been Angelo's godfather. But then Rick remembered his research in the archives of the *Gazzetta*. Angelo's uncle wasn't married yet. It would be logical that a married couple be godparents. Rick turned off the bright light but kept the phone in his hand. He aimed and clicked, and the flash momentarily lit up the page again.

"For your records, Mr. Rondini."

"Good idea."

Rick closed the book and returned it to its slot on the shelf. "Now to City Hall to find the actual birth record?"

"Lead the way."

They followed the instructions they'd been given, turning out the light and closing the door behind them, before retracing their steps back to the door off the altar. The custodian was not immediately visible, but when they stepped down onto the floor, he could be seen along the side wall, putting his broom to use with slow, deliberate sweeps. Rick walked over and thanked him for the help. When he turned back he saw Angelo standing directly in front of the crucifix, his hands clasped across his chest, head bowed. After a few moments he raised his eyes and he crossed himself slowly. Was Angelo Rondini a religious man? It was not something that had come up in the few days they had been together and perhaps, because of that, Rick assumed the man was not a regular at mass. But why assume that? Your faith was not something that you chatted about, especially with someone you had just met. From what Rick just witnessed, Angelo appeared to be a practicing Catholic...or had decided to become one again.

The temperature had dropped since they'd gone into the church. The sky was blocked by a pewter layer of clouds which stopped any beams of sun from reaching the ground. Rick and Angelo buttoned their overcoats and walked to the curb. A battered car passed in front of them, coming from the market. The man driving was arguing with the woman next to him, and in the rear seat a small boy looked through the car window, trying to ignore the dispute. His grim eyes moved quickly from Rick to Angelo to the church behind them. Rick watched the car as it turned off the street into a road through the fields.

They crossed the street to where Marco and the policeman stood next to their respective vehicles. Rick told the two men where he and Angelo were going next and the policeman gave him a loose salute, as if he didn't take this bodyguard duty very seriously. Marco, in contrast, was somber, reflecting the mood of his boss. The *Municipio* was only a few doors down, confirming that most community activity was conveniently located on this one street. Government, church, a bar, and a market—on this day, it was all a resident would need. On side streets, houses and the occasional two-story duplex had been built on acreage that had been open fields. There had to be a *pizzeria*, a requirement for a population this size, but likely it was somewhere on the periphery along with a small agribusiness or two. The people living in this town had to work somewhere; they couldn't all be public employees or pensioners.

The municipal building had a yellowed drabness that went

with its vocation. Two of the parking spaces in front of it, reserved for city vehicles, were empty. Of the other four, two held small sedans: a shiny red Mini and a Fiat *Cinquecento*. They were dwarfed by two pickup trucks next to them, their fenders and tires caked with dark mud. Rick and Angelo went up the steps, through the door, and into a large room that served as a waiting area. Wooden chairs, perhaps dating to the inaugural year, ran along one side, their line broken only by a door in the middle. Two men who were dressed like they belonged with the trucks, sat and talked quietly, each with an official-looking folder in hand. The opposite wall was taken up by two more doors and a long bulletin board cluttered with decrees, announcements, and other official government business. Rick wondered if anyone ever read them. Maybe, when people got bored waiting for their bureaucrat, they got up and wandered over. At the opposite wall from the entrance sat a man in a blue uniform. The desk in front of him was bare except for a telephone with a rotary dial, another vestige of the building's inauguration. Rick walked to the desk.

"Birth records?"

The man jerked a thumb toward a stairwell at the corner of the room. "Second floor."

There was no elevator, and Angelo took his time climbing the flights of steps, stopping at the top to catch his breath. The stairs had brought them to another room equal in size to the foyer directly below it, but with a lower ceiling. Here only a few empty chairs rested against the walls. There were more doors than on the first floor and they were all closed. The side of the room facing the street was made up of windows as well as a glass door that led to a small balcony, giving the room most of its light. The balcony must have been used at one time for political speeches, but that custom had gone out of fashion and now it served as a place to anchor the flag. Rick scanned the names on the door and found the one he was looking for: *Anagrafe.*

Followed by Angelo, he pushed open the door and almost immediately was stopped by a counter that ran the length of the room. Behind it were shelves filled with records, as would be expected in the office that kept track of the community's marriages, births, and deaths. He expected a cranky clerk to go along with the atmosphere of the place, but instead a woman appeared from behind the shelves, a kindly smile on her face. She was dressed in clerkly fashion in a blue skirt topped by a white blouse and dark cardigan sweater. Her glasses hung from leashes around her neck.

"Can I help you?"

"Thank you, yes," answered Rick. "We would like to look up a birth record."

She looked at Angelo and back at Rick, not understanding why the older man wasn't talking. "Doing some genealogical research? I get that on occasion."

"You could say so, yes. Signor Rondini is visiting from America, and he doesn't speak Italian. I'm assisting him."

"Ah." She looked at Angelo as if he was unable to speak at all, then turned back to Rick. "You wanted to look up a birth record? Everything is by year, of course, there is no way to search for specific names. Do you have the dates in mind?"

Rick told her.

"Interesting. There was a man in here recently looking for the same year." Before Rick could respond, she disappeared behind the shelves.

"No problem?"

"No problem. She's going to get the register from the year you were born." He decided it wasn't worth mentioning what she'd said. It was likely just a coincidence.

Angelo took a deep breath and leaned his elbows on the counter. "I had mixed feelings about coming to this town. It was something I had to do if I was going to return to Italy. My daughter insisted on it. But what I'm finding is a depressing village with not much past and a questionable future." He took off his glasses and rubbed his eyes. "Maybe I'm reading too much into what we've seen so far."

"You may well be, sir. This is a prosperous area. A bit drab, perhaps, especially on a day like this, but—"

"Drab? Tell me about it. This woman's the first person we've seen who smiled. But I suppose it's just as well. If it had been bustling and exciting, I might have wondered why my parents ever left."

They heard some noise from behind the shelves and the clerk emerged carrying four books that she eased down onto the counter. The word "births" was written in faded lettering on the cover of the top one, under which were two dates indicating the period covered inside. She brushed dust from her fingers.

"These are the four for that year." She pointed to the top of the stack. "This first one is from December of the previous year until mid-March. You can see how it's arranged." She smiled at Angelo. "You can take them to the end of the counter to read them. I'm sorry we don't have room in here for a desk."

"That will be fine," said Rick, "thank you." She returned to her hiding place and he slid the books down to the far end of the wood counter, under one of the ceiling lamps. The lighting was better than in the church archives, and he'd need it to read words that had lightened on the pages over time. Angelo stood next to him as he checked the dates on the covers and set aside the three not needed. "Month and day, when written, are switched in Italy. It will be in this one." He pointed to the dates on the outside and opened the book.

The pages were thick, and the entries written in the same elaborate script as they'd seen in the baptism records. Even if cursive wasn't being taught in the schools by then, the persons writing had been old enough to practice the old ways. Perhaps the woman who was helping them still did, but Rick doubted it. Everything on computers by now, even in a small town like Voglia. Like in the church, each page was carefully lined with columns. Date. Name of the child. Names and ages of the parents. Their places of birth and present residence. Rick explained the system as he turned the pages.

"Here it is. Rondini." Rick put his finger about halfway down the page.

Angelo adjusted his glasses and leaned forward to read. Suddenly he stiffened and bent his head closer to the page. His breath came in short gasps, like Rick had heard on the stairway.

"Mr. Rondini, are you all right?"

He ignored the question. "That's impossible. It just couldn't be."

Rick looked closer and realized what Angelo had read. There was his name, the A and R written with a flourish next to the birth date. In the next column, under the designation for parents, were two names: Enzo Rondini and Giuseppina Bardi.

"Why did they never tell me the truth?"

Chapter Eleven

Lexi shuddered. "Good Lord, that's horrible. What a way to find out you're adopted. Poor Angelo. Poor, dear Angelo." She and Rick stood in the doorway of her hotel room. "Why am I making you stand out here? Come in and sit down. I'm ready to go, I was just finishing up an e-mail, though that seems so unimportant now."

"He's pretty tough, Lexi. He'll sort it all out and get over it."

Her room was larger than his, and laid out differently. Unlike American hotels, built to order with every room a clone of the next, Italian hotels were often converted historic buildings like this one. Rooms had different sizes and shapes, each with its own charm. Lexi's had been rectangular, but when a bathroom was added it became L-shaped. Arranged around the space was a double bed, a couch, and a glass breakfast table with two chairs. One wall had a built-in desk with a comfortable leather chair. Lexi's laptop was centered on the desk next to a neat stack of papers, a legal pad, and pens, all under the light of a recessed lamp underneath the desk's shelving. Very neat and businesslike, as would be expected for Angelo Rondini's special assistant. He looked at the dresser near the bed, hoping to see a bottle of her perfume and was disappointed. It was in the bathroom.

He pulled off his overcoat, lay it over one of the chairs, and sat in the other. "What makes it harder to take, of course, is just who his biological parents were. Enzo Rondini, who Angelo thought was his uncle, is in fact his father, and his father is really his uncle. Enzo, who was not married at the time, must have talked his older brother and his wife into taking their child."

"And sending them off to America."

"I suspect they had been planning to emigrate before this happened. But with the same last name, Rondini, it must have been easy to take baby Angelo to the States as their own son. Enzo, even then, was ambitious, and didn't want the stigma of fathering a child when he wasn't married, though later he did marry Giuseppina. I recall reading the name Pina in the news stories of the time."

Lexi settled into the sofa, crossed her ankles, and stretched her legs. She was dressed in an off-white turtleneck sweater and black slacks. Gold rings again dangled from her ears. As always, her makeup was perfect, with just a hint of blush on her smooth, brown skin.

"Rick, I just realized something. Roberto Rondini was Angelo's brother."

"Exactly. He was coming to terms with that in the car as we drove back. Lexi, he was already depressed about his birthplace before all this happened. It's not exactly a charming town to begin with, and the weather didn't help. The discovery turned out to be the end to a perfect visit."

"What can we do, Rick?"

"I was hoping you would have some suggestions, though I'm not sure if there is anything we can do. You know him much better than I. Is he the kind of person who likes to talk things out with someone, or work problems out on his own?"

"More the latter."

"Then we leave him alone."

Lexi leaned forward on the sofa. "This couldn't have anything to do with the murder, could it?"

"No, I'm sure it doesn't. It happened so long ago." He closed his eyes. "Wait a minute."

"Rick, what is it?"

"Just thinking of something. Two things, in fact. I just said that what we discovered today about Angelo happened long ago, which is of course true. But my uncle said something when I first talked to him about the case and it just popped back in my head. People have long memories, is what Piero said." He closed his eyes again and rubbed them with his fingers. Then he opened them wide and smiled. "The kid in the car."

"What are you talking about?"

He fumbled in his pocket for his phone, scrolled quickly through the numbers and hit one. "I have to call Crispi." A voice answered on the third ring and Rick switched to Italian. Lexi watched.

"Inspector? This is Montoya."

"What is it?"

Mr. Personality, as always. "Can you check on something for me, or have that sergeant who is good with public records do a check?" When he got no reply, he continued. "When I was at the *Gazzetta* there was a story about the family whose land had been expropriated."

"You mean—"

"Correct, the same land, I'm quite sure. Could she check the name of that family? I'm interested in the person who owned it before foreclosure, before it was taken by the province and then purchased by Enzo Rondini."

"Montoya, that was fifty years ago. Is this connected to our case?"

Rick was tempted to revert to sarcasm, but resisted. "I believe it is."

Even over the phone Rick could hear Crispi's slow exhale. "All right, I'll get her on it, and call you back. Not sure how long it will take."

"I'm going to be out at the river, the memorial for Roberto Rondini, with my ringer turned off. Can you just text me the name?"

"As you wish."

"Thank you, Inspector." Rick was about to hang up when Crispi stopped him.

"Montoya, something else has come up, involving Francesco Guarino. Is he going to be at this memorial at the river?"

"Livia's husband? Yes, I assume so, if he's recovered from his accident."

"I'll tell you about it later. Is the corporal I assigned to you doing his job?"

It took Rick a moment to understand that he meant the bodyguard. "We're all still in one piece, Inspector."

"Glad to hear it. Don't say anything to your boss about Guarino. It may be nothing."

The call ended just as they heard a knock at the door. Rick and Lexi exchanged glances. "Come in," she called out.

Angelo opened the door, dressed in his overcoat, ready for the drive to the river. "Lexi? Did you hear back from—oh, you're here, Language Man."

Rick got to his feet, as did Lexi. "Mr. Rondini, Rick told me what happened. I don't know what else to say except that I'm so sorry."

Rick noticed that his boss was in better shape than when he'd seen him last. When they had arrived in the hotel, Angelo had walked slowly across the lobby, head bent, eyes staring at the floor. He stayed that way until Rick got off the elevator and the doors closed. Rick got to his room, checked his e-mails, and wondered what, if anything, he could do. Was it a good idea to leave Angelo alone, or did he need to talk it out? Only Lexi would have the answer, if there was one. That was when he'd walked up one flight of stairs and knocked on her door. Looking at the man now, it was evident that he'd come to grips with the news. Or put it away in some compartment to deal with later.

"Thank you, Lexi. It's been quite a shock. Not like anything I've been through before. I just got off the phone with Nikki, and as always, she was very supportive. She's the only one I can talk to about family matters since her mother died."

"I've unburdened myself on Nikki a few times," Lexi said. "She's a good listener."

"She wasn't very happy that I woke her up. In my state I'd forgotten about the time difference, but she forgave me when I told her why I was calling." He looked at Rick, as if noticing for the first time that he was present. "Do you think your policeman friend is going to discover who killed my brother?"

The question, and the tone of voice, jolted Rick. The investigation had risen to a new level of interest for Angelo Rondini, or focusing on it may have been a way to put aside the shock he'd received in Voglia.

"I just spoke with him and asked him to check on something that came to me as a result of our visit today. It has to do with the previous ownership of that tract of land."

"That damn land again? The Rondinis have owned it for decades, I don't see how that could be of any help in finding Roberto's murderer."

"Crispi thinks it might," Rick said, stretching the truth somewhat.

"No way. It has to be someone who doesn't want that land developed, or more likely wants it for himself. If property is involved, the issue is going to be money. I can tell you that from personal experience."

"That may well be, sir. But this thread should be followed and then checked off if it leads nowhere." What Rick didn't say, was that if his hunch was correct, among those gathering at the river to honor Roberto Rondini could be the very person responsible for his murder.

"It's getting late, Mr. Rondini." Lexi rose to her feet and picked up her coat. "We don't want to keep all those people waiting."

Thunderstorms had rumbled through the Trentino region the previous day, swelling the creeks that snaked through the steep hills surrounding the Lago di Garda. The streams dropped from cliffs around the lake, creating spectacular but temporary waterfalls. The water level rose, lifting the pleasure boats that had not yet been put into storage for the winter. At the southern end of the lake the shore squeezed into a funnel at the town of Peschiera, pushing the overflow from the rains into the start of the Mincio. The new river was allowed to meander for only a few kilometers. A short distance from the lake, canals began stealing from the main course, sending water east and west where it would be partitioned among farms and towns. Though diminished, the river kept flowing. At Borgetto, as it had for more than six hundred years, it passed under the bridge built by the Duke of Milan when the Visconti controlled the land on both banks. On the river ran, cutting through Goito before entering a nature preserve where birds—in air, perched and wading—watched it pass. By the time it lapped the outer edge of the Rondini property, the Mincio was calm and wide.

The Mercedes was not the first car to arrive. When it pulled into the open area above the river bank, followed by the police escort, Livia and Francesco Guarino were standing next to one of the dairy's Land Rovers, deep in conversation. She wore leather boots for the wet ground and a wool coat for the weather. He was bundled in a heavy overcoat, and his head was covered by a hat which conveniently hid any marks of his accident. It was not a friendly conversation. When Livia saw the other car pull in she said something to her husband and walked to where Angelo had opened his door and stepped to the ground. They embraced before she greeted Lexi and Rick.

"Uncle, the monument is beautiful, just perfect in its simplicity. It is so appropriate that it overlooks the river where my father spent so many hours."

"I'm glad you approve, Livia," said Angelo. "They did a good job installing it?"

"They came early this morning, and Francesco helped them place it." They all looked down at the patch of grass on which the column rested. "You can see that they put paving stones around it, which was a perfect touch. The inscription faces the river, as it should."

"So the fish can look up and remember their tormentor."

She laughed. "I never thought of that, Uncle, but yes, it's true."

Rick watched the exchange and wondered why her husband was hanging back when he should have come over to greet Angelo. Was it due to their argument? Or could it have something to do with the cryptic comment by Inspector Crispi about the man? Rick also wondered when Angelo would tell his niece, now a true niece, what he had learned that morning on the visit to Voglia. It had to come out eventually, but this was not the time to get into delicate family matters, what with the arrival of guests. And they were beginning to arrive.

The pickup truck that Rick had seen on two occasions drove up and parked several spaces away. From the driver's seat emerged Emilio Fiore, dressed in a leather jacket over jeans, like he had just come from feeding his cows. Carlo Zucari got out of the other side, dressed more formally, but with a practical pair of boots for the terrain. He opened the extended cab rear door and helped a woman step to the ground. Rick was surprised to see the face of Letizia Bentivoglio, and glanced at Livia who was watching the trio's arrival.

"Letizia was a friend of my father," she said to Angelo without prompting. "I don't suppose you talked to her last night at the Palazzo Te. We had a nice conversation and I invited her here today."

If Angelo put the name with the story of his brother's mistress, he didn't let on to Livia. Another car pulled up with the president of the cheese consortium and two other men Rick had seen the previous night. Livia excused herself and went to greet them.

"Is she who I think she is?" Angelo asked.

"Yes, Mr. Rondini," Rick answered. "I spoke with her last night, but she didn't have much to say. Certainly nothing that could help with the investigation."

Lexi made a small cough. "I noticed her last night as well. And we saw her having coffee with Zucari after dinner, didn't we Rick?"

"She's the one."

"Well, I'm glad she's here," said Angelo. "She obviously was important to my brother in his last days, and that's enough for me. Who are they?"

A light green pickup truck had driven up and parked with the other vehicles. Rick was too far from it to read the logo on the doors, so he decided it was either from another dairy, or perhaps a government entity. Two men got out whom he didn't recognize.

"I don't know, Mr. Rondini. Someone else Livia invited, I assume."

"Let's go down to the dock while Livia sorts it all out. It's her land, after all." He called to the driver, who was standing with the cop. "Marco, keep your friend from getting bored. There shouldn't be much danger for us with this group"

The driver nodded. "Yes, sir, I will."

The three of them walked down the gentle slope, stopped for a moment to look at the column, and continued to the river's edge. Angelo plunged his hands into his pockets and looked out over the water. On the far side a lone boat ran slowly along the shore, its motor barely audible. "Here we all are, coming down to the river, like some kind of story from the Bible. Everything happened here, next to this water, both the good and the bad. And now we're all back, like my brother somehow planned it this way." His smile was weary. "Let's join the others."

Everyone who'd been expected must have arrived, since Livia was inviting them to gather around the monument. Rick watched the policeman, who had been chatting with Marco, come down from the parking area and position himself on a small rise just to one side. It was a perfect place to stay out of the way while still keeping an eye on the Americans, as well as everyone else, indicating the cop was taking his assignment seriously. Nobody seemed to be surprised by his presence, or even notice it. They were too busy chatting with each other or admiring the clean, white stone of the column.

Rick looked at the gathering and wondered how long it would take Crispi to look up the name he'd requested. Maybe the records didn't go back that far, or had been lost in a fire. Records were always being lost in fires in Italy, which often was very convenient if they contained information that someone didn't want made public. He was doing it again, thinking like an Italian, something his uncle had been accusing him of lately.

A soft putter sound drifted over the scene before the mo-ped causing it came through the opening in the trees and approached the parking lot. Only Rick and the policeman seemed to notice, and they watched as a man parked, pulled out the key, and stepped to the ground. He wore a battered helmet which he unsnapped and pulled off with difficulty due to the quantity of hair. Placing the helmet on the seat, he walked briskly down the hill while trying unsuccessfully to push his hair into place.

"Look who's here, Lexi," said Rick.

Both she and Angelo looked up.

"That's the nut that was demonstrating at the gate," said Angelo. "Tell the cop to get rid of him, Language Man."

"Curiously enough, Mr. Rondini, your niece just noticed him and waved. I have to believe she invited him."

"I don't get it."

"We should get it soon," said Lexi, "she's about to start the proceedings."

Livia stood in front of the column with her back to the river. The invitees gathered on the other three sides of the monument, while Angelo, Rick, and Lexi stood behind her, back a sufficient distance so that Rick's interpreting would not be too distracting.

"Thank you all for coming," she began.

Rick placed himself between and just behind Lexi and Angelo, then went to work.

"We are here thanks to the generosity of Signor Angelo Rondini, who has put this monument here to honor the memory of my father." She turned and smiled at Angelo. "I could not imagine a more appropriate place. It was here that Roberto Rondini came when he wanted to forget the problems of the moment, and as you can see and feel, the tranquility of the river has the power to do just that. I recall one time when my father was starting to bring me into the family business..."

Livia spoke, and Rick translated in a low voice for Angelo and Lexi. When she was in the middle of her story, he felt the vibration of his phone, and without stopping his interpreting, he pulled it from his pocket. It was a three-sentence text from Crispi. When he was doing simultaneous interpreting, Rick put himself into an intense, concentrative zone; all that existed was the voice he heard in one language and the words in the other that he spoke in response. The message he glanced at on the screen of his phone broke his concentration. Angelo noticed and turned around.

"What's going on?"

"Sorry, Mr. Rondini." He pointed to the phone and kept his voice low. "The message came in from the inspector. It's not what I expected."

"Let me see." Rick showed him the small screen of his cell. Lexi bent to see it as well.

Rick whispered as he pointed. "This is the man who owned the land when it was taken by the government for unpaid taxes." His finger moved. "This is the name of his son, who was a boy at the time. Crispi did a check of this name and found that he died recently. And this last name is the grandson of the original owner and son of the man who just died."

Angelo's eyes darted from the phone to the people gathered around the monument. "That son of a bitch."

"Crispi is on his way," Rick said. "He'll probably be here before this ends."

"I want to get my hands on the guy before that."

"Mr. Rondini," said Lexi, her voice almost inaudible, "be reasonable. This is something for the police to handle."

To get Angelo's mind off revenge, if that was possible, Rick returned to interpreting Livia's remarks. She had finished the story about her father and was on a new topic.

"...the land that extends from the Mincio to the edge of our pasture land. It has not been used by my family for many years, but I have decided it is time to determine its future. I have received many purchase offers for those who wish to develop it in one way or another: luxury housing overlooking the river, a factory, a shopping center. I weighed all the possibilities and have made a decision."

The group was silent. The only sound, other than the low hum of Rick's voice, was the ripple of the river as it ran under the wooden dock behind them. Livia looked at the monument in front of her before going on.

"It was thinking about my father coming here that helped me decide what should happen to this land. I could not destroy the tranquility of this place with construction and development, it would be an affront to the memory of my father. Instead I will be donating the land to the Mincio River Nature Reserve, so that it can revert to its most natural state, and be available for the enjoyment of the public."

She smiled at the two men who had arrived in the green truck, and they began to clap. They were joined by an enthusiastic Domenico Folengo, after which came the more subdued applause of the others. The expressions Rick saw on the faces of the invitees betrayed their opinion of her decision. The men from the cheese consortium exchanged glances, now understanding that a large amount of acreage would not be used in competition with other dairies, and the equilibrium of power within their organization would remain stable. The two men from the nature reserve were still clapping as they exchanged words. Fiore and Zucari showed only grim frowns and ignored each other. Letizia Bentivoglio had a tearful smile and kept her eyes on the column inscribed with Roberto Rondini's name. Francesco Guarino, unlike the others, displayed only stunned surprise. Was it possible that Livia had not told her own husband beforehand? She waited for the clapping to subside and continued.

"I would like now to ask the person we can thank for this beautiful memorial, Angelo Rondini, to say a few words." She turned. "Riccardo, can you do the interpreting, *per favore?*"

If Angelo was surprised by the invitation, he didn't show it. He and Rick stepped forward and Livia moved to one side. The faces on the others showed curiosity. All of them, save the invitees from the nature reserve, knew who Angelo was, and of those, many had met him. Despite that, he was still a curiosity in the closed circle that was any Italian city. That he had been born here just added to the exotic quality of the man.

"We are here today," he began, "to remember Roberto Rondini. While our gathering is about him, I cannot help but tell you about how my life has been changed by his death. As many of you know, I never met Livia's father, and that will be one of my greatest regrets until the day I die. But I have him to thank for bringing me back to the place where I was born. I should have done it earlier in my life, I know that now. But it isn't too late for me to reconnect to my roots, and to my family."

While he listened to the Italian, Angelo squeezed his niece's hand. The only sound was Rick's voice, until the faint bleat of a siren floated over the fields toward the river. Lexi noticed it and looked anxiously at the people gathered around the stone column. Angelo apparently heard it as well, as his next words indicated.

"Regretfully, Roberto's death was not an accident." He paused and waited for Rick to interpret.

The reaction from the group was immediate. They stiffened, exchanged puzzled frowns, but stayed silent, no doubt wondering what was coming next from the American.

"And now we know who was responsible."

Rick turned to his boss. "Mr. Rondini, do you really think this—"

A sharp cry of pain came from where the policeman had been standing, causing everyone's head to turn in his direction. The cop was on his knees, a stunned look on his face. Blood seeped around fingers pressed against a wound on his forehead, but he was alert enough to reach for his holster with the free hand. The holster was empty.

Marco stood above him and waved the gun at the crowd, but his eyes were on Livia.

"You think you're so noble, donating the land to the people," he said in a quivering voice. "But you can't give away land that doesn't belong to you." His eyes darted to the stricken faces of the others. "Enzo Rondini stole it from my grandfather. Her father knew. Yes, Roberto Rondini knew the whole sordid story. And yet he came to my father's funeral, so what was I to think? Perhaps the man had some decency, something that his father lacked. Perhaps he was ready to make amends for stealing this land from my grandfather. But when I came here—to this very place—to talk with him, he laughed at me." He looked nervously back at the line of trees which separated the river from the Rondini property as the gun wobbled in his hand. His eyes moved from person to person but ended on Livia's face. "You were my last chance. Surely you would see things differently. But now I know I was wrong, you decided to give the land away, land which rightfully belongs to my family."

The sound of the siren had grown stronger. Rick calculated that Crispi was passing the gate of the dairy and would be appearing within minutes. Which might be too late. He started walking slowly toward the driver, holding up his hands.

"Marco, don't do this. No one here had anything to do with taking that land. It was decades ago. Everyone here is innocent."

"Stay where you are, Riccardo." The hand shook as he gripped the pistol. Again he looked quickly back, hearing the siren. His voice, which had been a plaintive wail, now turned icy cold. "The police won't get me, I promise you that. But there is some unfinished business I have to take care of."

He raised the pistol and moved its barrel between Livia and Angelo. His eyes darted from one face to the other, trying to decide which to aim at first. Lexi took advantage of the hesitation, grabbed Livia by the shoulders and pushed her to the ground behind the column. Marco's reaction was immediate. He jerked the gun in their direction and the barrel exploded. The bullet hit the column and small chunks of stone flew into the air. Everyone fell to the ground and instinctively covered their heads. Rick had dropped to one knee on his bad leg and winced in pain. He looked back and saw that Lexi and Livia huddled, unhurt, behind the column.

The sound of a second shot echoed across the water.

Marco began swaying. The gun was still held tightly in one hand, but his arms had dropped to his sides. His unfocused eyes rolled skyward as the pistol slipped from his grip and fell to the ground. He clawed at a dark red spot below his collar, then looked in disbelief at the blood on his fingers. Slowly his knees bent, and he crumpled to the ground.

Rick looked back. Angelo stood stiffly, arms extended and legs spread, like he was on a firing range. The small pistol was pointed at the body of the driver. Only when Rick reached Marco did the pistol disappear into Angelo's overcoat pocket.

Two police cars burst through the opening in the trees.

● ● ● ● ●

"Angelo's got a concealed-carry permit, Rick."

"Somehow I doubt it's valid here in Italy, Lexi. But since Crispi's man was lax in allowing Marco to grab his gun, and your boss saved the day, the inspector may look benignly on the transgression."

"I hope so. Angelo never goes anywhere without it. Another advantage of having one's own airplane."

Rick glanced at the memorial, where the farm manager and Letizia Bentivoglio stood reading the inscription. She was holding tightly to Zucari's arm, and her face was streaked by tears as she stared at the letters etched into the stone. Her hand reached out and touched the cold surface when Zucari noticed Rick watching them. Gently but firmly he led her from the column toward Rick and Lexi.

"That was very courageous of you to try to stop him from shooting," said Zucari.

"I wasn't successful," Rick answered.

"Never the less, my *cugina* and I are very appreciative of your effort." She nodded silently, tugged at Zucari's arm, and they walked away quickly.

"What's the matter, Rick?" said Lexi. "You look stunned."

"Zucari and Letizia Bentivoglio. They're cousins. I thought…"

He was interrupted by the brusque appearance of Emilio Fiore. Livia's neighbor ignored Lexi and spoke to Rick. "Well, Montoya, your boss didn't get what he wanted, did he? A nice international contract would have been so nice, an excuse to fly over here and eat in our restaurants." He pointed a calloused index finger at Rick's chest. "But I would have preferred even a shopping center to this insane decision by Livia. If only Carlo and I could have talked her out of it. We didn't care who got the land, as long as it was used for cattle. Now nobody is happy except those eco-freaks." He shook his head and strode off.

Rick turned to Lexi. "He's not happy about the donation," he said.

The invitees milled around, talking in low voices. They studiously averted their eyes from the prostrate figure of an unconscious Marco Bertani. One of the policemen who had arrived with Crispi was applying first aid as best he could, after having covered the bleeding driver with a blanket. In the distance another faint siren could be heard, this one that of an ambulance.

After tending to the fallen man, Crispi had spoken first with Livia, since it was her property, then with the shaken policeman who gestured nervously as he talked and held a bandage to his head. Then the inspector had pulled out his cell phone and spent at least ten minutes in conversation before striding toward Rick. Lexi saw him approach.

"I'd better let you two talk."

"Thanks, Lexi." He watched her walk quickly to Angelo, who was standing with Livia and her husband.

Crispi did not bother to shake hands. He glanced again at the man on the ground, looked out over the water, and then faced Rick. "This place is cursed, Montoya. She told me she's going to turn it into a nature reserve, but I'm thinking nobody will want to come here. One person killed and his murderer shot, in almost the same spot? They'll be afraid to get near this shore."

"Or they'll come out of morbid curiosity."

The detective nodded. "I suppose you could be correct." He paused and rubbed his chin. "I just had a long conversation with my boss and explained to him what happened."

Rick studied Crispi's face, and as always it revealed nothing. "You told the *questore* what Mr. Rondini did?"

"Of course. He was pleased he'd made the decision to allow Mr. Rondini to be armed, after those threats."

It took an instant to understand, then Rick smiled. "I had forgotten that."

"So had the *questore*. It took some convincing since his first reaction was to prosecute your Mr. Rondini for illegal possession of a firearm. But I reminded him of another investigation I've been doing."

Rick couldn't resist. "Lando up the windmill again?"

"No."

Still no change of expression. The man was a robot.

"I refer to that illegal gambling operation," Crispi said. "You may remember one of my men said something to me when we had lunch."

"I remember," said Rick. "But I don't understand how that would convince your boss to look the other way with Mr. Rondini."

"Let's just say that the *questore* himself is very fond of games of chance. He was pleased when I told him that the investigation into the local operation will be going nowhere."

Crispi may not have all the social graces needed in office politics, Rick decided, but he knows how to work the system. Uncle Piero will be pleased.

"I will not give Mr. Rondini the details behind the decision, but he will be very appreciative."

"It also affects Signor Guarino."

"Livia's husband? You have lost me again, Inspector."

"Signor Guarino also enjoys the occasional wager. More than occasional, apparently. He was rather heavily in debt."

Rick glanced over at Francesco Guarino, who was talking with one of the men from the cheese consortium. "So his injury may not have been from an accident?"

Crispi's answer was a shrug.

The ambulance pulled up and turned off its siren, but the flashing lights stayed on. A woman in white carrying a small bag got out of the passenger side and ran down to where Marco lay. Two men dressed the same followed seconds later, bumping a stretcher on wheels down the hill. The gathered group, ordered to stay by Crispi, was being interviewed by the inspector's men. They had avoided looking at the man who had been shot, but now stopped and watched the emergency crew work. The policeman who had worked on the driver walked to where Crispi and Rick were standing.

"He's in bad shape, sir, but they can probably save him. I didn't see a slug, so it must still be lodged in his upper chest.

The shooter was a good marksman, but if he'd aimed just a bit lower, the man would be dead."

"You did well, Corporal. Now help the others take statements from the witnesses. Just the Italians."

"Yes, sir." He walked to the group. They were still watching the medical technicians work.

"I assume you'll be talking to Rondini and Signora Coleman, Inspector. Do you want me to interpret when you do?"

Crispi pondered the question. "Your statement should be enough," he said finally.

The EMTs lifted Marco to the stretcher and carefully strapped him in.

Rick thought back to when the man had met him at the train station. Nothing in the way he'd acted that day, or since, had betrayed what must have been simmering inside. Even as he resorted to violence against Angelo, Marco kept on playing his part, holding out hope that the Rondini family would finally make amends for the sins of the past. Was that hope so unreasonable? But Roberto Rondini's daughter had other plans for the land, and when that became clear, the explosion was inevitable.

Rick's thoughts were interrupted by the voice of Crispi.

"Tell me something, Montoya. What made you think that the previous owner of the property could have a connection with the murder? It was, after all, half a century ago that the land changed hands."

One man pulled the stretcher while the other pushed from behind, and they started back up the incline toward the ambulance. Their colleague walked next to it, keeping her eyes on the ashen face of the man wrapped the blanket. Crispi was the only one not watching Marco being taken away. He had turned to stare out over the water, which had become choppy thanks to a light wind. After a few seconds he looked back at Rick, who was deciding how to answer. Tell him about seeing the boy looking up from the back seat on that street in Voglio?

Mention the old newspaper photograph of Marco Bertani's father at about the same age, staring at the camera, perhaps on the same street?

"It was just a hunch, Inspector. My uncle told me that some crimes have roots going back many years. That made me think of it."

"Your uncle is an excellent policeman, Montoya."

The late afternoon sun had dropped below the level of the wall, casting a long shadow over the gravestones and making the temperature colder than it had been when they'd gotten out of Livia's vehicle. But at least the high wall sheltered them from a wind that blew over the fields around the cemetery, slowed only by the occasional line of trees. Winter was upon the Po Valley, and with it had come gray skies and shortened days. Snow, infrequent on the flat lands, would soon build up in the mountains to the north, a white cloak from the foothills to the Austrian border.

Rick and Lexi stopped just inside the gate and watched Angelo and Livia walk together to the grave of Roberto Rondini, she holding tightly to her uncle's arm. In her other hand she held a small bouquet. She knelt and placed it among the wilted flowers from the funeral, still arranged around the headstone. When she got to her feet, Angelo put his arm around her and began speaking quietly in her ear. They both looked down at the grave as he spoke.

"He must be telling her now," said Rick. Lexi gripped his arm as they watched.

Livia suddenly looked at her uncle, but he kept his eyes on the fresh grave. Her expression was one of shock, but it soon melted into a bitter smile, and she looked at Angelo's face as if seeing it for the first time. She reached up and touched his cheek, causing him to turn toward her. Her fingers moved around his face, like a blind person meeting a new friend. They stood over Roberto's grave for several minutes before he grasped her arm and they turned toward the gate.

After one step Angelo paused, took a breath, and looked down at two grave stones. With difficulty he got to one knee, rested his hand on the stone marked Giuseppina Rondini, and closed his eyes. When he opened them, he stared at the letters on the next grave for several minutes. He struggled slowly to his feet with the help of his niece, crossed himself, and the two of them walked arm in arm to the gate. Outside the wall, the nearly horizontal rays of the setting sun joined them together into a single, long shadow stretching over the rich soil of Lombardy.

Chapter Twelve

Angelo was his thoughtful self again on the drive from the hotel to the airport. Other than a crack about hoping that Renzo, the new driver, wouldn't try to kill them, he remained quiet in the comfortable back seat of the car that had picked them up just after dawn. Rick had his usual front passenger position, and Lexi sat behind him, clicking her fingernails on her tablet's keyboard. The day was clear and sunny, as if Mantova was telling the three visitors that they should stay longer. "There is more to see," the castle called out when they drove past it, "and my city is giving you such nice weather to help you enjoy it." The lake glistened as they drove over the causeway on their way to the *autostrada*. After taking the toll ticket, the car glided down the ramp and roared over to the left lane, passing a slow-moving truck like it was parked. The wine red Maserati Quattroporte acted like it knew about the Mercedes and wanted to put it to shame on the highway. The engine adopted a throaty growl after being taken through the gears and settling into cruising speed. The trip to Verona's Villafranca Airport, the driver had told Rick, was only about thirty kilometers, which at that hour would take twenty minutes. The way the Maserati was passing everything on A22, Rick thought it might be fifteen. He checked the clock on the dashboard when they arrived at the gate to the tarmac, and he was correct.

The airplane was parked in the same place. It's door was open, and through the cockpit window the pilot could be seen doing his pre-flight check. As the car drove up one of the flight crew appeared at the doorway and turned to alert the crew that the boss had arrived.

"I have to make a call to Livia," said Angelo as the driver started to open his door. They were the first words he'd uttered since they'd pulled into the street in front of the hotel. He got out, took a cell phone from his pocket, and walked toward the tail of the plane as he dialed. Rick and Lexi, standing next to the car, watched him stride away. They were both dressed for travel, Rick in blue jeans and a sweater under leather jacket, she in the same pants suit she'd worn when he'd watched her walk down the steps of the plane just a few days earlier.

"He's already back into his business mode," said Rick.

"He was never really out of it, Rick, even with all that's happened." She looked up as two crew members came down the steps. "There's something you never told me, Rick. What was it Marco shouted just before he got off that shot?"

"I didn't tell Angelo, either, come to think of it. Marco yelled that she had no right to give away the land since it didn't rightly belong to her, that her grandfather stole it, and that she was his last hope to make amends. He also said that Roberto had laughed at him. That must have happened when he confronted Roberto at the dock."

"And that enraged him enough to commit murder."

"I expect that was the scenario, yes. If Marco survives, the police will ask him."

They were interrupted by the arrival of Angelo, as well as one of the flight attendants ready to hoist the luggage up the steps to the plane. The new driver popped the trunk.

"By the way, Language Man. The driver is going to take you all the way to Rome."

Rick held up his hands. "I appreciate the offer, Mr. Rondini, but if he drops me at the train station in Verona, that will be fine."

"No, it's done. Call it an extra thank-you for your services. In addition to the outrageous fee I'm paying you, of course."

"I appreciate it." Rick glanced at the trident logo on the front of the Maserati. "With this car he could have me home in time for lunch."

"Better than airplane food, I'm sure. Now if you'll excuse us, we have a plane to catch."

Angelo and Lexi's bags were being taken up the steps, and Renzo was about to close the trunk when Lexi stopped him. She walked over, pulled out a large shopping bag, and handed it to her boss.

"What's this?"

"Your gift to Nikki. With all that was happening yesterday I thought you might not remember to pick up something for your daughter. It's her size and color."

"You're a lifesaver, Lexi. I talked to her last night and told her to start planning a trip, that she has to get to know her Italian cousin. The shopping here will give her even more incentive to visit." He turned around and faced Rick. "She said she wanted to see Rome, too, by the way. Maybe you could show her around, Language Man."

Lexi, who stood behind Rondini, shot Rick a big grin.

"I'd be glad to, sir."

Rondini took in a deep breath and looked up at the mountains where the sun sparkled off the distant snow. He reached out his hand. "Thank you for all you did, Rick. If you ever need a job back in the States, let me know."

Rick was momentarily without words. It was the first time Angelo had called him by his first name. "It was a pleasure working for you, Mr. Rondini."

"Come on, Lexi. Say your good-byes and let's get the wheels up." He got to the top of the stairs and gave Rick and the driver a presidential wave before going inside.

"He doesn't say that to just anyone, Rick."

"What, Lexi? Ask them to take care of his daughter?"

"Well, that too. I meant offering you a job. You're going to love meeting Nikki."

"You won't tell her anything bad about me, will you?"

"Only the good things, I promise." She put her arms around him and kissed him on the cheek. "Good-bye, Mr. Montoya."

He returned the kiss. "That would be *arrivederci*, Ms. Coleman."

Clutching her tablet bag, she hurried up to the door, waved, and disappeared. A crew member retracted the stairs and pulled the door closed just as one of the engines came to life. Then the second engine turned over with a high-pitched whine, and a ground crew member appeared and removed the chocks from the wheels. Sun reflected off the metal body of the plane, causing Rick to shade his eyes as he watched. He was lost in thought for a few minutes while the plane slowly began to move, then he pulled out his cell phone, checked the time, and turned to the driver.

"Renzo, if by some chance we can't make it all the way to Rome by lunchtime, there's a restaurant I know just off the *autostrada* near Orvieto that specializes in grilled meats."

"I certainly wouldn't want to get a speeding ticket, Signor Montoya."

Ten days later, at a few minutes before one in the afternoon, Rick made his way down a cobblestone street near the Chamber of Deputies. It was sunny, but a chilly front had dropped down off the Apennines and was holding the Eternal City in its grasp. The cashmere scarf around his neck felt good. As always, he looked forward to lunch with Commissario Fontana. Uncle Piero invariably had some fascinating story of his police work that he shared with Rick, and was a good listener if Rick needed advice. There was no one better than a policeman to explain Italians, and specifically Romans, to a newcomer, and though Rick spent much of his youth in Rome and spoke perfect Italian, he still had much to learn about what made the locals tick. It was an education that would never be complete.

Piero's choice of restaurant that day was non-traditional for their periodic lunches. Its menu featured regional specialties from around the country, brought in fresh daily, most famously *mozzarella* from the Campania region around Naples. Unlike their usual lunch spots, the place was extremely modern in décor, stainless steel and glass to the extreme. As Rick noticed when he pushed through the doors, the clientele was also younger than at the other restaurants. Roman yuppies sat at a long polished-wood bar, but instead of eating sushi they sipped wine and speared pieces of cheese and cured meats. He looked past the bar and saw his uncle sitting at a table next to the window. Piero got to his feet and gave his nephew a kiss on both cheeks, in the Italian family tradition. He was dressed more staidly than usual, a dark wool suit with a white shirt, the tie a conservative print. Perhaps he wanted to contrast himself with the youthful clientele of the place, including Rick who wore a blazer without a tie.

"I ordered a Langhe," Piero said, picking up the garnet wine bottle on the table. "Since we'll be eating *mozzarella* and *prosciutto*, it should be a good match."

"Perfect." Rick watched the wine flow into his glass. "Some good wine and cheese is just what I need. I've never been to this place, but heard a lot about it."

Piero glanced at his nephew's face, noticing faint circles under his eyes. "I'm glad you finally found the time to have lunch with your uncle."

Rick took a long sip of the wine. "I had a backlog of translations to do, and to make it worse, scientific articles. They're the most tedious. So I've been at my computer most of the day and into the night working on them. And I had a few last-minute interpreting jobs I had to squeeze in."

"You do look tired."

Rick rolled his eyes before scanning the menu. "Let's do the *mozzarella* sampler, I've heard it's the way to go in this place."

"And some *prosciutto*," said Piero. "They have their own producer of *San Daniele*. And a few artichokes. After that, if you're still hungry, we can decide." He waved over the waiter and gave him the order. "Now tell me what really happened up there. The report I saw from Crispi didn't give the impression it was complete."

Rick fortified himself with a bite of crusty bread and another sip of wine before giving his uncle a description of the investigation. He tried not to leave anything out, since he knew Piero would be interested in all the details. The policeman did not interrupt, but Rick knew he would have questions when he was finished.

He was just about done when the waiter arrived with their order and put empty plates in front of them. A rectangular white platter had the three unadorned *mozzarella* balls, and on a wood board lay paper-thin slices of reddish-pink *prosciutto*. In a bowl sat two small artichokes in oil, prepared Roman style.

"This one is the *delicata*," said the waiter, pointing to one of the balls. "It is sweeter than the middle one, the *intensa*, which has a stronger taste. The third is the *affumicata*, with a smoky flavor. *Buon appetito*." They thanked him, and after he departed decided to go from sweet to smoky. Each of them cut off a slice of the first and put it on his own plate, along with some of the *prosciutto*. The *carciofi* would wait.

"Your *capo* is quite the man," said Piero, after a bite. "But I wouldn't have been happy if someone involved in one of my cases was found to be carrying a weapon."

"Do you think Crispi did the right thing?"

"By closing an eye to it? Since your Mr. Rondini was an American, and one you said knows your ambassador, Crispi avoided a monumental headache by finessing it. But what fascinates me is how he handled it with his boss. It's a side of Crispi I hadn't seen before."

"Do you know the *questore* in Mantova, Zio?"

"I do." Two words, but Piero's tone of voice told Rick volumes about the Mantova chief of police. "He will be retiring soon, Riccardo, but don't tell that to Crispi. Which do you think is best?"

Piero's question referred to the *mozzarella*, since they had tasted pieces from all three, and eaten half the *prosciutto*.

"The smoked is definitely the winner. But they all melt in your mouth like pudding."

"I agree." Piero took two more slices of *prosciutto*, one of the artichokes, and another piece of bread. "Did you tell your boss about the gambling problem of his niece's husband?"

"No. I didn't think he needed to know, and he had enough on his mind. My guess is that Livia will deal with it. Just in the few days I was there I could see her changing, taking charge, becoming the head of the family. Francesco will be brought into line, I would be willing to bet on it." Rick put a piece of *prosciutto* on his fork. "No pun intended."

"What fascinates me," said Piero, "is that the plot of land was never used."

"I've thought about that myself," said Rick. "All those years ago Enzo Rondini may have bought it simply to demonstrate that he could, to show everyone that he had the power and the money, and leaving it fallow just added to that impression. At the time he was starting to have higher political ambitions, so acquiring land was the perfect way to show he was a force to be reckoned with. After that he may have lost interest."

"Or felt some guilt?"

"From what I read about him in the newspaper archives, he wasn't the kind of person who felt guilt, but one never knows what's in someone's head." Rick took the other artichoke. "The question is whether Enzo's son Roberto knew the whole story of the land, since it was only recently that he started thinking about selling it. That was about the time he appeared at the funeral of Marco's father. "

"That's a bit bizarre."

"Yes and no. The man at the newspaper archives told me someone else had been in doing a search on the Rondini's, and I suspect it was Roberto Rondini himself. His lady friend had told Crispi he had been doing a lot of thinking about his parents and his own mortality. He must have read about the land episode in the newspaper archives and found out that the descendants were not only still around, but one of them had just died. So he went to the funeral, perhaps to clear the air after all those years."

"If that was his intention, it backfired. Your man, the driver, must have found out who he was, wasn't happy, and then stalked Roberto, ending in a confrontation at the river."

"That's the scenario I came up with too."

Rick had more wine and looked out the window at a dark Mercedes passing slowly along the narrow street. "What bothers me in all this is why I didn't suspect Marco. I was so focused on all the other suspects—the neighbor, the manager, Livia's husband, even the demonstrator—that I didn't see what was right before my eyes. Every time something happened, from the first threatening note on the windshield, to the falling cheese, he was there, and yet it didn't cross my mind he could be involved."

Piero wiped up the oil from the artichoke with a piece of bread and popped it in his mouth. "Hiding in plain sight, so to speak."

"It's a cliché, *Zio*, but it's true. I've gone back over the days in my mind and recalled other things. Like when Marco dropped us at the church that first morning, mentioning that he'd been to a funeral recently, and later Crispi told me that Roberto Rondini had been to one as well. That should have at least made me wonder. And a couple days later Angelo made a comment in the car about how he was going to tell Livia to sell the land just to annoy Folengo, the demonstrator. He was joking, but our driver heard it and must have taken him seriously. What happened immediately after that? Someone tries to push thousands of pounds of cheese down on us."

Piero took the final slice of the first ball of cheese. "A waste of good Parmigiano-Reggiano."

"Especially since we escaped relatively unscathed." Rick had not told his uncle about the slight injury to his leg, which was now back to normal.

"*Zio*, I may not have mentioned about Marco trying to run us down."

Piero was about to take a drink of wine but stopped before the glass got to his lips. "No. I don't believe you did."

Rick recounted their exciting walk back from the restaurant. "Once again, I didn't see the obvious," he added when he'd finished. "Angelo had said that people at the reception suggested restaurants near the hotel where he could take Lexi to dinner."

"So you concluded that someone who was at the reception, who knew he was going to dinner on foot, was the one who tried to run you down."

"Exactly." Rick splashed some wine in his glass and drank it. "Which brought me back to the same list of suspects since they were almost all at the Palazzo Te. Instead it was Marco, who had been given the night off."

"And decided it would be a good opportunity to run Angelo down, though I'm not clear why the American was in his sights in the first place. What was the threat?"

"At first I thought it was because he didn't want the land developed, and Angelo appeared to be pushing her toward doing that. But then it occurred to me that Marco may have considered that Angelo could have some claim on the land."

"As a cousin? I don't think so. The property would have gone to the deceased's daughter."

"Ah, but when we went to the registry office in Voglia, the clerk said someone had been in checking on the same year's records. I would bet that was Marco. He knew the truth, that Angelo was in fact Roberto's brother. When Angelo said he wanted to go to his birthplace, Marco feared that Angelo would find out and try to claim the land for himself."

"So better to get rid of him that night rather than let him see the birth record the next day."

Rick's reply was a thoughtful nodding of his head. A minute

passed before Piero spoke, and the words jolted Rick out of his thoughts.

"Have you talked to Betta since you've been back?"

It was no secret that Piero thought highly of Betta Innocenti. She was the first of Rick's romantic attachments that he completely approved of, though he would never try to influence his nephew one way or another in such matters. More importantly, Piero stayed away from a discussion of Rick's relationships during those infrequent phone calls with his sister—Rick's mother—no matter how much she prodded him. Rick was grateful for his uncle's discretion.

"I talked to her once. She said she was working day and night on a new case with the art police. When I told her I was busy with translations she seemed almost relieved."

"How did that make you feel?"

"You're sounding like a psychiatrist, *Zio*."

The policeman drained his wine glass. "Sorry. It's better for us to talk about a funeral in Mantova."

"I agree. Which reminds me of a detail I may not have told you, about the case. A key detail, and I must give you credit for it. Something you said when we talked on the phone nudged my mind in a new direction which, as it turned out, helped solve the murder."

Piero carefully folded his napkin and placed it next to his empty plate. "And what would that have been, Riccardo?"

"You said people have long memories."

Commissario Fontana smiled and called for the check.

The Wines

For the readers who may be planning a trip to Mantova after reading this book, or would like to look in their local wine shop for some of the wines Rick drinks, here is a bit more information.

In one of the meals with Lexi, Rick orders an **Oltrepó Pavese Pinot Grigio.** The grapes are grown, as the name indicates, on "the far side of the Po" River from Pavia, a picturesque town famous for its medieval atmosphere and university. Besides Pinot Grigio, the Oltrepó appellation can be found on a number of red and white wines, including Chardonnay, Malvasia, Moscato, Barbera, and Cabernet Sauvignon. Production of DOC wines in this geographic area is the third largest in Italy, after Chianti and Asti, but the quality matches the quantity.

At the lunch with Angelo and his niece, they order **Lambrusco Mantovano**. Unfortunately, Lambrusco, which is more commonly associated with Emilia-Romagna than Lombardy, gets a bum rap from many American wine drinkers. This is unfortunate, since a dry Lambrusco, ruby red and lightly sparkling, is a wonderful accompaniment to many a meal. Also unfortunately, it is hard to find a good one in the States, but if you do, you will not regret it.

Rick's uncle orders an unnamed **Langhe** red for their meal at the end of the book. The Langhe is an area of rolling hills in south central Piemonte, the region which has Turin as its capital. Some of Italy's finest wines come from the Langhe, including perhaps the most famous, Barolo. But when you see the name Langhe on a bottle it can be one of various varieties, both red and white. The Langhe area, which does not get the tourist invasions like Tuscany and Umbria, is the place to go in the fall when you can sample both the wine and the truffles. Tasting shaved truffles on a cheesy gnocchi, along with a hearty red, can be a life-changing experience.

Mantova is on the eastern edge of Lombardy, but there are more Lombard wines than Rick could ever drink in one book. From the northern part of the region is **Valtellina**, noted in the second mystery in the series, *Death in the Dolomites*. Mantova is also close enough to the Veneto region, with its **Soaves, Bardolinos** and **Valpolicellas**, that they would be commonly found on wine lists in the city. They also show up in the third Rick Montoya book, *Murder Most Unfortunate*, which takes place in Bassano del Grappa, in central Veneto. That region also produces the best **Prosecco**, the bubbly which seems to find its way into every Rick Montoya mystery, including this one. Fortunately, Prosecco is available everywhere in the States.

I should note that in this book, as in others, Rick often orders the house wine, available in all but the highest-end restaurants in Italy. The house wine is usually local, reasonable, and good. You will seldom go wrong by ordering the *vino rosso* or *vino bianco della casa.*

Mille grazie to my good friend, John Myers, the knowledgeable owner of 80 Twenty Wines in Pueblo, Colorado, for his advice and assistance.

Author's Note

Many people have asked me where the best food in Italy is found. Such a judgment is subjective, of course, but that doesn't stop me from answering. What I tell them is to get a map of northern Italy and draw lines connecting three cities: Parma, Cremona and Mantova. That area in the heart of the Po River Valley produces a spectacular array of farm and dairy products, and over centuries has created memorable regional dishes using them. Many of my best culinary memories were made inside that triangle, and my wife and I still talk about dishes and restaurants from the area. The Lombard city featured in this book is especially rich in its gastronomic tradition, and as I have done with regional specialties in my other books, I've included foods unique to Mantova on these pages.

But the draw for the visitor to Mantova—as well as to the other cities in the area—is more than culinary. Its history and art, which are really inseparable, come at you from all sides, blending with the medieval atmosphere that permeates most of the downtown area. We have the Gonzagas to thank for that, since the dukes ran the place for three hundred years and were patrons of some of the most talented artists of the time, such as Raphael, Giulio Romano, Alberti, Mantegna, and Rubens. The Gonzaga court was also famous for the school run by humanist Vittorino da Feltre for both boys and girls, noble as well as poor. Much of the Gonzaga action took place in the massive complex that includes the Palazzo Ducale and the Castello San Giorgio, now a museum. It is inside the castle where Rick, Angelo, and Lexi see Mantegna's work on the walls and ceiling of the Bridal Chamber, one of the great masterpieces of the Renaissance. The Palazzo Te, which is featured in another scene of the book, is also a museum that should not be missed by anyone traveling to the city. The Gonzaga summer residence shows off Giulio Romano's then-controversial Mannerism in both architecture and painting.

Three of the restaurants where Rick eats in this book are real places that I had in mind when writing. His and Lexi's first dinner was at Il Cigno Trattoria dei Martini, which does two local specialties—pumpkin ravioli and capon salad—to perfection. It was the first place I dined at on my first visit to Mantova years ago, and we've been back many times since. Il Ponte in Goito is another excellent restaurant, with views of the river either through their picture window or from tables outside in the summer. And the place where Rick and his Uncle Piero lunch at the end of the book is Obicá, which has two locations in Rome as well as in other Italian cities. Be warned, however, that once you eat their fresh *mozzarella*, you will want to throw rocks at other *mozzarella*.

There's a lot of cheese in this book, and most of it is Parmigiano-Reggiano, which chef Mario Batali rightly calls "the undisputed king of cheeses." If you are curious to see more about how it is made, the producers consortium website, parmigianoreggiano.com, has an excellent video along with facts about the history and traditions of their product. I thank the consortium for information that was so helpful in writing this book.

As always, I am indebted to my wife, my most trusted adviser on food and fashion, for her support, ideas, and constructive criticism. My son, Max, once again gave me advice, this time on his favorite subject of cars, both German and Italian. And a thank you to my good friend, Bill Bode, for explaining the

To see more Poisoned Pen Press titles:

Visit our website:
poisonedpenpress.com
Request a digital catalog:
info@poisonedpenpress.com